Tomorrow Unfolds

A Survivor's Adventures in Latin America

*By the author of the bestselling
"Tomorrow Will Be Better, Surviving Nazi Germany"*

Walter Meyer

Copyright © 2004 by
Walter Meyer
Austin, Texas
All rights reserved.

Meyer, Walter, 1926–

   Tomorrow Unfolds: a Survivor's Adventures in Latin America / Walter Meyer

   p. cm.

   ISBN 1-56870-512-3

   I. Latin America—XXth century history.   2. Meyer, Walter, 1926– .
   3. Latin America—society & customs.   4. Andean region—society & customs.   5. Latin America—geography.

   Library of Congress Control Number: 2004093544

Production manager: Matt Lesher
Printer and binder: RonJon Publishing, Inc.
Typefaces: Gill Sans Light, Impact

To my children and grandchildren.

Contents

Preface: the Holocaust as precursor to my days in Latin America 7
Acknowledgements 13
The Stowaway 15
In the City of Favorable Winds 27
Life and Death in a Park 35
Work as an Artist 41
The Shirt on my Back 47
Meeting actor John Carroll 53
A Dose Of Wrestling Cures Poverty 63
Crooner at the Zanzibar 77
Welcome to Salta 89
The Tobacco Rancher 95
Race Improvement and Spider Wars 107
The Breathing Black Cloud 115
Superwalter in Salta 125
The Bronco Rider of Salta 133
Mines, Mummies and Mary 147
The Smuggler of Time 157
The Bloody Train Ride to Bolivia 169
My Last Days in Bolivia 181
Life in La República del Perú 195
My First Days in the U. S. of A. 211
To Düsseldorf via the Golden State 229
The Texas Two Step with Horses 253

Preface: the Holocaust as precursor to my days in Latin America

Some people are born to be servants, bootlicking obsequious thralls of the omnipotent 9 to 5 schedule, while the brazen, bellwether leaders of the world opt to corral and shanghai life by the horns, riding fearlessly from one audacious adventure to the next. Without a shred of doubt, I fit most the latter crowd. From the brutality of the Nazis upon 6 million helpless European Jews and other so-called heretics to the more recent incalculable genocide between Tutsis and Hutsis in Eastern Africa, little in our raging, apocalyptic world unfolds without man's contribution, whether it be for good or bad. Throughout my 78-year-old tumultuous life to date, I have chosen to lead - a medal-winning Hitler Youth swimmer in Europe, owner of several successful enterprises in South America and a proud earner of a PhD at the University of Texas at Austin - albeit stumbling on too many occasions to realistically count.

"From whom did you inherit so much gypsy blood?" my father once asked me during dinner.

"I think I know the answer to this one," my mother offered. "Walter is very different."

"What do you mean?" *Pere* inquired, frowning and setting his forkful of sausage aside.

"I wanted to make love in nature, away from the city and traffic," she began, smiling and literally beaming with pride. "I dragged your father into a beautiful forest. That's where you were conceived. That's why you're so different."

Of course, my mother was only chaffing about the perdurable effects of radically alternative lovemaking on her offspring, but I am truly convinced that my father was most veracious in his assessment that indomitable gypsy blood does so ruinously course though my energetic veins.

Do I now regret any of the dare devilish episodes in my life? Certainly! First of all, as God Almighty so has it, one cannot undo deeds that have long come to past. If such retrospective powers were in any way attainable, I'd be relentlessly rewinding my temerarious days as I sit to remedy many a life folly instead of toiling desperately to record them lest my clock heave its last toll.

Secondly, I truly believe there is futuristic meaning to whatever good or bad that men do. For instance, I often wish I hadn't killed a man. However, in retrospect, there is little need for guilt for the deceased malefactor in question - once a gaping sore upon the earth - is perhaps better off that way. This philosophy mimics the concept of the bright light at the end of a discouragingly dark tunnel. Proof of this undeniable fact abounds in my life experience, first committed to writing in my memoir "Tomorrow will be better: Surviving Nazi Germany," narrating my life from birth in Düsseldorf to incarceration in prisons and concentration camps as a teen to my escape via ship to South America, whence this book begins.

It was 1943 and Düsseldorf was being bombed steadily. We were an industrial city, and therefore a primary target of the Allies. The city went bizarre lengths to protect its industrial infrastructure, stashing French prisoners of war in the basement of a factory near my house to deter the bombers from hitting it. The French men, alone and trapped in the home of their enemy, yet facing attack from their own allies, fascinated me. My adventurous spirit would sometimes lead me to steal away at night to talk to the men through barred basement windows. I could hardly make out their faces in the obscure darkness, but I could very well imagine what they looked like - haggard like starving vultures and tired, frightened, but the bravest of men. I eventually became the source of ample grub and war information for the physically and spiritually starved men. Quite predictably, their questions evolved around the war: Had America entered the war? Would they be released soon? What were the conditions in France?

One night, after a brief visitation with the Frenchmen, I strolled to a café in downtown Düsseldorf to meet up with my fellow teenage buddies from the *Edelweisspiraten*, a subversive, anti-Nazi prankster group that did anything it could to derail the Nazi system. Our pranks ranged from deflating Nazi officers' tires to fitting condoms around their tail lights. As adolescents, it was the best we could do. We were racking up the balls for another billiard game when the sudden wail of an undulating siren severed our conversation.

"Air raid!" someone yelled.

The planes swooped through minutes later, leveling invaluable buildings that had been standing for centuries, and scattering debris on the streets. An hour later, the bombing ceased. We tiptoed outside to witness the post-bellicose wreckage. I still remember how fascinating it was to wander about the newly bombed city; the charred remains of statues and blocks of concrete forming the bulk of a land of irrevocable chaos, similar only to imagery of some exotic planet. Nothing is as you remember it, almost as if the bombs had created a new city on the ashes of the old.

On King's avenue near the café, my friends and I walked through a small field of broken glass that had once been the façade of a large shoe store. We expeditiously snapped up as many shoes as our deep coat pockets could carry, and headed down the street to Adolf Hitler Square to inspect our loot under the faint, bombed-out streetlight. As was always the case, people oozed out of a nearby bomb shelter past us.

"They're all lefts," my friend cried.

Fresh from the bomb shelter, an elderly lady in bedraggled clothing sauntered past us and I seized the opportunity to relieve myself of the shoes. I pressed them toward her, but she wouldn't take them. She kept shaking her head and pushing away.

"Take them," I urged. "They're good shoes."

"Leave me alone!" she yelled, attracting the attention of a nearby policeman.

"You! What do you have there!" he yelled.

I started running. At that moment, one period of my life had effectively culminated, and another darker period had only just commenced, beginning in the Düsseldorf police station and continuing unchecked through confinement, disease and ultimately the Holocaust. How I had gone from being a member of the Hitler Youth, a paramilitary, Boys Scout-like, Nazi military recruiting machine, to being thrown in a concentration camp is still beyond me. The turbulent details of this horrendous experience is amply narrated in my first memoir, "Tomorrow will be better: Surviving Nazi Germany," for which this publication is a sequel.

Today, when I narrate to fellow friends and associates events of my time spent in a German concentration camp during World War II, I often get questions like: "Are you Jewish?" or, more positively, "Oh, so you must be Jewish?" Of course, my surname "Meyer," of Hebrew origin, could easily be Jewish and always seemed to give me away wrongfully. Many simply sneered and cast their heads aside in doubt for they were fully convinced that a non-Jew could never have been imprisoned in Nazi concentration camps.

It is the world's most unfortunate subterfuge that the Holocaust has become an almost exclusively Jewsh chapter in history. Many are still oblivious to the regrettable fact that thousands of French, Czech, Italians, Germans, Polish, Austrians, Jehovah Witnesses and Gypsies were also persecuted and wrongfully imprisoned. A plethora of publications and Hollywood, with its convincing performers, have shed light on the Jewish Holocaust experience, establishing worldwide awareness on this grim episode in human history.

The story, however, has yet to be fully told. Most people are acquainted with Dachau, Auschwitz, Belsen, Sachsenhausen, Buchenwald and Ravensbrueck concentration camps when indeed Germany and its occupied countries had more than 2,000 such camps. Only a few made headlines. All were equally atrocious. In my camps, Ravensbrueck and Sachsenhausen, 20 percent of all inmates were Germans and Austrians (Austria had been annexed and its citizens were considered Germans), other nationalities, and 8 percent were Jews. Some of the camps had a majority of Jews, notably the infamous Auschwitz.

Known as the Hetzlager (the rush camp), the men's camp of Ravensbrueck was the grim headquarters for many smaller camps (Aussenlager) in northeast Germany. Thousands worked in camps owned by large corporations such as Siemens and Heinkel. The Holocaust was a world-class mess with the fingerprints of the many so-called civilized nations of the world all over it, particularly the United Kingdom and the U.S.A, both of which folded their arms and watched in silence, often contributing directly and indirectly to the mass slaughter. Without the negligence and assistance of these culpable Allied powers, Hitler would not have succeeded with his "Final Solution," and millions of humans would still be alive today.

To understand the Holocaust in the fullest fashion, I strongly recommend "Warning and Hope: Nazi Murder of European Jewry," by William Samelson and "Holocaust Conspiracy: An International Conspiracy," by William R. Perl.

Many friends ask: "Do you think there might be another Holocaust?" to which I respond with a firm "Yes," given the pessimistic content of daily news. However, I choose to be an optimist, one who realizes that horrors such as the Holocaust do not have to happen.

"Education, not quantity but quality of education," I often explain, is the solution to a repeat show.

Today, at my advanced age, I feel extremely fortunate to enjoy my beloved wife and partner for life and the growth of my little children: Asai (6) and Paul James (3). I pray that they will go through life without being subjected to wars and senseless international disputes.

Winding from Europe through the major nations of South America and eventually to the United States, this book is about adventure, resilience and struggling for acceptance in a land where most looked and spoke differently. It is about the coming of age of a man who had seen it all, but is still searching, blind to the many hidden trappings of life. While nothing can ever surpass the difficulty of my Holocaust experience, many of my travails in

South America came pretty close. If there was but one thing positive about my concentration camp experience, it was that it toughened and readied me for storms ahead.

I hope the health gods continue to bless me so I may complete my third memoir. Even though this publication has a few gory stories, my experience in the Americas will give the savvy reader ample opportunity to laugh.

Acknowledgements

I thank those who helped me along the way and provided me with kindness and consideration.

To Remi Bello, I offer my gratitude. Without his editorial assistance, the manuscript would still be dwelling away in the cellars of my computer, awaiting many changes.

Thanks to the many who encouraged me to write and tell the story.

I greatly appreciate the many suggestions and advice I received from my friend and comrade, Dr. William Samelson.

Matt Lesher shepherded the book through production. I thank him and his lovely wife Teresa Shu for their able assistance and abiding friendship.

Jeff Williams, a friend and ultra-talented graphic artist, took the time to design the cover for this book. Many thanks to him as well.

Many thanks to my friend Jos Baker, the reknowned writer and editor in Capetown, South Africa for reading the manuscript and recommending that the book be printed.

There are many who encouraged me, listened to me, gave me suggestions. There are my children and grandchildren.

Finally, I thank my life companion and mother of our small children, Asai and Paul James (PJ). Without her, only God knows where I would be and what I would do.

The Stowaway

We will either find a way or make one. - Hannibal of Carthage.

I met Chris in Antwerp, Belgium in December, 1948. He worked as fourth assistant engineer aboard S.S. Parkhaven, an old coal ship on which I stowed away from Europe to South America.

Chris was about 26 years old and clean-shaven, the kind of man who would certainly make chief engineer in a few years. During the tumultuous trip, we became close friends, and he repeatedly helped me avoid deportation. Thanks to him, I made it all the way to Brazil, Uruguay and, eventually, Argentina.

Now it was the summer of 1949, and I stood patiently awaiting him in the industrial port of Montevideo, Uruguay. When we arrived in coastal Montevideo, it looked welcoming and reminiscent of many European cities, lavish in its 18th century colonial architecture. But, now, after being rejected by a contact I expected to harbor with provisionally, I couldn't wait to make tracks of the diminutive nation.

"You can wait here and return with us to Europe," offered the captain of the S.S. Parkhaven, noticing my disappointment. "But, I'm sorry I can't take you to Buenos Aires"

His calculated words stabbed me like a million pins. This meant I had to concoct a strategy to stow away again. My longtime friend Chris was my only savior.

I paced the quay smoking cigarettes and hiding in the monstrous shadow of the seventy-five hundred-ton Parkhaven. I tossed my butts into the still water beneath the boardwalk, and stood mesmerized watching the discarded butts stick together and rotate viciously in a small eddy next to the wooden pillar. Squawking black crows swooping about the port grounds for morsels of grub symbolized prognostication, birds of ill omen. But I paced on, holding out for more favorable fortune, like a stranded pirate looking to sea from some coconut-infested island.

Suddenly, at three o'clock in the morning, Chris appeared out of the gloomy shadows, signaling to me. He was as handsome and athletic as any uniformed man can be; his crooked smile undoubtedly a lady magnet. I sauntered across the slipshod loading dock and straggled him cautiously below the decks and into the belly of the ship. The dark, oven-like and unbearably irriguous belly was no hiding place for a man.

"A man is defined by how many choices he has," my father fondly said.

Employing his definition, I had ceased to be a man the moment I reduced myself to one choice: Reaching Argentina by any means necessary.

Skillfully, Chris guided me past the temporarily empty crews' quarters, down to the unusually quiet engine room and through a maze of dark, narrow passageways lined with jutting insulation pipes. Eventually, he halted and pointed at a tiny, dark crawlspace beneath the ship's ever-active boilers.

"You hide in here under the furnaces," he said, in his rich Dutch accent. "It'll get very hot, so take your clothes off."

He slipped on a mild frown, and eyeballed me intensely in anticipation of my observance of his order. Chris was not chief engineer yet, but he might as well have been for he had mastered the commanding tone.

I stood, shocked like a once faithless man who had just seen a miracle, staring at the spot, and wondering how my brawny, adolescent body would fit into such a cramped space. Then came the voices of drunken men above, returning from surrounding bars to their rightful quarters. They were boisterous and unruly, like college freshmen on a first night out.

"I bet you the watch commander will soon arrive to discipline them," Chris warned, pointing at the hiding place. "You had better do as I say."

Quickly, I obeyed Chris' captain-like orders and embarrassingly stripped down to my dingy underwear. I rolled my foul-smelling shirt and pants into a tight bundle, which I curtly handed to a seemingly amused Chris, beaming with a clownish smile.

"What are you laughing at?" I cautioned.

"Nothing," Chris replied, cringing as he fought to rid himself of his smile. He was on the bursting verge of laughter, his forced-shut lips reverberating like those of a trumpet player.

"I'm about to risk my life here, Chris. You find my condition suitable content for comedy?"

"No, not at all," he said. "I'm sorry, it's just that you look really funny in your underwear. Forgive my taste in humor."

Chris was right. In retrospect, I looked quite impish in my diaper-like, off-white homemade underwear, secured around my waist with a blue safety pin.

Walter and Lovey, the ship's coal trimmers

The black-threaded stitches on the white briefs were noticeably wriggly; the backside too wobbly and spacious for even a man with the biggest of buttocks.

I had held on to the incommodious underwear more as a twisted souvenir than for adolescent masochism. Thus, a piece of clothing that Chris found insignificant and jocular, was a reminder of where I had been in life. I didn't find it funny.

A current of hot, dry air overwhelmed my face as I wiggled into the hellish hole. Once beyond the tight threshold, I waited for my eyes to adjust to the pitch darkness. The tunnel ended at a flat iron wall, whence I turned my head around to face Chris.

All I could ascertain in the now distant shadows was the silhouette of his brawny torso at the mouth of the tunnel. His blonde-haired head was virtually invisible but for the whites of his eyes, glowing like moons on his weather-beaten face.

"Alright?" he asked, in a faint whisper.

"I liked the propeller shaft better," I whined.

A small cubicle above the ship's propeller shaft had been my hiding place on the S.S. Parkhaven for lengthy periods during our previous trip from Antwerp to Vitoria, Brazil.

The dry heat slowly began to dehydrate my mouth. I swallowed hard, and braced myself for a tumultuous ride.

"I'll be okay. Come and get me when it's safe."

"You stay out of sight until inspection is completed," he ordered. "I don't want trouble with the captain, and he doesn't need trouble with port authorities."

Chris slammed the door shut. A gloomy darkness suddenly overcame my new bedroom. Noises once insignificant and inaudible were now amplified and eery. The rubbing of my pants against the shaft's steel surface now sounded like a saw working its way through some robust log of wood. Every wink and sigh crackled and bellowed, each distinct enough to be counted. My breath gushed like the grandest of tornadoes; every subtle fart now parallel in deafening sound and asphyxiation as the most lethal bomb.

I waited patiently until the 6 p.m. whistle blared. Then the ship trembled and lurched forward. The hollow whir of machinery was familiar to me; it had a lulling but scary effect.

Soon my eyes began to fail me, and my tongue tumefied like yeasted dough. As the torturous heat became unbearable, I felt death creep upon me like a thief in the dark, an experience I had brooked many times before. This time, however, solitude was my only refuge. Desperate bodies had besieged my prior incarceration in the dreary and inhumane Ravensbrueck Concentration Camp. This time, I was only panicking.

Soon my body adjusted to the heat and I sprawled there, filling my lungs with warm air thinking how relatively comfortable this coffin-like little nest had become. I envisioned myself in my mother's womb, surrounded by the soothing warmth of her belly. Then I pictured myself buried alive, dirt being shoved on top of me, but unable to call for help. I wondered if the dead felt the warmth of compost and decay as they nestled in the bosom of the earth. Was my deceased brother content in his grave, still sporting his infuriating smile?

My mother always had a special craving for the beautiful Edelweiss, a flower graced with white wooly leaves that predominantly grows along far-reaching rocky crevices in the Alps. On vacation to the Austrian Alps, my brother Paul Meyer, Jr., ever eager to win my parents' approval and favor, swore to return with the cherished flower.

It rained heavily on Paul's last day of vacation, and the guide, with whom Paul had resided, advised against mountain climbing for the treasured flower. Paul insisted. Indeed, he stumbled upon a plant after climbing just approximately 900 feet. This was unusual for the Edelweiss is known to inhabit much higher terrain. Eager to reach one more flower, Paul bravely jumped over a gorge.

He slipped.

I vividly remember my brother's mangled face when his grotesque body arrived a few days later at the funeral chapel at the cemetery in Düsseldorf. He had biffed several overhanging rocks as he plummeted, and his face was unrecognizably distorted. His lips were puckered, as if gesturing for a perpetual kiss. I remember gawking at his disengaged jawbone and imagining him masticating sideways like a cow.

My mother or "*Mutti*," as I referred to her in German, ran her fingers along the shattered craters of his skull. She bent over him and whispered something.

The pallbearers lodged Paul in a coffin that tapered at both ends like an Egyptian sarcophagus. They had difficulty bearing the coffin aloft because the longtitudinal spacing wasn't even, and the four men carrying the foot-end had to take baby steps to avoid stepping on each other's heels.

Later, our parents tossed dirt onto the coffin, marking the last time we saw Paul Meyer, Jr. However, not a day passed without my folks weeping and lauding his name. A lone picture of him stood atop the piano with his face smiling at us. Every time I failed at school or gave the wrong answer at the dinner table, my mother would glance at Paul's picture and sigh. It was as if I had stolen his birthright. Even in death he was loved more.

A bead of salty sweat trickled along my lips into my mouth, jolting me from dreaming. I began to suspect Chris had forgotten me as I drifted in and out of a restless sleep. My clownish underwear was drenched with sweat; my constricted testicles slick and itchy. From the changing shadows, I guessed it had been about 9 hours since Chris had deserted me.

I shoved myself against the metal sides of my coffin; unsuccessfully trying to relieve my restricted, numb arms by holding them above my head. My fetal position proved inescapable.

"How much longer to Buenos Aires?" I wondered aloud.

Then, I smiled half-heartedly, rejoicing a little that I had secured a place to stay once I arrived in Buenos Aires. I remembered Julio, an officer I had met on an Argentine ship in Antwerp, handing me a scribbled-on paper with his grandmother's address.

"You're welcome to stay with us in Buenos Aires. I should be at home by the time you arrive there," he said, after learning that I was destined for anywhere in South America. "Now, she's a real model. So try not to rape her."

"I shall do my best to restrain myself," I replied, returning the humor.

And, so it became that I chose Buenos Aires, Argentina, out of a hundred South American cities, as my favored destination.

I had barely fallen asleep when searing abdominal pain awoke me. It was as if death was flashing himself to me again, but I only needed to urinate, the pressure on my bladder creeping up to my chest. I gasped desperately for air, and, after thrashing myself around, eventually found a position that diminished the agonizing pain. I dosed off again.

When the nearby engine rattled to a screeching halt, I snapped out of my slumber with a sudden gasp. The placental drone in the lullabying womb where I hid had been like the massaging heartbeat of a mother to her child and, suddenly, I was deprived of it.

I was immediately terrified by the sheer vastness of the S.S. Parkhaven for now I could hear tinny voices on the deck above. Then there was knocking, banging, and suddenly a heap of warm soot descended upon my bare chest and limbs.

Apparently, the crew was extricating the furnaces of soot and raking the boiler grates. Black snow disgorged onto my head, into my mouth and eyes.

At first, it was primitively amusing, the warm dust and flakes reminded me of my continued existence. However, the hot soot began to insulate my skin, overwhelming me. I was literally being buried alive!

I began to panic from the suffocation that ensued. If I remained in the tunnel, I would die before birth. Invoking every ounce of potency I had stashed within my feeble self, I started belly-crawling through the canal. The small reservoir of air left in the hole diminished each second as more soot came pouring in.

"Get that pile over there!" one man yelled from above.

Then a heavy heap tumbled onto my back, squelching all movement, and sputtering black dust everywhere. No more breathable air. Pitch darkness. I was officially suffocating to death. The irony sickened me; I had survived a bloody Nazi concentration camp only to die on a harmless cargo ship.

I pulled forward for what I was certain was my last try. Then, my head hit something. Had I made it to the access hatch? I delivered several desperate punches to whatever it was my head had hit. It popped open. Air! I crawled halfway through the threshold before passing out.

Face down and covered in soot, I awoke to a crew of men clamoring over me.

"We got us a nigger stowaway!" one of the men yelled in disbelief.

I stood naked to the world, save for the black soot, which, momentarily, kept the crew from recognizing me.

My surreptitious disguise was soon uncovered when one of the men grabbed a water hose and sprayed me down. I shivered from the cold, stinging spray while the men laughed as they witnessed my blackness melt away and my skin turn pink. I'd been caught for the second time on the same ship!

Soon after we departed Antwerp, the purser, acting on a tipoff by some of the sailors, who had spotted me climbing in and out of my first hiding place, searched for and caught me snoozing in a bunk bed. Then Chris was forced to squirrel me away above the ship's propeller.

"What a horrible ordeal that was," I thought, as I wondered what my punishment would be this time.

"What a damned nuisance!" one of the men yelled. "Don't you ever learn a lesson?"

I glanced at each sailor for a friendly countenance, but found none. It dawned upon me that the captain would soon be briefed. Sailor's law had it he would promptly inform Argentine authorities of my presence. I was fully dogged in my wish not to return to Europe.

Acknowledging that I posed neither threat nor peril, the men flippantly returned to their duties while one was dispatched to notify the captain. I trailed him, climbing to the captain's cabin. Upon arriving on the uppermost deck, I detoured and sprinted for the starboard railing. I threw a rope ladder over the edge, and descended to ten feet above water. Then, I let myself drop.

Sporting bomb shelled faces, the men on the deck pointed animatedly at me as I bobbed in the water.

"There are sharks," they shouted, their voices laced with a reasonable amount of concern.

Two tugboats were getting rigged to haul the S.S. Parkhaven into port. As I swam in between them, the pilots yelled, "*No se permite nadar aquí!*" (swimming is not allowed here) I smiled mischievously, disregarding their Spanish warnings against swimming in the murky waters.

There was plentiful litter in the water and, as I swam, debris smacked my thrashing legs on several occasions. I cringed every time expecting a flesh-ripping shark bite. As soon as I was certain my safety was secure, I splashed on, scanning the ocean ahead of me.

Then I spotted a ship about a mile away clearing customs and securing dock space. I swam to it, making long breaststrokes just as I had been taught during my Hitler Youth days. That was before I was deemed an enemy of the Third Reich and condemned, with 12 million others, to noxious concentration camps.

The rubbish bobbed around me: oil, seaweed and dead fish turned slimy and purple, asphyxiated to death by man's deleterious waste. The large waves buoyed me aloft enough to spot the behemoth ships anchored in the bustling port of Buenos Aires. I picked the best looking of the docking ships and vigorously swam my way to it. From its flapping flag (red with a blue cross outlined in white that extended to the edges), the ship was undoubtedly Norwegian.

The men on the S.S. Parkhaven did not bother giving chase. I guess they figured I'd get arrested wherever I was heading.

Nevertheless, my arms parted the water like stabbing shovels, indicative of an inexplicable burning desire to reach the Norwegian ship, and, subsequently, Argentine soil. My contrivance was set: I would purchase some very well-needed clothes and then visit Julio's grandmother in town. He had assured she would house me until I found work.

As my wild imagination and energetic arms drove me closer to my destination, I envisioned making a fortune and sending a boastful letter home. The words in the letter danced on the splashing water before my eyes. "Dear *Mutti* and Dad," it would read. "Today I met the President of Argentina. He has asked me to work for him. I will either live rich or be poor and political. I'll start a revolution for which my face will grace paintings on buildings. I'll be famous and recognized."

After reading the letter, I imagined my parents' faces would beam with pride. The thought alone energized me. Being an athlete, I propelled myself through the water like a shark hunting its prey. I must have been the fastest man alive. I had competed and excelled at several swimming championships in Europe. Had the 1942 Olympics not been cancelled, a 16-year-old Walter Meyer would have been selected to represent Germany. With each ribbon and medal I brought home, perhaps *Mutti* and Dad would have shifted Paul's picture more to the edge of the piano.

Eventually, the ultra-blonde Norwegian crewmen spotted me, and tossed down a rope ladder, their light-colored eyes glistening at the ardent thought of perhaps reigning in a wreck survivor. The flush of sunlight against their milkish skin, made the sailors seem somewhat angelic, their bodies encased in glowing halos. I had finally made it to Argentina, and "angels" were with me.

I felt a salty liquid trickle into my mouth. But I was not crying, it was the filthy ocean.

I boarded the Norwegian ship with fervent enthusiasm, but danger loomed. I could sense it. Armed with rifles and vicious scowls, several uniformed police and immigration officers marched the port scouring for rascal stowaways like me. One of them glanced my way, but I ducked furtively and speed-walked to the gang of friendly-looking sailors aboard the ship's deck.

The sailors' countenances bore a relieving mixture of joy, bewilderment and admiration, having witnessed me swim approximately six miles through oil and rotten debris to their ship. I could feel the officer's stare raise hairs on my back as I walked gingerly toward the welcoming group, each step taking an eternity.

I began hugging and kissing the sailors as if I were one of them. Then I turned around and smiled generously at the officer. He fell for my trick and pursued other interests. I heaved a sigh of relief. One of the men handed me a towel and scouring soap, and some clean clothes.

"Get rid of that oil and grease and then you can tell us about your adventure over breakfast," said one sailor in English, as another ushered me under the deck to a bathroom.

I spent an eternity under the warm shower, ridding myself of the burdening grease of the past and ushering myself into the relieving freedom of the New World. Then, properly dressed, I joined the men on the ship's deck for breakfast.

"You look like you haven't eaten for weeks," one of the men joked, as he plopped a mountainous heap of food and a cup of coffee in front of me. "Is coffee okay?"

I nodded thankfully.

While I craved a good meal, my appetite failed me halfway through the plate for my stomach had shrunk markedly during my stay in the S.S. Parkhaven's belly. The curious sailors asked many questions, most of which I replied with a nod and a full mouth.

"Where are you from?" one man asked.

"How did you get here?" another inquired.

I pointed at the S.S. Parkhaven, by now approximately three miles away, being slowly hauled into port by a tugboat.

"You swam all the way from there?" asked another sailor in disbelief.

Soon the men were celebrating me like a hero.

An hour passed before the S.S. Parkhaven finally docked nearby. I waited patiently until the coast was clear, and then bid farewell to the friendly Norwegian sailors. They seemed somewhat disappointed to see me leave.

"Come back and visit us," offered one sailor, as I disembarked and strolled toward the S.S. Parkhaven.

"Sure," I said, still shocked by the sailors' kindness. "Good tidings!"

I noticed the captain standing atop the Parkhaven's bridge. He seemed rather stunned to see me.

"How in the world did you get here?" he asked, suspiciously.

"Swimming," I replied with a mischievous smile.

The captain smiled, shaking his head in disbelief.

"You know, you're welcome to come with us," he said. "I could use a tough, die-hard survivalist like you."

"I appreciate the offer, captain, but I have reached my destination," I replied, shaking his hand. "Thank you for having me so far."

"Good luck," he concluded, before returning to his quarters.

Chris was preparing to leave his cabin when I knocked on his door.

"Sir, accompany me to my new home, sir," I said, saluting him jokingly.

He instantly dropped his chores, and soon we were on our way into Buenos Aires, the City of Favorable Winds.

In the City of Favorable Winds

On February 2, 1536, Spanish conquistador Don Pedro de Mendoza arrived to populate Rio de la Plata lands. Mendoza christened the city Espíritu Santo and named its port Nuestra Señora del Buen Aire, which was later renamed Buenos Aires, the city of favorable winds.

It was January 24 1949. I had no immigration papers, spoke no Spanish and knew only one person in Buenos Aires: Julio, whom I had met in Antwerp, aboard the Argentine ship El Gaucho. His right hand missing an index finger, Julio had scribbled his address on a scrap of paper: "*Calle Las Heras 54.*"

I hadn't the slightest clue where Las Heras Street was in the monstrous sprawling city of six million Spanish-speaking residents, but worry was least on my mind. Adrenaline pumped through my youthful body as Chris and I cruised from the port toward Retiro Railroad Station, traversing exciting new terrain along the way.

The rhythmic sound of Spanish was thrilling, so were the gorgeous Argentine ladies clad in elegant multihued chic - I figured I'd get to them later. The atmosphere was fresh and appealing, including the policemen's gaudy uniforms, their hats graced with white extended neck covers to prevent scathing sunburn. Older tenement houses or conventillos stood out among more modern Romantic-style and art nouveau architecture from the Old Continent.

We passed the rowdy Retiro Railroad Station, and stopped at a busy corner where streetcars frequented, many of which were covered with blaring advertisements.

Buenos Aires' history is quite colorful. While it was founded in the 16th century, it remained a village until the 18th century creation of the viceroyalty. Juan José de Vértiz, the first viceroy of the protracted transformation, went on a modernizing spree during his reign, installing street lamps, cobblestones and Argentina's first printing press. First arrived the Italians and the Spanish, the majority of whom were poor farmers. Afterwards came the Jews, Poles, Croats, Czechs and Ukrainians, among others. By 1895, 72 out of every 100 Buenos Aires inhabitants were foreigners.

Like most gullible Europeans inspired by renowned 19th century Romantic artists like Karl Bodmer and George Catlin, both faithful recorders of the lost Mandan tribe of North America, I had subconsciously envisioned South America to be underdeveloped and hopping with savage Indians. I was wrong. Human and vehicular traffic was torrential, and Buenos Aires' Victorian architecture was eerily similar to that which adorned European skylines. My heart skipped beats, as I stared into the horizon, marveling that I had finally made it.

As I stood mesmerized by the sheer modernity of Buenos Aires, a midnight-blue convertible with large fins stretched out behind it, pulled up to the curb. The driver, a young Latin man with a bushy mustache, smiled at us. I stared back at his reflective aviator sunglasses.

"English?" he asked.

A distorted reflection of my six-foot frame bounced off on his silver lenses. My physique, convoluted by the concave lenses, accentuated a contorted, troll-like face. I returned a half-hearted smile to the friendly stranger. Tall, blond and casually dressed, I must have resembled one of many gringo sailors abound in Buenos Aires. I wasn't surprised he'd singled me out as a foreigner. To the Argentines, anyone with blue eyes and blond hair was considered a gringo or gringa.

"Where are you headed?" he asked.

"*Calle Las Heras*," I replied. "Could you please give me directions?"

"Nonsense," he insisted, waving his hands animatedly. "No directions, get in and I'll take you there." Chris and I jumped into the back seat.

The Latin man's overt friendliness made me skeptical. My grotesque depictions against his concave lenses reminded me of Gothic witches gleaming into a dark future cast by a shimmering bowl of clear water.

Chris nudged me, jolting me out of my daydreaming, and I momentarily chastised myself inwardly for envisioning such a pessimistic future. How could my fortune run afoul in a civilized city blessed with nice folks like this mustachioed man?

"What are you thinking about?" Chris asked.

"Just strategizing how I'm going to get to all these colorful ladies at once," I lied. "Have any ideas?"

Having survived Nazi concentration camps, I was a master at elevating my spirits against all odds, but I flinched again as another glum thought raced through my mind. What kind of a man or darkness lay behind those sunshades? I sensed rocky travails in my new home of Argentina, and I braced myself well for it.

If my suspicions were erroneous, then Argentina must be the friendliest place on Earth, I thought, as the car lurched forward. Where else in God's harum-scarum, misanthropic world would an absolute stranger confer a ride upon a sojourner who was in all probability penniless?

Ten minutes later, Chris and I were standing outside *Calle Las Heras* 54 on the outskirts of Buenos Aires. The two-story duplex had a defining steep staircase, which set it apart from the other houses on the block, stacked next to each other like murdered sardines in a can.

The mustachioed driver bade us auspicious fortune as he drove off.

"Remember, this is the city of favorable winds," he said, the spiky hairs on his upper lip dancing animatedly as he spoke. "I hope the winds blow you in a most favorable direction."

"So far, I've been the recipient of all the luck one person can ask for," I replied. "Thank you for wishing me more."

I ascended the stairs and rang the doorbell.

"I'll wait down here," Chris said, respectfully allowing me some privacy.

An elderly woman in her sixties jerked the door open. Clad in a lose-fitting dress, her hair was streaked with gray strands and pulled back into a neat bun. She held the door ajar enough to squeeze her face through.

"*Si?*" she asked.

I was subtly surprised to encounter her at the door for I'd expected to meet Julio. "*Eh, Julio aqui?*" I asked, forcing a few words of Spanish.

In German schools, we were taught Latin, French and English, but never Spanish because of Europe's sustaining German-English-French illogical ethnocentric pact. I regretted that now.

"*Julio no está aqui. Está viajando, va a regresar dentro de un mes,*" (Julio is not here. He is traveling and will return within a month) she said, shaking her head vigorously.

Her hurried words were simply indecipherable for me. "Sorry," I said and, as the mustachioed man in the blue convertible had asked earlier, "English?"

"Ah! *Inglés?*" she said, motioning me in, denoting further proof of Argentine hospitality. I spoored her through a narrow hall and into a living room dominated by a dark blue sofa and a hanging jumbo print of the Holy Mary cuddling an *au naturel* baby Jesus.

The old woman persisted to jabber in Spanish as if I understood every utterance.

"*No hablo inglés, pero mi hijo, el hermano de Julio, él lo habla, momentito,*" (I don't speak English, but my son, Julio's brother, he speaks English, just a minute,) she said, jetting out of the living room.

I glanced around the dark room confused, wondering if she left to bring me something to drink or fetch Julio. Soon she returned with a man who resembled Julio, at least his strong build and prominent nose. He shook my hand firmly.

"I am Julio's brother Roberto," he said, in accented English. "My grandmother says you're looking for him."

I nodded, ecstatic that he spoke English.

"He gave me this address," I said, handing him the paper Julio had scribbled his address on. "He said I could stay with him here."

"His ship doesn't return until next month," said Roberto, looking surprised. "You can come back later and then talk to him."

"Where can I stay until then?" I asked, getting worried and remembering my earlier ordeal with the mustachioed man and his "futuristic" shades.

"Oh, you have no other place to stay?"

"No," I said, hoping he would sense my desperate condition and proffer me an invitation to stay for at least a day or two.

"How much money do you have? There are some inexpensive hotels in the city."

"I don't have any money," I said, whimpering pathetically. "I was planning on finding work soon. I am an excellent swimmer, maybe I could give lessons at a club."

"Try the *Club Gimnasia y Esgrima*," he snapped. "It's a little ways out of town, but it might be worth the try."

His cosmetic suggestions, aimed solely at getting rid of me, stung my self-pride repeatedly like an African worker bee protecting its queen. He scribbled the address to the fencing gym on the same scrap of paper on which Julio had written, and politely showed me to the door. I thanked Roberto and his grandmother.

I was homeless again.

Chris must have discerned the disappointment on my face as I descended the stairs. My relaxed demeanor had disappeared and I felt edgy.

"Come with me to Parkhaven," he said, trying in vain to comfort me. "You are always welcome there."

Despite his pleas, I accompanied Chris to the Retiro Station, and hugged him goodbye. He had become a valuable friend to me.

"I can't thank you enough," I said. "I wish you good luck in your aspirations to become chief engineer."

"Now that I've met you, I'm questioning if I'm worthy enough to be a leader on that ship," he said, giggling lightly. "I've never been as impressed by a person's sheer will and determination. Thank you."

We shook hands. I never saw Chris again.

After my emotionally excruciating separation from Chris, I ambled through the city, weaving through urban streets, nostalgic churches, shops and suburban lots. Despite being the capital and main port of a former Spanish colony, the porteños (as the residents of Buenos Aires still call themselves) had more Italian and German names than Spanish, and their buildings and cultural traditions oozed a history of steady European immigration.

I felt like I hadn't traveled more than 6,000 miles to South America. In the 1940s, Buenos Aires, in its structures, layout and flair, could realistically have been Berlin, Milan or Paris. But I was not in Europe, and the peculiar differences peeked out at me from dark shadows and creepy alleys.

I developed a dreamy paranoia as I travailed the wide avenues, suspicious of porteños who, only a few hours ago, had seemed so amicable. Their smiles now looked like evil leers. Their alien language buzzed in my ears like a poisonous snake ready to strike its vulnerable prey.

"*No hasta miércoles, hasta lunes,*" one man yelled. "*Cada semana los lunes!*" (Not until Wednesday, until Monday, every week on Monday)

On a tiled sidewalk, across the street from Don Enrique Restaurante, two men stood arguing aggressively, saliva flying from their mouths. I found it quite amusing that the man yelling highlighted every expletive sentence with a clap. The other man remained relatively stoic choosing to offend with, to my understanding, obscene gestures, which infuriated his opponent even more. I entertained myself for a while, watching them banter like teenage girls.

Suddenly, I was in the middle of mass human traffic, busy pedestrians hustling by on either side with luggage, wooden crates or pushcarts. I rotated in one spot hoping to catch as many faces as possible, expecting to recognize somebody. I only disappointed myself.

Eventually, as darkness loomed, pragmatism kicked in, and I began strategizing for a place to sleep, some food and money. I stared into a murky puddle of stagnant water on the curb. My twisted reflection reminded me of the grotesque caricature of my body on the mustachioed man's dark shades. The pessimistic prediction was real, I thought. I snapped away from the puddle of water, took a deep breath and focused on summoning some courage for the daunting task ahead.

I stopped anyone on the street, hunting for an English, French or German speaker. Finally, I ran into a thirty-something-year-old Englishman. He looked elegant in his conservative coat and tie.

"Do you know where I can find work as a swimming instructor?" I asked.

"It's not likely," he replied. "Private clubs wouldn't hire you, but try the *Plaza Italia*."

Plaza Italia was a complex of myriad office and residential buildings, a portion of which formed an entrance to the enormous Parque Palermo, spotted with joggers and small kiosks.

"People who need day laborers go by there to pick up a few men for temporary work," he said. "Here's a quid for the bus."

I thanked the Englishman and did as he instructed. With the cash newly afforded me, I boarded a luxury bus to Belgrano, a posh northwestern Buenos Aires suburb, and disembarked when the bus conductor yelled, "*Plaza Italia!*"

I glanced around, expecting to discover lengthy queues of laborers scouring for employment. There were no such queues; just a few elderly couples strolling with their pets.

I sat on the closest park bench, contemplating my dismal future on an empty stomach.

Life and Death in a Park

The gem cannot be polished without friction, nor man perfected without trials. - Chinese Proverb.

At the center of *Plaza Italia*, encircling shade trees cast long, speckled shadows on the dry grass and skinny sidewalks. A suspect caravan of sluggish, horse-drawn carriages circumvented the plaza's perimeter, which was decorated with a colorful variety of stores tucked beneath apartments.

The carriages, armed with curtained cabins, taxied clockwise within the plaza, like Olympic relay runners. I noticed movement behind the caliginous curtains even though they were conveniently drawn. Men loomed within the foxy carriages.

"What a bizarre Argentine custom," I thought. "Well, different countries, different customs."

Suddenly, one of the carriages stopped, and a twenty-something-year-old man jumped off. He glanced around furtively, adjusted his ruffled jacket and fled the plaza. Then an older man quickly approached the carriage, and slipped through its flowery curtains. Lo and behold, the merry-go-round procession commenced.

"Aha!" I said aloud, like a prophet in revelation.

The carriages were seedy bordellos on wheels.

Soon after the customer clambered in, the stagecoach rocked and the walls shuddered, the mischievous couple inciting a short-lived illegal sexual earthquake. I even caught a climactic groan or two when the carriage throttled by me.

As I marveled at the ingenuity of the 'vendors,' the thought of seeking employment here, luring potential customers into the square for carriage owners, sped through my mind. However, while I enjoyed my many trivial sexual relationships with numerous ladies over the years, I revered women too much to engage in the crude marketing of their flesh.

As I strayed away from the circle, a 1931 Ford police car halted in front of me.

"*Qué está haciendo aquí?*" (What are you doing here?) the younger officer asked.

Guessing the officers were investigating my strolling about a park so late, I shrugged my shoulders and lifted my hands to the sky.

"*Buenos Aires!*" I yelled.

In English, "Buenos Aires" means "favorable winds."

The officers laughed hysterically and permitted me to proceed. Luckily, they overlooked the customary identification check. I was identityless.

That night I slept behind shrubby, protective bushes in the park, proximal to the statue of a tongue-wagging dog reminiscent of a boxer I once owned. It was a clear night and I lay on a cushion of leaves staring through wiry branches at the glowing stars. I picked out the various constellations to fascinate myself, but was soon disappointed. The usually conspicuous Leo, configured like a menacing lion, now looked misplaced and non-threatening. Lupus the wolf and Ursa the bear were both positioned differently in the sky, at least from what I was accustomed to in Europe. Was this because seasons had changed or because I was now situated on the opposite side of the planet? After laboring my brain with constellation trivia, I lulled myself to sleep with the melodic thudding of carriages circumventing the nearby plaza.

Screeching noises and the morning's usual commotions awoke me the next day. The sun was uncomfortably luciferous; I was sweating profusely, and my moist, sticky hair plastered my forehead. Soon the ambient noise became unbearable; men yelling, hammers banging and car engines revving. I stumbled toward the din, gradually dabbing sleep from my dreary eyes.

After walking a few hundred yards from my uncomfortable 'bedroom,' I stumbled upon the world-class Buenos Aires Racetrack, location of the renowned Grand Prix Buenos Aires, encircled with bleachers, kiosks and overarching trees.

The track was spotted with racecars and their gleaming drivers. In the immediate background, mechanics playfully revved throttles in rapid crescendo. A crew of aptly-dressed men neatly stacked cushioning, contact-friendly straw bales on the edge of track curves. Beyond the track, hawkers erected makeshift hotdog and soda kiosks. Presumably in preparation for the Grand Prix, some of the drivers lapsed around the circuitous track, yelling gleefully at the conclusion of each test-run.

The Grand Prix racetrack evoked memories of my obstreperous German childhood, during which car-racing superstars Rudolf Caraciola and Bernd Rosemeyer dominated the popular sport. I recall neighbors returning from car-racing events with Rosemeyer on their tongues. One could blame them not. Rosemeyer had gained a notoriously popular reputation for deadly speed, while maintaining his exultant status as crowd favorite for his happy-go-lucky, ebullient personality.

I froze on the track's lip, staring at the test-drivers whiz by innocently. Something about their ethereal demeanor was reminiscent of the sad countenances that my neighbors bore upon returning from a Rosemeyer-Caraciola, Auto Union vs. Mercedes Benz exhibition duel on January 27, 1938.

In his opening exhibition race for Benz, Caraciola had set a 268 kph record, placing considerable pressure on his long-time rival. It had been predictably windy when Rosemeyer climbed into his Auto Union closed cockpit special, and jetted down the Autobahn in Frankfurt, which was the starting point for the exhibition race. Rosemeyer had been traveling at more than 270 mph when his automobile caught a crosswind and somersaulted, hurling him into a tree, and thus his untimely death.

"May the thought that he fell fighting for Germany's reputation lessen your grief," proclaimed Adolf Hitler, in a radio address soon thereafter.

Hitler's resonant words rang in my head, waking me from my daydreaming. I walked across the track toward a group of men building stands and offered my assistance.

"*Trabajo, comer,*" (work, eat) I said, in my brutally broken Spanish. After indulging in a few rounds of uncontrollable laughter, the men heeded my request for food in exchange for work.

"*Buen provecho,*" (Enjoy the food) one of the men said, handing me a bun.

I added "*buen provecho*" to my infinitesimal list of Spanish language pleasantries, and watched the practice races free from a kiosk. Afterwards, the men handed me a few bales as makeshift shelter.

My luck was getting better.

Two days later, the Grand Prix was in full swing, and I savored every minute. The perilous speed at which the automobiles circumvented the track and the drivers' daredevil courage fascinated me. They made dizzying tight turns and ruthlessly cut each other off at narrow straightways, huddling together like schools of fish as they jockeyed violently for positioning, which was king in this sport of death. Their daring maneuvers and die-hard persistence appealed to my potent sense of adventure.

The Grand Prix Buenos Aires lasted several days. The soft qualifying races were first, then the preliminaries (the so-called separation of men from boys) and the ultra-competitive finals. Being both pathetically homeless and jobless, I meticulously acquainted myself with the favorite drivers and their signature racecars.

The French standout Jean-Pierre Wimille, known as the uncrowned king of the forties, was particularly aggressive on the track, and soon became a hero to the fans, like Rosemeyer was in his heydays. Daring to the adrenaline-hungry, beer-chugging men and handsome to the many ladies clutching race schedules for later autographs, Wimille incited the most vociferous cheers during the qualifying and preliminary races.

During the finals, the fans were on their feet, cheering and waving frantically as he maneuvered between two cars in a deadly zigzag that galvanized him into second place. Like a sorcerer with death trapped in his pocket, Wimille dangerously veered left and then right, gaining on the oblivious Italian in first place. Aided by a favorable turn and a prodigious burst of speed, the third-placed German nudged closer to Wimille. Soon, all three racers were locked side-by-side as they barreled balefully to the bottlenecked straightaway. The rigid congestion of sparking racecars, scraping metal of each other's fenders, loosened none as the drivers careened to the curve. The horror-struck crowd congealed in utter quietude as the unfortunate inevitable unfolded.

Wimille was clipped from both sides. His car suddenly veered off-line, hitting a tree and turning his Gordini upside down. The crash fractured his scull and the 41-year-old died almost instantly.

Grand Prix staffers flagged the race to a screeching halt. Emergency crewmen scrambled to remove barricade bails, which had once served to safeguard the drivers, but were now barriers to the very audible incoming ambulances. The police commenced attempts to disperse the shocked crowd, but nobody moved. Many fans sat stunned, their eyes fixated on Wimille's body as paramedics cut it loose from a smoking seatbelt. From my nearby kiosk, I witnessed medics strap the grotesque and lifeless body - if I may call it that - to a gurney.

It was not the first time I had whiffed the putrid smell of burning flesh.

Then the silent ambulance taxied away. Certainly, there was little need for celerity or blaring sirens. Having confirmed Wimille's death, the hushed fans laggardly departed their seats; policemen ushered them through a back gate away from the carnage. Aware of my pitiable financial predicament, I stalled until everyone departed, and began scouring under seats for lost change. I picked up a few pesos.

I helped dismantle stands for a little more cash. Soon I was alone again, a proud resident of a bale home. I resorted to shameful begging, stopping anyone who looked European.

"I've just arrived in Buenos Aires, can you please spare a donation," I plead, as people hurried by. "I've been mugged and left with no money!"

Some threw a peso at me, but many simply sneered, and sped past me like I was either invisible or infected with the plague.

The more time I spent as a destitute in Buenos Aires, the more unimpressed I was with the city's mock European architecture. Even the residents now looked dissimilar from the exotic, Latin models I'd earlier perceived. But, I consoled myself with the pleasant weather, which was important to a man sleeping behind straw bales under the watchful eye of a poorly-caste bronze dog.

I begged at various food stands for leftovers.

"*Banana, por favor,*" (Banana, please) I stuttered.

The owners chuckled, but eventually handed me softened *plátanos* (bananas), bruised irrevocably by skeptical shoppers who'd pinched the rinds. In exchange for morsels of food and *leche* (milk), I cleaned stalls. Needless to say, I quickly added leche and plátanos to my limited Spanish vocabulary. One Friday, I accumulated quite a feast: Four bananas and a pint of cold milk. I considered purchasing a Spanish dictionary!

However, after wolfing down the meal, my stomach cramped. The pain was overpowering, and I could barely stand. I alternated bodily positions, but all failed to suppress the sharp stomach pains and the overwhelming dizziness. Soon, to the chagrin of numerous bystanders, I was puking in the street so violently I popped several blood vessels in my cheeks. My eyes began to fail me. I sank to the curb, spitting out morsels of gooey banana still lodged in my mouth.

An eloquently dressed, British-looking businessman, probably in his sixties, had witnessed my convulsions from the sidewalk, but offered no assistance. He turned red as a beetroot when he realized I'd noticed him.

"Can you spare a peso for a man down on his luck?" I asked.

The man rushed off in a huff, and disappeared into a posh restaurant.

I was down and out, but favorable winds were near.

Work as an Artist

The mother of the useful art is necessity. - Arthur Schopenhauer.

One sunny afternoon, from the proceeds of extensive dishonorable begging, I purchased numerous drawing utensils at a ramshackle art store in downtown Buenos Aires. I was most determined to begin cashing in on my artistic talents.

Out of constant youthful boredom, I sketched my first portrait at the tender age of 11. It was an ink portrait of my tall, lanky grandfather, who had a stately but weather-beaten countenance. Elated that he'd discovered the next Albrecht Duerer, my art teacher rushed me to the Academy of Fine Arts in Düsseldorf, where I first studied life drawings. At eleven, the sight of naked women posing for adolescent artists was staggering. All too often, I caught myself nervously erasing and redrawing depictions of breasts and Mt. Venus pubic areas.

"Walter, you're not allowed to create shadows by blotching pencil marks with your finger!" my professor had once yelled, as I had innocently resorted to such natural tactics. "You either use a pencil or charcoal, no finger!"

The professor's barking reminded me of my father's abrasive commands; I didn't like it much. Due to further estrangements with my bearded, weird-looking teachers, I dropped out of the academy two months later, but not before attaining considerable training, which has proven invaluable over the years.

Hunting for the perfect subject to sketch, I strolled into a conservative bistro, where local well-to-do businessmen routinely converged at approximately 11 a.m. for aperitivos or appetizers. The formally dressed waiters scattered aperitivos, consisting mostly of vermouth, and miniature plates loaded with potato salad, cheese, chips, chunks of beef, shrimp, peanuts and other Argentine delicacies. I sat at an empty table near three chatty businessmen.

One of the gentlemen, blessed with a strong jawline and an aquiline nose, seemed the perfect fit for a sound portrait. The waiter eyed my tattered attire suspiciously as I placed my aperitivo order. Even though I was flat broke, it was my risqué way of remaining optimistic that I'd earn some money.

I began sketching the attractive businessman unbeknownst to him. The characteristic stare at my subject, and subsequent sketchpad scribbling, soon caught the fellow's attention. He approached my table, and peered at my sketchbook. I had become versed in Spanish well enough to nod agreeably when he inquired, "*Podría comprar el dibujo cuando lo tiene terminado?*" (" Could I buy the drawing when it's finished ?")

Upon returning to his table with the portrait, the gentleman and his colleagues chattered positively about my artwork, smiling and nodding agreeably. Soon another suited man from the table approached me, requesting that I sketch a portrait of him too. I obliged. As soon as I completed one portrait, another anxious customer waited in the flanks. I earned a few bucks and aperitivos were free.

Visiting the restaurant daily became pleasantly rewarding. The waiters could care less and the guests welcomed me with open arms. New customers seemed inexhaustible. Many insisted I sketch portraits from photos, my expertise exactly. Of course, every day afforded a fresh opportunity to acquire new Spanish words.

During my travails to and fro the restaurant, I mastered the bus and streetcar schedules. Mimicking Argentine youthful exuberance, I hung onto jam-packed buses with a foot on the board and a hand on the door handle. Such reckless rides were free.

Armed with a few pesos and a quasi job, I gradually took favor to the city's name, "favorable winds." However, I remained amply perturbed by my filthy clothes and pungent body odor. I hadn't taken a bath in weeks. That, I hoped, the winds would soon change. The sketching allowance was sufficient to live by. Yet I still resided in my makeshift "hotel" at Parque Belgrano.

After a month, I decided to look Julio up again. I wondered if he'd returned from his sailing tour. I found *Calle Las Heras* by streetcar this time. Julio's grandmother answered the door. Void of a smile or greeting, she ushered me in, and called for Julio. He had indeed returned, and I reckoned my sorry days at "Park Hotel" were over, at least for now.

Julio was just as delighted to see me as he was during our brief friendship in Belgium. His Latinesque brown eyes lit like minute stars, and his signature smile added more spark to his attractive, muscular stature.

"How are you?" Julio asked, gesturing for a bear hug. "Has my country been good to you?"

"*Estoy muy bien, gracias*," (I'm very well, thanks,) I replied.

Upon my initial reply, Julio froze in his tracks. A flurry of dreadful "Park Hotel" images flashed across my mind in response to his suddenly sullen demeanor. I feared the worst.

"*Argentina es muy generoso conmigo!*" (Argentina is very generous with me) I enthused, hugging Julio firmly like it was my last.

"I didn't know you spoke Spanish?" he barked.

Julio spoke sternly like a secret agent interrogating a helpless criminal. I wondered what it was about my Spanish that bothered him, and began strategizing remedies to our sudden estrangement. "Park Hotel" was my darling creation, but I could use some clean sheets and a bath, I thought.

"I've learned the language easily," I replied, wondering why he was more concerned that I spoke Spanish than that I was alive. "My French definitely helped."

I could tell Julio wasn't convinced. He rolled his eyes at me with utmost suspicion.

"Do you think I'm stupid, Walter?" Julio yelled. "Nobody learns a language that fast."

My recurring efforts to convince Julio proved futile, but he agreed to temporarily play host until I secured employment. Apparently, he wasn't as amiable as I'd perceived him to be in Belgium. But, I complained little.

My residence with Julio commenced on rocky terms and persisted in that manner for weeks to come.

Eventually, Julio and I were virtually congruent, even though he never wholly accepted that I spoke no Spanish when we met in Antwerp, Belgium four months prior to our reunion. He unabashedly accused me of fibbing, doubting that I was an avid linguist. Initially, I forgave his abrasive demeanor in exchange for a place to rest my head every night. But my patience soon expired, and I toiled relentlessly to secure employment and a place of my own.

One morning, Julio introduced me to a sign shop owner, which led to my temporary employment as a poster painter for the Buenos Aires subway system. I lost the job in two weeks when the manager discovered I had no papers.

Soon I was in the innovative business of recycling, yanking rusted nails out of used wooden boards. Predictably, that job lasted as long as there were boards. Periodically, I sketched portraits, mostly of children, for many proud, doting parents.

Walking a neighbor's dog Diana each morning brought in only a few pesos, but it was worth the reacquaintance with canine life. I had once been an avid dog aficionado. Walking Diana to empty her bowels every morning invoked skills I had acquired from Ret. Police Officer Schuster, a Düsseldorf neighbor, who schooled me informally in dog training when I was twelve. Every afternoon, Schuster strolled by my house, accompanied by a mismatched, but adorable, pair of a large German shepherd and a black poodle.

"Can I walk with you today?" I asked, starving for adventure as I returned from school one day.

"Yes, you may," Schuster said, smiling as usual. "This is Alf, the big coach, and Hexe, the trainee."

I've loved dogs ever since that adventurous walk.

Despite our occasional indifference, residing with Julio was rather fascinating. I'd never eaten so much beef. Almost every dish in Argentina was cattle-related. Actually, it got rather monotonous.

I also learned to drink wine with soda. To make this peculiar practice convenient, a large soda bottle stood perpetually at the center of most Buenos Aires dining tables, carbonated and under pressure. A small dispenser atop the bottle allowed guests to squirt soda into their wine glasses. Being a German, I considered the wine-soda mixing tradition an insult to good wine.

In the evenings, I often sat outside Julio's home, observing yet another bizarre Argentine tradition. Oddly, a favorite pastime in Buenos Aires involved residents perching in front of their houses in pajamas, reveling cool evenings. That the practice was questionably odd made it something to look forward to.

Eventually, the sofa on which I slept at Julio's house had to be surrendered. One morning, I stumbled through the hallway to the bathroom, clad in only underwear. Julio's grandmother saw me stagger by her doorway. That was it! I was banished from the house at sunrise. Since Julio had departed on another Trans-Atlantic trip, I had no companion on the issue. Besides, grandmother was the boss - she made all the rules.

In her overt aggressiveness and eagerness to dictate, she reminded me of Adolf Hitler. In my youth, I fought against the Reich as a member of *Edelweisspiraten*, a political organization that did anything it could to derail the Hitler Youth, a paramilitary organization designed specifically to wean German youth to the Wehrmacht (German Army). Our rascal tactics included deflating tires and dressing bicycle tail-lights with condoms to embarrass Hitler Youth officers. How I wished such pranks could have availed me of grandmother's Hitlerish dictatorship.

I was on the vicious streets again.

After scouring Buenos Aires for days, I happened upon a park bench on which I sat and meditated without disturbance. Each time I came close to depression, I reminded myself of my tumultuous, but glorious past, and of the prisons and concentration camps, but eventual freedom.

At 16, I considered suicide numerous times whilst in solitary confinement at the infamous Rockenberg Prison near Frankfurt, Germany - by all accounts worst than most concentration camps - as punishment for a third attempted escape.

After a lengthy, bloody horse whipping session, two brutish prison guards threw me in a dark, diminutive solitary cell with a daily menu of six ounces of bread and a pitcher of water. As they did the previous two brutal confinement sessions, they returned 28 days later, after I had shed 25 pounds. Had there been anything sharp in the cell, I would have slit my wrist a thousand times. God knows I tried for I still bear the rugged scars sustained from scratching my wrist against blunt walls.

Such gory memories brought a painful smile to my crackling, dirty face. Even without food, abode and clean clothes, I was markedly better off than then. I mustered the will to live, and sprang from the park bench.

"Tomorrow will be better," I said aloud, bouncing down the street.

Indeed, the next day brought the most pleasant change.

The Shirt on my Back

The fortunate circumstances of our lives are generally found at last to be of our own producing. - Oliver Goldsmith.

It was a foggy Friday evening in Buenos Aires. During my short-lived residence with Julio, I had made a few invaluable friends, who seemed eager to ensure my success. One of them, Gustavo, invited me to a party in Vicente Lopez, an upper class Buenos Aires residential suburb.

A small, relatively inexpensive hotel was my abode at the time. For an incommodious fortnight, I had switched hotels every other night for the scrupulous managers would refuse me accommodation for more than two consecutive days without papers.

I had a single meal everyday. I was broke.

I owned one dingy, tattered shirt, which I wore daily, toiling in the brutal heat. I was certain the party would attract the cream of Buenos Aires' crop, clad in the finest of designer clothing and chic. My host Gustavo was one of Buenos Aires' wealthier bankers. He seemed the perfect key to a gleaming future of employment and possible residence. I wished not to embarrass him.

So the shirt had to be washed. Pressed for time, I scrubbed only sections of it visible to all: The collar, cuffs and breast.

I threw on a concealing coat and boarded a microbus, one of Buenos Aires' most intriguing tourist attractions, graced with vibrant paintings that frequently celebrated Argentine culture and history. The bus chain owners often competed for the prettiest, most colorful vehicles, which typically attracted the most passengers. Each bus bore the name of a saint. An avid artist, I patronized the microbus that boasted the most professional artwork: *Santa Maria* (Holy Mary).

Unlike the raucous streetcars, I loved the more tranquil microbus ride. The streetcars rattled annoyingly with their tight-shut, claustrophobic windows.

The microbus screeched to a halt near Gustavo's mansion. I pranced down the street in optimistic anticipation. Free food and drink awaited me.

The house was colossal, and its architecture, like most of Buenos Aires, was nostalgically European. The flat roof, undecorated walls and rectangular shape was reminiscent of chalet villas one sees scattered about small villages in Southern Europe, except Gustavo's house was surrounded by equally lavish houses, demarcated from each other by chest-high masonry walls.

An aggressive stork-like bird, which screeched loudly as I hesitantly approached the front door, guarded Gustavo's house. Apparently, the tico-ticos were Argentina's most popular "watchdogs" at the time, their ear-splitting squawking the perfect alarm against unexpected intruders.

I skirted around a tico-tico, and rang the doorbell.

"Well, it is Walter, my painter friend," Gustavo said, as he ushered me in. "Please come in. We've been expecting."

"Thank you."

Gustavo, a rather handsome thirty-something-year-old Argentine of Italian heritage, walked me to the living room, adorned with awesome floor-to-ceiling windows. Gustavo's diverse guests stood in small groups chatting. I could hear the castanet-like clicking of women's heels prancing about the parquet floor.

"Walter, pretend the house is yours tonight," Gustavo said. "Remember, this place is packed with wealthy and well-connected business owners, so you should leave with at least five good job leads if you work hard."

"I will secure a job before the night is through," I said. "I assure you."

"That's good," he replied, patting my shoulder. "There is nothing more inspiring and satisfying than a man with confidence. That's rare these days."

Comforted by Gustavo's encouraging words, I asked one of the waiters for a glass of wine, and pounced on a large table, laden with mouth-watering cheese, fruit, pastry and caviar. Intent on hiding my ravenous hunger, I scouted the table like a buzzard circling its deceased meal. After stocking my belly full of appetizers, socializing was next. Even though my German accent distorted my Spanish pronunciations, I could hold my own during most conversations. The tipsy guests couldn't care less anyway.

As the evening aged, the liquor flowed, and the atmosphere got increasingly casual. Soon the living room was an active dance floor of sweaty, drunken couples. I jealousy watched other men rip off their suits. Mine had to stay on, of course, but with all the dancing and subsequent body heat came unbearable discomfort.

Sweat accumulated on my brow as I ogled a scantily dressed David, one of Gustavo's close friends, do an energetic, seductive tango move on an attractive lady whose light dress clung onto her voluptuous body, revealing her sexy curves. I winced in attraction for it had been long since I'd been with a woman. As David slid his knee into the lady's crotch, it became utterly obvious to me why tango was banned in Germany during Hitler's reign.

"Come on Walter, what are you still doing in your coat?" David yelled, over the loud Carlito Gardel tango record.

I was the only one still wearing a coat.

"It's warm and you're among friends!" David said, returning to his obviously impatient tango partner.

"Yes, Walter, you're no longer in formal Europe!" she said, smiling seductively. "Relax and join us!"

"I'm more comfortable in my coat!" I was lying. The heat was unbearable. I was trapped in an embarrassing dilemma.

"I can't, Gustavo," I later explained. "The parts of my shirt that you see are the only parts that are clean."

"Why would you only wash the visible parts of your shirt?" Gustavo asked.

His discernibly loud laughter caught the attention of several inquisitive guests, who quit dancing and moved in on the action that Gustavo and I had roused. As soon as he broke the news of my controversial shirt, the guests were guffawing so hard I couldn't help but join in.

"Why not just put on a clean shirt, Walter?" David joked. "Is this how things are done in Germany?"

I giggled at his superficial suggestion.

"No, this is the only shirt I own."

Walter in Buenos Aires at age 23

David and the other guests laughed boisterously, not out of cruelty (for they were all prosperous people), but I guess it never occurred to them that a person might own only one shirt.

I sensed good fortune when Gustavo patted my shoulder confidently.

"Walter, keep your coat on if you want, but we'll still see to it that you get a job so you can buy all the clothes you like," he said, turning to the crowd. "Right everyone?"

The crowd yelled a collective, "Yes!" some nodding in agreement. Soon the guests rained gifts and goodwill on me like it was my 21st birthday party. One bloke handed me a business card scribbled with directions to a nearby film studio. Argentines were avid moviegoers, thus the studios stayed prolific, constantly seeking well-paid temporary workers.

David's attractive tango partner strutted towards me, and handed me two folded, pressed shirts. Her glossy lips parted slightly as she smiled seductively.

"She has the lips of a champion, doesn't she?" Gustavo asked, grinning boyishly.

"I guess so," I replied.

"Are you kidding me?" he asked. "I bet she gives the world's best fellatio. Think about it. Anybody with lips as supple as hers must be heaven-sent for such sexual purposes. You think God would have blessed her so for no practical reasons, you know, for good, able men like you and me?"

"I have no comment," I replied giggling.

"What do you mean you have no comment? As pleasurable as it is, I'm willing to bet you remember your first time quite well."

"No, I don't."

"Of course, you do!"

David joined the conversation.

"What are you guys talking about?"

"Hello, David, thank Jesus you're here," Gustavo said, pulling David into whispering distance. "You remember your first time right?"

"Don't listen David, he's a little drunk," I warned.

"That's fine, Walter," David insisted, turning to face Gustavo. "First time doing what?"

Gustavo stuck the rim of his dripping beer bottle into his mouth, and slid his lips up and down the slippery, saliva-covered neck. David gasped in shock.

"You know, I've seen you in bad drunken state before, but this, by far, is the worst," David said, turning to leave.

"Come on, David, you're being a bad sport!" Gustavo said, tugging David's shirt. "Do you remember?"

"Okay, okay, yes I do!" David conceded, smiling curtly. "Are you happy now, you filthy drunk?"

"How long did it take for you to come?" Gustavo asked.

I immediately burst into the most hysterical laughter I had had since my childhood days in Germany, so much so that my gut hurt.

Gustavo and I were in tears of joy at David's expense.

"Very funny, Gustavo," David barked, pouting like a tantrumming child as he darted off in a befitting rage.

Soon the lady and I were entangled in a sexy tango lesson, which drenched my new shirt in sweat. I wondered how her lips felt, but never found out.

"Don't thank me, my friend; I take care of my guests," Gustavo said, as I departed later that night. "That's the way it is here in Argentina."

The appealing film studio employment leads led me to the most unexpected prize.

Meeting actor John Carroll

All the world's a stage, and all the men and women in it merely players. They have their exits and their entrances; and one man in his time plays many parts. - William Shakespeare.

I had met Roberto at Gustavo's party. He had offered me what I deemed the strongest job lead in Martinez, a wealthy residential and commercial Buenos Aires suburb. Film studios abounded on the outskirts of Martinez, where I hoped to secure temporary employment as a handyman on a movie set.

By the age of 12, I had developed strong aspirations to become a movie star in Germany, which boasted a prosperous film industry.

In the 1920s and 30s, film directors Friedrich Wilhelm Murnau, Fritz Lang and Ernst Lubitsch produced my favorite classics: "The Blue Angel," "Nosferatu" and "M," thought-provoking dramas often laced with sexual themes and subplots.

One summer morning, my dad and I were outdoors in our lawn fixing the dog's kennel, which had been ruined by a rainstorm the night before.

"Dad, I've made up my mind," I announced, as my dad hammered nails into the kennel roof. "I want to become a movie actor and director."

"A film director?" my father yelled, waving the hammer in my face. "I'll never let you become a peddler of sex and such filth!"

Thus, my father, a self-proclaimed moralist, squelched my film acting and directing dreams, which, in retrospect, may have been a subtle blessing in disguise. Under the ultra-conservative Nazi regime, most notable directors and actors were forced into exile, stifling the motion picture industry for decades. So my acting and directing career would have been squelched nonetheless.

Following Roberto's instructions, I boarded a bus to Martinez, a small town near the scenic Tigre River.

An emotionless, uniformed guard stood by the studio entrance like a Royal Guard at the renowned Birmingham Palace in London.

"*A ver, qué quiere?*" (What do you want ?) he yelled sternly.

"*Busco trabajo,*" (I'm looking for work ?) I replied confidently.

My words seemed magical. Perhaps sensing my German accent, the guard promptly referred me to a middle-aged German named Max. Sporting a Hitleresque mustache and a snug safari suit, Max approached the gate grinning.

Like a teenage boy on his first date, my heart skipped a hundred beats at the prospect of speaking to a fellow German.

"*Verstehen Sie bitte, ich muss unbedingt Arbeit finden,*" (Please, understand, I need to find work) I said, explaining that I was in dire need of employment.

"*Sprechen Sie englisch?*" (Do you speak English?) he asked.

When I nodded, Max pointed at a tall, handsome brunette exiting the studio. It was John Carroll, the famous Hollywood movie star. Alongside gorgeous female co-star Adele Mara, Carroll was in Buenos Aires shooting John Auer's "Los Vengadores," an action movie that was never released theatrically. Also starring in the multilingual movie were Argentine actors Roberto Airaldi, Osvaldo Miranda, and lady heartthrob Fernando Lamas.

"Excuse me, Mr. Carroll, Max sent me over," I said. "He said you may have some work for me. I can paint, sing and write."

Silence. Carroll continued walking like he hadn't seen me.

"I'm a very hard worker," I continued. "I'll do anything."

"Oh yeah," Carroll said, cracking a smile. "That's what the last guy said until I told him to clean my ..."

"Oh, John, must you digress again," Adele interrupted, before veering off to her car.

While I appreciated her Samaritan interruption, Adele was a little too late. Even an idiot could have filled in the last word to Carroll's abrasive statement.

"Alright, follow me," Carroll barked.

The word on Carroll, I later discovered, was that he was nauseatingly conceited, narcissistic and moody. Thus, his co-stars could barely get along with him. With such an irrevocably putrid attitude, it was rather remarkable that Carroll was cast as the lead star of more than 20 Hollywood movies.

Carroll and I clambered into Max's impeccable 1936 Cadillac, idled by the studio's back door with the motor running. Max drove; John and I rode in the back, both of us as stiff as corpses.

Our destination was the large and impressively manicured Martin Estate, which John was leasing while shooting the movie. The estate was graced with an apple-shaped swimming pool and access to the picturesque Tigre River, which attracted hundreds of kayaking, picture-taking tourists annually.

John Carroll's home

"Well, congratulations, Walter, you're my new personal assistant," Carroll said non-challantly, as Max parked the Cadillac in front of the mansion.

Carroll was a man of few words, but I felt discomfited that we conferred not my salary nor the specifics of my employment. I figured once I began work at the presumably fun-filled studio, I wouldn't care. As it turned out, I didn't. Even though I never drew a salary, Carroll was a generous tipper.

I commenced work immediately, arranging Carroll's personal belongings whilst on the set, supervising other servants at the mansion and organizing corporate parties. One of my favorite responsibilities was exchanging U.S. dollars for Argentine pesos in the heart of Buenos Aires. Organizing a party was always a pleasurable opportunity to paint table centerpieces with colorful floral designs, bringing the usually drab furniture to life.

One day, while wolfing down a spoon of gumbo, Carroll, a Louisiana-native, noticed one of my unique centerpieces. He immediately requested that I sketch a portrait of his friend Commander David MacCampbell, the U.S. Congressional Medal of Honor holder and Navy attaché at the U.S. Embassy in Buenos Aires.

Walter with his portrait of Commander McCampbell

MacCampbell's famous World War II squadron became known as "The Fabled Fifteen" after setting records in Japan for the most airborne planes shot down (318), the most aircraft destroyed on the ground (348), and the most aircrafts destroyed in one day (68), nine of which MacCampbell shot down himself.

I painted an arresting life-size watercolor portrait on an abandoned ping-pong table. For a presumably hardened war hero, MacCampbell was exceptionally pleasant and soft-spoken.

"I certainly hope you can make it to the States someday," he said. "We could use more able men like you."

MacCampbell's encouraging words inspired an end product that was so successful that similarly striking artwork of Carroll's other party guests soon ensued. One of the portraits was of Carroll's lovely fiancée Lucille Ryman, who had unexpectedly arrived one searing afternoon from the United States. Lucille was sister to Herb Ryman, one of Disneyland's prominent designers.

"Walter, call me Lucille," she had insisted the first time we met.

Consistently humble and friendly, Lucille seemed an exact opposite to John Carroll, who was forever moody.

One day, while driving to a shoot, John shocked me.

"Walter, would you like to return with me to the United States?" he had asked, breaking a protracted silence.

"Huh?" I replied, struggling to find the appropriate words.

"You heard me."

"I'd love to, sir," I replied, mustering some enthusiasm. "That's my greatest wish."

"Well, let's go to the American Consul in Buenos Aires and see what we can arrange," he said, to my utter surprise and delight. "Tell Max to have the car ready in the morning."

"I certainly will," I stammered.

Pedestrians gawked as we drove into Buenos Aires the next day in the old, but well-kept Cadillac semi-convertible. Some lady fans waved animatedly at Carroll as we drove by. He returned a characteristic rehearsed smile, and waved half-heartedly.

Virtually everyone at the American Consulate recognized and worshipped Carroll. Even the American Consul, Mr. Guerra, greeted him with utmost respect. Needless to say, we jumped the queue.

"I want my assistant, Walter, to return with me to the United States," Carroll asked Guerra. "Is that a problem?"

Carroll's question was the bane of my future. It felt like a million years passed before Guerra replied. Had I been 78, like I am now, I might have had a heart attack.

"I'm sorry, John, but I would have to put Walter on a German waiting list," Guerra said. "It could take up to seven years for him to become eligible for an immigrant visa."

Carroll pried Guerra insistently for an exception to the strict rules, while I babbled the Hail Mary prayer repeatedly in the immediate background. I doubted that She was listening for I could not recollect the last time I had attended church.

To my utmost mortification, Mr. Guerra remained steadfast.

"Walter, why don't you keep in touch; things may change, you never know," he said, trying to comfort me, albeit unsuccessfully.

I detested his consolations, akin to pouring salt on an open wound, more so than the initial rejection.

"Goddamn bureaucracy!" Carroll yelled, as he slammed the Cadillac door. "The Second World War is over, it's time to move on, you fucking idiots!"

Carroll turned to me, and patted my shoulder uncharacteristically.

"Don't worry, Walter, I'm certain I can make something happen once I'm back in the States."

"Sure, I appreciate your concern."

Carroll's generous offer lightened my sorrow momentarily, but acute pangs of realism soon set in once I reminded myself of Carroll's unpredictable and non-promising character. His empty words reminded me of my father Paul, an aficionado of German sayings.

"You talk a lot when the day has twenty-four hours," he would say. I never paid any attention then, but the saying made perfect sense now.

Fernando Lamas was a young actor when I first met him on the "Los Vengadores" set with Carroll. He certainly was not the Latin lover for which he later became Hollywood famous. Lamas had hoped to storm Hollywood as an actor and director. He roomed and swam the estate pool with me.

Rumors had it that he and his wife were mired in marital problems. As one might expect, he was a smooth-talking conversationalist; his pleasant voice charmed many, especially the ladies.

On the set one day, I overheard Lamas seek from Carroll parlous advice on how to gain access into the United States and Hollywood.

"Fall from your horse and break your arm," Carroll snapped, smiling sarcastically. "That'll keep us from meeting the production deadline here. You'll then have to travel to the States to finish filming there."

A few days later, Fernando did in fact fall from a horse, and "break his arm in two places." His sham casts, inscribed with condolences by his many "friends," certainly fooled everyone. As expected, he couldn't finish shooting his part in Argentina. Pressed by a cumbersome deadline, the director decided to culminate filming in Hollywood, and soon departed with the bulk of the cast to America.

Three weeks later, Lamas left Buenos Aires for Hollywood after his arm had "healed." He later married famous swimmer-turned-actress Esther Williams, and became an award-winning actor and director. I never saw him again.

I accompanied Carroll and Lucille to the airport on the sunny bright day that they departed for Hollywood.

"As soon as I get to the States, I'll talk to my attorney about your situation," he said. "He'll figure out a way to get you a visa. Don't worry, I'll get you to the States soon."

As I waved goodbye to Carroll and his fiancée, I envisioned, with a pounding headache, returning to an unpropitious life without a king size bed and a home to cover my head.

In Carroll's absence, I frittered a week away with sweet Carmen, one of the maids at the mansion. Carmen took excellent care of me, so much so that she wound up expecting a marriage commitment. Since matrimony was not in my paramount plans, I escaped her and took brief residence with

Jorge, the estate's gardener. He lived in the gardener's small shack with his wife and three children.

Everyday, I spent many laborious hours collecting leaves and absterging walkways in exchange for the couch at night. Jorge could certainly not afford to pay me, but the family shared the small food they had.

"In memory of Mr. Carroll, I would like to tell you a joke that he once told me," I said at the dinner table during dessert one rainy evening.

We were having *dulce de leche con queso*, finger-length bars of evaporated and sweetened milk dipped in mellifluent cheese.

"You being a master of dirty jokes, I'm not sure I want to take the risk of such pleasures with my three kids at the table, Walter," Jorge warned, swatting a fly from his last bar of dulce de leche.

"Don't worry, Jorge, it's as clean as a whistle," I assured. "Plus, the kids won't pick up a thing anyway. May I?"

"Sure."

Jorge's wife winced at his approval. I proceeded.

"After having their eleventh child, an American couple from Louisiana decided 11 was enough because they could not afford a larger bed," I started. "So, the husband went to his veterinarian, and told him that he and his cousin didn't want to have any more children."

Mimicking their parents, the three kids giggled behind their palms.

"Hey kids, be quiet!" Jorge warned. "Go on, Walter."

"Anyway, the doctor told him that there was a procedure called a vasectomy that could fix the problem, but that it was expensive. The doctor said a less costly alternative was to go home, get a cherry bomb, light it, put it in an empty beer can, then hold the can up to his ear and count to ten."

"I know where this is going," Jorge's wife said.

The entire family was teary-eyed in surmounting laughter, and I had yet to narrate the most humorous.

"No, you don't. Anyway, the American said to the doctor, 'I may not be the smartest man in the world, but I don't see how putting a cherry bomb in a beer can next to my ear is going to help me.' 'Trust me,' said the doctor. So the man went home, lit a cherry bomb and put it in a beer can."

"Oh my God, Mister Walter, what happened to him," whined Jorge's genuinely concerned 13-year-old daughter, denoting the rest of my audience's sudden transformation from cheery to lugubrious demeanor.

"Listen, and you might find out," I replied, smiling mischievously. "He held the can up to his ear, and began to count with his free hand. 'One!' 'Two!' 'Three!' 'Four!' 'Five!' Then he stopped, placed the beer can between his legs, and continued counting on his other hand."

Silence.

"This procedure also works in other backward American states like Alabama, Oklahoma, Mississippi and Arkansas," I concluded, nervous that my joke was for naught.

The family was completely benumbed, as if still awaiting my humor. It had long come and gone, and yet they sat calm, rubbernecking me like a frazzled trapeze artist caught in a crumbling circus act. I felt miserable. The joke had been belly-slapping hilarious when John Carroll had told it.

Then, suddenly, after protracted silence, Jorge relieved my anguish. He started cachinnating, spewing morsels of dulce de leche across the table in the process. Then his wife followed, and then the children, as a consolation prize.

"That's much better," I said, heaving sighs of relief. "I was just starting to doubt your intelligence."

"Even though it took me a while to process, that was a good one, Walter," Jorge conceded, dabbing tears from his eyes. "I've heard before that Americans aren't that smart. I guess this is proof."

When the powers that be eventually leased the mansion out again, the new renters brought their own management staff, which meant we all had to vamoose. Jorge and his family packed up and moved to Buenos Aires, hoping to find employment.

John Carroll's former studio managers knew me quite well, so I soon secured a job as janitor at the film studio near Martinez. The pay was meager, but I found sleeping solace in the many abandoned, yet still lightly furnished sets. I resided there for weeks, hoping to hear from Carroll.

"I have your visa for the States," I repeatedly imagined Carroll would say in his letter, which never arrived.

One day, a studio guard caught me sleeping in the property room. I was promptly fired.

It was time to move on.

I headed back to Buenos Aires, and sketched at *Plaza Italia* for pocket money, praying daily that Carroll would leave word with Mr. Guerra once the visa was ready.

In the meantime, my livelihood nosedived.

A Dose Of Wrestling Cures Poverty

Amusements are to virtue, like breezes of air to the flame; gentle ones will fan it, but strong ones will put it out. - David Thomas.

Buenos Aires offered ample financial opportunities as an artist, yet my stay there was rather brief. I went scouring for a job at the film studios again, but found nothing. A wiry female secretary with a snappy attitude ordered that I return in a month. I figured I'd try back in two.

As I stormed out of the fruitless studio, I ran into Jorge's sociable cousin, Alfredo, whom I had first met while quartering at Martin Mansion. Unemployed, impecunious and audacious, Alfredo and I had a lot in common. We decided to chat over dinner.

"Do you like *lucha libre* (freestyle wrestling)," he asked, gleaming with enthusiasm as he wolfed down a mouthful of *salchicha* (Argentine hotdog).

"Yes," I replied. "I encountered the finest Graeco-Roman wrestlers in Europe, while traveling with the Hitler Youth swimming team in Germany."

"Well, I have one extra ticket," Alfredo enthused. "My cousins didn't feel like going."

So it came to be that I became the lucky recipient of one ticket to see a slate of *lucha libre* fights in downtown Buenos Aires.

I munched on my *salchicha* as we boarded the bus to Luna Park, an arena fervently popular for featuring freestyle wrestling matches. It was near the Retiro Railroad Station, which ignited teary-eyed memories of my arrival in Buenos Aires and Chris. I wondered how he was doing in Europe. I often missed him. Luna Park was plastered with full-sized macho posters, and rabid fans hustled their favorite wrestlers for autographs. *Lucha libre* was apparently a highly favored sport. I was thrilled, and could care less about a place to sleep that chilly night. The largest and most menacing posters were those of *Hombre Montaña* (the mountain man), an enormously large man that looked more like a gorilla.

Our seats were conveniently close to the ring. A few boastful wrestlers in tight spandex costumes mounted the podium, yelling gesticulatively. In between their guttural roars and the screeching microphone, I lost perception of their speech.

"He's insulting and challenging another wrestler," Alfredo explained. "He promises to make pudding out of him."

Then came a few pretty models with large boobs clutching boards that advertised upcoming rounds and fights. A short rotund referee boarded the ring and soon thereafter the barbaric wrestlers. I felt like I was sitting in a deadly bullring. The wrestlers were the enraged bulls, pinned with sharp *banderillas*, darts with streamers attached stuck into the neck and shoulders of a bull by eager *banderilleros*.

The first bout featured a masked wrestler *El Indio*. His opponent *Vikingo* sported a scruffy beard and long blond hair. I mused at the heavyweight men flipping through the air like 80-pound trapeze artists. The crowd roared sonorously as *Vikingo* hurled his opponent over the ropes. The referee promptly whistled the fight to an end, and awarded victory to *El Indio*, hoisting his limp arm in the air. In protest, *Vikingo* grabbed the ref by the shirt and shook him vigorously. After much ado, *Vikingo* departed the ring in a huff.

"How in the world can he be the winner when he's barely conscious?" I asked.

"Apparently, it is against *lucha libre* rules for a wrestler to throw another over the ropes," Alfredo clarified. "You'll figure it out as the night progresses."

Two more fights ensued before the main bout. It was *Hombre Montaña* vs. *Hermanos de la Selva*, two brawny brothers who resembled indigenous Indians from the heart of the Amazon jungle. When *Hombre Montaña* approached the ring, the audience roared rabidly. He wore black knee-length boots and a colorful cape on his broad muscular shoulders. The mountain man looked menacing with his long dark hair bound with a colorful bandana.

I glanced at my fight schedule: "*Hombre Montaña*: 430 pounds." The concrete floor under our nearby seats trembled vigorously as he clambered over the ropes. After strutting across the ring thrice, he subsequently folded his cape neatly and placed it in his corner.

As was necessitated by *lucha libre* rules, one Indian remained in the ring while the other was relegated to a corner behind the ropes. Wasting no time, the Indian kicked *Hombre Montaña* in the mid-section sending him writhing on the bouncy canvass. Taking advantage of the big man's frailty, the Indian delivered another firm kick. This time the mountain man grabbed the Indian's leg and threw him into the air. The Indian yelled, stumbled to his corner and tagged his partner. *Hombre Montaña* waited confidently.

The energetic Indian dove for the big man's legs and befell him. Sensing seemingly inevitable victory, the smiling Indian dragged *Hombre Montaña* to his partner. They tagged again, and one Indian leapt over the ropes, pinning the big man to the sweaty canvass. The unfaithful audience quickly switched sides, and began roaring for the brothers.

Things didn't look good for *Hombre Montaña*, Argentina's most popular wrestler.

Suddenly, as if summoning strength from his own demise, *Hombre Montaña* clutched and snapped the Indian's arm. Then he laggardly rose to his feet to the crowd's resonant chants of, "*Hombre Montaña!*" He grabbed the Indian by his ankle, swirled him around a few times, and hurled him at his unsuspecting partner, who subsequently biffed the concrete floor outside the ring. Both Indians lay helplessly, one on the canvass and the other on the concrete, as the ref counted to three. Surprisingly, the Indian in the ring rose to his feet on the second count, while his partner hustled back to his corner.

The referee restarted the bout. What ensued was an absolute repeat show. *Hombre Montaña* picked up the Indian, swirled him around thrice above his shoulders and threw him at his partner. This time the Indians seemed unconscious. The referee counted them out, and hoisted *Hombre Montaña's* right arm. The audience went wild as the mountain man conducted his characteristic victory dance. After the encore event came some minor fights, all properly staged.

I wondered why men clamored to see other men get pummeled. The absurd spectacle was reminiscent of Roman gladiator fights where unfortunate slaves waged unfair battle against 250-pound lions.

"*Te gustó?*" (You liked it?) Alfredo inquired as we departed Luna Park.

"*Sí, mucho,*" (Yes, much) I assured him.

Near the large exit was a job advertising sign that read, "*Se necesita masajista. Informes en la oficina al lado.*" (Masseur needed. Inquiries in the office next door)

"What is a *masajista*," I asked, as we walked through the exit doors.

"A *masajista* is a masseur," Alfredo explained.

"Thank you."

The ad ignited an interest and I committed to investigating the job opportunity the next day.

"Why do you ask?" Alfredo inquired curiously.

"Nothing, I was just wondering," I lied.

The light blue signature Buenos Aires sky spilled a ticklish drizzle on my adolescent face as I arrived at Luna Park the next day, murmuring to Holy Mary for employment. The sign the night before had tickled my fancy so much that I drooled at the prospect of becoming a masseur. It was the second time I had prayed in a month. Mary had forsaken me when I had sought assistance with Mr. Guerra, the American Consul, in my quest for a visa to Hollywood. Hopefully, She was listening this time.

"*Buen dia,*" (Good day,) I said, greeting the beautiful, zaftig secretary seated behind the Luna Park reception desk.

"*Buen dia, en qué le podemos servir?*" (How can we help you ?) she asked, ogling me seductively.

Clad in a snug bright red dress-suit that caressed her eight-figure attractively, Mona, as her name badge plainly indicated, was gorgeous with her pony-tailed, pitch-black hair and full lips. She was a walking red rose; I loved her scent.

"I saw the sign; I'm here to apply for the masseur job," I said, returning a coquettish stare of my own.

Sensing that I had bitten her flirtatious hook, Mona ogled further, sizing me up, examining my every bodily contour and curvature. I felt her eyes rip the shabby clothing of my chest and thighs. I wondered how soft her lips felt.

"Do you have experience?" she asked, halting the slight erection I'd begun to develop.

"Yes, I certainly do," I replied confidently.

The Hitler Youth swimming team had an eminently seasoned staff masseur Hans Giessen, who eventually trained Germany's kayak team in the 1968 Mexico Olympics. In Nazi Germany, grocery welfare coupons, which one could conveniently exchange for rationed bread, meat and fat products at any grocery store, were key to daily existence for the poor and underprivileged. However, there was a stinging catch. To obtain treasured coupons from the stingy welfare office, one was required to furnish extensive proof of employment. So, at the age of 20, I signed up as Giessen's apprentice. My impeccable six-month, unpaid training under him was exceedingly invaluable for it won me numerous jobs over the years. Giessen later became one of Germany's most successful homeopaths.

"It's hard work, you know," Mona offered. "And the pay is not very good."

"Well, tell me a little about the job and the compensations?" I asked.

"I love your accent," she said, rekindling her flirtation.

"Thank you," I replied curtly, getting impatient.

Her seductive stare felt good, yet uneasy.

"I'm sure you'd do just fine, but you must talk to the manager first," she said. "I hope to see you later."

Mona was really flirting now, but I didn't mind at all.

"The manager will be with you in just a moment," she said, fumbling with some paperwork while sneaking a few more peeks.

I promptly returned her smile, certain I'd see more of her.

The burly, rotund manager stomped into the reception area slamming his office door behind him. Edi was a big, bald-headed and dark-skinned former wrestler.

"Please sit down," he said.

With his perpetual smile and raspy chuckle, Edi was rather affable and munificent for a man who once earned a living pummeling other wrestlers. A plethora of his championship belts and plaques graced the office walls.

While Edi sorted paperwork with Mona, I ensconced myself in the reception area armchair, patiently awaiting my interview, which ended up being unexpectedly straightforward and concise.

"We expect you here every day from 9 a.m. to 2 pm," he instructed. "The massage table is in the large room behind the ring. You'll be expected to perform four massages everyday. After 2 pm, you can have lunch in the cafeteria behind this office. We'll pay you 10 pesos an hour and lunch is on the house. Does that sound okay?"

I had never heard a man talk so fast, but I caught the impressive "10 pesos an hour." Mona's earlier warnings now seemed laughable.

"May I see the facilities?" I asked. "I haven't done that many massages in such a relatively short time. I would most appreciate it if I could experiment a bit. You know, to see how things work out?"

Edi deemed my suggestions fair, and set my first assignment for Monday morning. It was Friday.

"I look forward to working here," I said, trying hard to impress my new employer. "May I ask one more question?"

"Of course," Edi said, his rosy face beaming with enthusiasm.

"Would I be allowed to watch the wrestling matches with my friends?" I inquired, recalling my earlier hilarious experience watching fan favorite *Hombre Montaña* pound the two Indian brothers.

"You may bring two friends," Edi replied. "The men at the gate will recognize you."

Edi asked Mona to record my name and address. She smiled, delighted to heed the task for a golden opportunity to resume our conversation.

"Are you married?" she asked, as Edi shut his office door behind him.

"No, thank God," I said laughing aloud.

"How long have you been in Buenos Aires?"

"Since January."

"I'd like very much to show you around our lovely city," she offered, leaning over her desk, revealing sexy cleavage. "Would you like that?"

"Forgive my brazen forwardness, but are you married?" I asked, enjoying her bosom display.

"No, thank God!.... Do you have plans for Sunday?"

"No," I said.

"Well, why don't we meet at Retiro Station on Sunday at 2 pm," she said decisively, like she'd planned the date two weeks ago. "Does that sound okay?"

"I'll be there, come rain or shine," I assured.

I bounced out of the building whistling a Lily Marlene tune with a smile glued to my face. Ten pesos sounded splendid, and the prospect of dating even more so.

"Were all Argentine women flirtatious like Mona?" I thought to myself, as I boarded the streetcar to Alfredo's nearby house.

If anyone deserved to hear the good news first, it was Alfredo, to whom I felt indebted for introducing me to Luna Park. At dinner, I divulged my favorable fortune to his hospitable family, but kept Mona classified information. The two teenage boys were particularly thrilled about free wrestling matches. Alfredo's brother, an outbound salesman, had travelled on some long-distance sales call, so I harbored temporarily in his lavishly furnished bedroom.

It was 2 pm on a limpid Sunday, and I paced Retiro Railroad Station scouting for my date. She arrived five minutes late, sporting a tight, flowery dress that accentuated her slim, attractive body. I craved to touch her voluptuous breasts, which looked rather appetizing under her scanty dress and discernable bra. Her firm boobs were undoubtedly genuine for they bounced smoothly as she cat-walked towards me. We strolled around the station holding hands like teenage lovebirds.

"You look beautiful," I started. "I'm sorry I don't have a camera."

"*Gracias, muchísimas gracias, es Usted todo un caballero,*" (Thank you, thank you a lot, you are quite a gentleman) she said, praising my courteous words.

Being called a gentleman amplified my arousal for Mona. I couldn't wait to be alone with her, away from the faceless walkers-by and chirpy pigeons; away from all that kept us uncomfortably aloof.

We sauntered through Plaza San Martin, a lush, peaceful square named after General José de San Martin, who spearheaded Argentine independence from Spain in 1816. We sat underneath the imposing statue of the general riding a horse and clutching a stately sword.

"May I kiss you?" I asked, as I felt a warm paste hit my nose.

It stank. As Mona giggled away, I looked up, and spotted a couple of pigeons fraternizing atop the general's outstretched arm.

"Not here, silly, let's go to my apartment," Mona said, pointing at the pigeons.

There I stood, red with embarrassment, even as Mona's heartening words only rekindled a fiery sexual crave between us, as I dabbed the pigeon droppings from my face with tissue.

"Let's go, I crave to kiss you," I said 15 minutes later. "Very badly indeed."

"I didn't know Germans were so hot-blooded," she said giggling.

We left Plaza San Martin via cab, for which Mona seemed perfectly at ease paying. I wasn't, and informed her so.

"Once you make money, you pay for the cab, okay?" she said emphatically.

"Okay," I replied, feeling relieved. I didn't have the money anyway.

Mona's miniature apartment was spotless. A medium-sized, sparingly furnished living room bled neatly into the dining room, which in turn flowed into the small kitchen. A life-sized Molina Campos painting, depicting a Gaucho riding a horse, dominated the living room back-wall.

"Would you like something to drink?" she asked, as she casually flung her scarf on the couch.

"No, thank you, I feel like eating and drinking you."

"My God, are you German or are you a Gypsy?"

"Both," I joked. "I'm the perfect sexual mutt."

She laughed sexily. I was aroused already.

"Well I'd like to take a bath," Mona whispered, as she pushed the play button on the record player.

It was another sultry tango song by Carlito Gardel, who seemed rather trendy in Argentina.

"Why don't you join me?" she suggested.

An idea had never sounded so wonderful. As I planted kisses on her supple neck, we stumbled to the bedroom where we aggressively undressed. I was darn correct about her breasts, graced with firm pink nipples, and complimenting her body quite fittingly.

The heated lovemaking began underwater in the bubbly bathtub, and culminated in Mona's queen-sized bed. I was in paradise. After the sexual pleasure and subsequent climax, we sprawled under the sheets naked, whispering pleasantries to each other like lovers generally do.

"You must be hungry, it's been a long afternoon," she said sliding from underneath the sheets to her closet.

There was ample warmth and concern in her voice like a doting mother to an infant.

"A little bite won't hurt," I said. "But don't go through any trouble."

"No trouble at all," she said smiling.

I cringed in frustration when Mona threw on an opaque robe and strolled to the kitchen. Dinner was ready a few minutes later. I guessed the menu right: Beef. Ravenous from energy-depleting lovemaking, we wolfed down crackers with meat out of a can. Mona served wine without soda.

"You needn't drive all the way to your friend's house tonight," she suggested. "Why don't you spend the night with me; here you're closer to Luna Park.

I hesitated, remembering my many impressions upon Edi.

"I'll prepare a nice breakfast for you in the morning?" Mona said.

How could I not accept her tempting invitation? We made passionate love again and, quite exhausted, I slept deeply near Mona until about 7:30 a.m. when presumably she silently rose to prepare breakfast. At approximately 8 a.m., I felt a tender kiss on my forehead.

"It's time for breakfast, *mi amor* (my love)," she whispered. "Remember, you need to be at work at 9 a.m."

We had coffee and *pan dulce* (sweet bread), and boiled eggs.

"Would you like cream and sugar," she asked.

"Just a little sugar and a little cream, please."

I had difficulty comprehending the fortunate string of events, spanning from meeting Mona at her office to making sweet love for the first time in weeks. Now a delicious breakfast? Was this Holy Mary's way of answering my prayers?

It felt like I had been dating Mona for decades. She was compassionate, considerate and big-hearted. This was too much for a young homeless man. But Mona wasn't cognizant of my condition, and I kept it that way.

Leaving for work was a mountainous task. I was tempted to make love all over again as Mona kissed me goodbye, but the new job was waiting, and Edi was too nice to disappoint.

"Be careful," she said.

I arrived at Luna Park at 8:55 a.m.

"Come with me," Edi said. "I'll introduce you to some of the wrestlers, your clients."

I trailed him to the "Workout Room," furnished with a massage table fixed in the center of the room. Behind the table stood a row of hissing showers, out of which several nude heavyweights soon clambered. The wrestlers seemed at peace naked to the world.

"*Buen dia (good day), this is Walter, our new masseur,*" Edi said. "Please be nice to him."

One of the wrestlers, sporting dark Latinesque hair and a moustache, was exceptionally muscular and tall. His arm was the size of my waist, and he spoke with *mucho gusto* (much pleasure), perhaps signifying leadership status.

"Have you figured out the order of things here?" Edi asked the imposing wrestler. "Who's first?"

"Rico's first, then Bruno and then I, Carlos," he said. "Guapo is last today."

After Edi left the workout room, a disrobed Rico mounted the massaging table. How the flimsy board had supported such elephantine bodies is still a profound obscurity to me.

Work began. I corralled a stack of towels and a bottle of fragrant oil from a small shelf near the showers.

My massaging session with Rico began with his limbs, each the size of a healthy ten-year-old. He heaved little sighs of comfort as I worked his back. Then it was flipping time. I tossed a towel over his private parts as he made the swift turn. He whistled contentedly as I kneaded my hands from his broad shoulders to his King Kong-like hairy chest. A foot massage concluded the session.

The sessions lasted 45 minutes. That afforded me a 15-minute interlude to relax between clients.

"*Muy bueno, gracias,*" (very well, thanks) thanked Rico.

Bruno was next, and then Carlos.

"Apply more pressure," Carlos yelled.

Of course, this meant I had to throw on my entire body weight, but even that was insufficient for the huge wrestler.

Guapo was last in line. I wondered why he was named so for Guapo meant "pretty boy." Indeed, he was an Apollo. Chest high and ripped all over, Guapo strutted to the massage table showing off his beautifully proportioned body. His black hair was impeccably combed. Despite being handsome and cocky, he was rather kind. After the massage, he invited me for lunch.

In the cafeteria, I ran into Mona at one of the tables, chatting with another lady.

"*Buen dia*," I said flatly, giving little indications that we knew each other intimately. She understood.

The lunch was more like a dinner, slabs of meat hanging over the plate, potatoes, gravy and vegetables.

"*Buen provecho*," Guapo said, giggling at my startled demeanor. "We big boys need lots of nutritious food."

The waitress returned with a tray of *dulce de leche con queso*, an Argentine delicacy, and a small mug of strong espresso.

"You'll grow while you're here, and you'll eat more," Guapo said, humoring my discomfort.

"*Hasta mañana*," I said, as I dragged from the table at lunch's end.

I had never eaten so much.

Mona tugged my shirt as I marched out of the building.

"Why don't you come to my place later?" she plead.

"After massaging four huge men, I need some rest," I explained. "Let's wait until tomorrow."

Mona was understanding so I boarded the bus to Alfredo's place, and snoozed from 6 p.m. until 6 a.m. the next day.

The next few workdays were a carbon copy of the first. The wrestlers were surprisingly nice and the food was manageable. I longed to cash my first paycheck.

I spent my weekends with Mona, who spoiled me rotten.

"Mom and dad, I'm doing great," I wrote in my usual weekly letter to my parents. "There's no reason to worry about me."

One Friday night, I took Alfredo's generous family to Luna Park for a slate of *Lucha Libre* wrestling matches. The boys seemed highly impressed that I knew the wrestlers personally.

Three random events derailed my comfortable course, leading to my resignation as masseur of the heavyweights and untimely separation from Mona.

Guapo was a sympathetic listener to my many horrific adventure stories. On several occasions, he offered to take me out dancing but I declined, all to spend more time with Mona instead. One day, during one of our massage sessions, Guapo had an erection and motioned to embrace me. I backed off politely.

"You need a cold shower," I yelled.

He apologized.

"Don't worry, I understand," I said.

In Germany under Hitler, the Gestapo would've arrested Guapo for his homosexual behavior. The Third Reich had routinely persecuted and wrongfully imprisoned homosexuals in hostile concentration camps.

One day, Mona invited me to visit her parents in La Plata, west of Buenos Aires. Her offer sounded too much like a marital commitment. I struggled to explain my feelings.

"There's an important man from America visiting me this weekend," I lied. "Remember, I told you I was waiting for a visa to the States."

Once again, Mona understood.

"We'll do it some other day," she replied.

Alfredo's traveling salesman brother returned earlier than expected. I was homeless again.

The next day, I resigned at Luna Park without explanation. Of all the heavyweights, *Hombre Montaña*, the ferocious gorilla who turned out to be a very soft-spoken gentleman, was my favorite. The stocky men were superb athletes and fine actors. I knew I'd miss them all, but I never returned to Luna Park.

For the weekend, I revisited the Zanzibar Nightclub, a posh hangout spot I once frequented with John Carroll. My thoughts were with Mona, and I was often tempted to call or visit her. I never did.

New adventures awaited me.

Crooner at the Zanzibar

Both music and painting add a spirit to devotion, and elevate the ardor. - Lawrence Sterne.

The ritzy Zanzibar Nightclub, located in Buenos Aires' picturesque downtown, was true heaven on earth, at least so John Carroll and I concluded after visiting thrice together.

Zanzibar was strategically situated on the ever-active corner of Córdoba and Maipú streets. For a relatively inconspicuous hole-in-the-wall, the Zanzibar drew more than its fair share of diamond-wearing, high-caliber customers. Adorned with a high-arching decorative ceiling, the club's small rectangular space featured a podium with a piano, a curved bar and nine tables.

Three days after suddenly fleeing Mona and Luna Park, I found myself swinging into the night-crawler enclave for some action.

It was comforting chatting my sacred mother tongue with Zanzibar's two German-Argentine waiters. While my Spanish had become near impeccable, the opportunity to speak German brought back golden family memories. Grotesque pictures of excruciating concentration camp life flashed through my damaged, yet healing, youthful mind as we chattered away.

Zanzibar was popular for featuring a solo singer every night. As I strolled into the club, an attractive black man in his thirties, Charlie, broke out in soulful love-singing as he stroked the grand piano animatedly. Charlie's voice was so angelic, lucid and melodic, he sang without backup. A breathtaking voice often won Charlie more than the characteristic boisterous applause, for, like inevitable clockwork, he swung out of Zanzibar very night with a different gorgeous chic clinging to his strapping arms.

I envied Charlie's good fortune.

My new residence was a small shoddy hotel near the club, so I visited often. One night, to the utmost disillusionment of a discontent lady-laden audience, Charlie simply failed to show up, the small raised stage disappointingly vacuous. The club's good-looking manager, Monica, who had previously turned down several of my advances, cringed visibly as displeased customers trickled out of the club. Without Charlie, a few loyal customers idled at their tables drinking. They could certainly do that at presumably two hundred other joints in town.

I was young, mischievous and adventurous, so I clambered onto the stage and grabbed the microphone to the perceivable chagrin of the audience.

My singing training began in Düsseldorf when I was only 15. One chilly winter morning, local opera singer Helmut Krebs, a close friend of the family, had paid my parents an unexpected visit. He had overheard me singing and whistling in the shower.

"Walter has a promising voice," Krebs said, as I had scurried across the living room to my bedroom. "Would you mind if I gave him some singing lessons?"

My parents had obliged, and so it was that my singing training had begun. The moment of truth came three months later when I stood onstage facing a stern-looking panel of judges preparing to sing Franz Schubert's "*An die Musik,*" an undulating, utterly challenging song.

I was nervous, so was my voice.

The test, for admission into *Hochschule für Musik* (Music Conservatory), Cologne's prestigious conservatory, had been designed to specifically separate men from boys, Germany's future outstanding soloists from the many less popular choir members.

I only made the choir, and thus quit my short-lived singing career soon afterwards.

My singing has been restricted to parties with fellow drinkers, reveling drunken camaraderie, since that disappointing March afternoon in Cologne.

The Zanzibar Nightclub had virtually become my home, so I had easily memorized three key ballads in Charlie's extensive repertoire. I bobbed the microphone before bellowing out the romantic lyrics to Frank Sinatra's "Night and Day" in my schmaltzy, baritone voice.

The audience swooned in jaw-dropping awe as my voice sailed saliently across the club. The stage was eerily dark. Thus, I could not seek approval from spectators' countenances, but I accepted silence as encouragement. Soon I was bowing out courteously as the patrons applauded.

No sooner had I sauntered off the stage, did the lights flicker back on.

"Walter! Walter! Walter!" the crowd yelled, encouraging me to proceed.

I sang "Heartache," a lady favorite, and concluded my brief stardom with a golden oldie number that began with the line: "I love you for sentimental reasons."

"Sing another one," one woman yelled. "What are you waiting for?"

Descanting away like a canary on a borrowed stage felt rewarding, but the obnoxious fans made me blush.

"What the hell," I whispered to myself.

I sang "Night and Day" again. Emboldened by the subsequent rabid applause, I added Marlene Dietrich's famous melancholic love song "Lilli Marlene" in German. Singing the tune's high discant notes reminded me of gorgeous sex symbol Dietrich, an utterly famous German-American actress and singer, belting the Lilli Marlene lyrics: "Outside the barracks by the corner light, I'll always stand and wait for you at night," to sex-starved, drooling American troops in North African and European bases during World War II.

"If she had nothing more than her voice, she could break your heart with it. But she has that beautiful body and the timeless loveliness of her face. It makes no difference how she breaks your heart if she is there to mend it," writer Ernest Hemingway once wrote of Dietrich.

After warbling "Heartache" a tiring third time, I laggardly returned to my seat. Drinks were on the house.

"Walter, why didn't you tell us you had such a marvelous voice," Monica whispered, eyeing me seductively. "Would you like to sing every night, to me?"

I squirreled away her flirtatious requests for later.

I returned nightly as Charlie's opening performer. The routine was simple: I sang my three songs repeatedly, added "Lilli Marlene" as an encore, and introduced Charlie.

Unruly sailors traveling through Buenos Aires would often demand that I belt out more tunes. Unbeknownst to them, my repertoire was rather limited. To the drunken sailors, however, I simply chose not to perform what they wanted to hear. Their animosity often boiled over, and they would occasionally swear.

"Fuck you!" one yelled. "What are you, a tape recorder? Sing something else!"

The salary at the Zanzibar was little, but sufficient to cover my hotel room. When the opportunity arose, I slouched at a table, and sketched hasty portraits for customers.

My stardom and sudden financial freedom was rudely disrupted when la policía arrived on the scene.

One night, a hefty Englishman stomped into the Zanzibar Nightclub during my singing performance. Soon he was drunk.

"Sing Lilli Marlene in English, you bloody Nazi," he yelled, discontent with my German belting.

When I continued descanting, he screamed derogatory comments.

"Fucking Nazis think they can fuck up everything. Now South America?" he yelled, tossing his empty paper cup on-stage. "Why don't you go back to Germany, you bloody piece of shit!"

Since my Nazism experience involved being an inmate in shuddersome concentration camps, I certainly did not appreciate being called a "bloody Nazi." The Englishman's foul language intensified as I walked off the stage. He was pestering for a fight, and I was more than willing to dish out one.

We stepped outside.

The tall, obese Englishman looked like he weighed 250 pounds. Under normal circumstances, I was no match for him, but he was amply sluggish, and too bleary eyed from alcohol to present much of a threat.

"Go home before you get hurt," I warned, using a little psychology that only infuriated him even more.

I riveted a firm punch to his jelly-like gut, expecting him to remain standing as the equally mountainous villains often did in numerous action movies. But the Englishman slumped to the ground helplessly like a crumbling stack of cards.

It was my easiest fight.

"I'll pay you back," he groaned, resisting my attempts to alleviate him to his feet. "Watch your steps!"

Disregarding his hollow threats, I returned to sketching portraits for my waiting customers.

"What happened Walter?" one of the waiters asked, as I bounced back to my table.

"I had to teach the man a lesson," I boasted, as they giggled sonorously.

Two police officers apprehended me as I walked out of the Zanzibar at 2 a.m. later that morning. Soon I was in the police station under intense interrogation.

One of my interrogators was Captain Gomez, a rather handsome man in his forties, who, like most Argentine men, seemed more concerned about his looks than he perhaps should have. His greasy black hair was neatly combed, complimenting his impeccably clean uniform. Captain Gomez' every other sentence was preceded with a light pat on the coif like a model or politician in front of flashing cameras.

"What is your employment at the Zanzibar Nightclub?" he barked.

"I draw portraits for customers," I replied. "I'm an artist."

Like I had uttered words from a magic book, the questioning ceased, and the officers began whispering to each other.

"Can you do a sketch of me?" Captain Gomez asked, breaking the silence and grinning apologetically.

"Do you have any special requests?' I asked, sensing that my artistic training had saved me once again.

"Make me look like a German officer," he said, sinking into a chair across the interrogation room.

Decorated with cross-chest leather straps and long collared trench coats, the Argentine police uniforms were eerily similar to Wehrmacht attire. I met the captain's request effortlessly; other police officers soon followed. Desperate to secure my freedom, I portrayed each officer exactly as he wished.

I was the 'artist in residence.'

"It's rather early in the morning, and I'm a little tired," I suggested, three hours later. "Can I return some other time?"

My leading question was petrifying. Would Captain Gomez rightfully resume his interrogation? Would my labor be in vain?

"Of course, of course," the captain said, looking askance, to my utmost relief. "Would you like some coffee?"

Sipping the smoking-hot espresso gingerly, I glanced at the dusty ticking clock. It was noon, much later than I'd expected. Neither one of the officers had recounted my arrest. I wisely elected not to remind them.

Captain Gomez walked me to his patrol car, and dropped me off at the hotel.

"Visit when you're in our area again," he said, as I climbed out of the patrol car.

I was incognizant that I'd be forced to return there soon.

Three days after my initial visit to the police station, I was rooted in a front-seat at a cinema on Corrientes Avenue, Buenos Aires, intensely watching a dubbed John Wayne Western.

I chuckled listening to John Wayne 'speak' Spanish. The movie was near-end; in its climax to be exact. I sat there, patiently waiting for Wayne to aggressively apprehend the senseless bad guys.

Suddenly, a rough hand caressed my thigh. Lo and behold, the burly, dark-haired man seated next to me was putting a seductive move on me in the dark.

I slid away twice, but the hand followed me each time. Eventually, I lost my patience, and slapped the man's face. An elder lady behind us screamed, drawing the fixated stares of an entire theater.

When a young police officer arrived at the scene a few minutes later, the movie was still playing, albeit unnecessarily. The audience was now watching the homosexual and I bicker like teenage girls. Our fracas was certainly more interesting entertainment than 'Spanish-speaking' John Wayne killing his hundredth villain.

"*Qué pasó*,"(What happened) the young officer inquired, holding back tears of laughter.

I relayed my story hurriedly, but the officer insisted on lugging me to the police station. The presumable homosexual pressed no charges, and conveniently disappeared.

It was sheer luck that our destination was Captain Gomez' station, at which I was once the 'artist in residence' for "beating up" the Englishman.

I walked into the station, immediately noticing my drawings pegged onto the bland yellow walls. I took solace in the fact that a few of the portraits were nicely framed.

A few minutes later, Captain Gomez saw and recognized me.

"*El artista*," he exclaimed, motioning for an embrace. "What brings you to our station again?"

When I narrated my cinema "love story," Captain Gomez and other passers-by roared in laughter.

"Gay men like German men," Captain Gomez warned facetiously.

The police officers got their fill of late-night humor and I learned a new Spanish word: *puto*, Argentine slang for a gay man.

The officer from the cinema requested a portrait of himself. I obliged. Experience had taught me to skirt the policemen's good side. I was never asked for identification papers.

I was still an illegal resident of Argentina.

"Goodbye, be careful with the gays," Captain Gomez joked, as I shut the door to the police station.

I was free again. Sex was on my mind.

I resumed work at Zanzibar uneventfully. As usual, I sang my three introductory songs and added a few German tunes.

I figured the time was ripe to follow-up on Mónica's earlier flirtations for I often caught her staring while I was on-stage. In her stunning aristocratic beauty, Monica reminded me of Mona except Mónica was older than I. Her round, brown eyes sometimes met mine, followed by her characteristic seductive wink. I craved to pursue that mischievous wink, but was a little too shy. Was she encouraging or teasing me?

At approximately 3 a.m. one dreary Saturday morning, after Maria had departed the premises, Mónica and I toiled in the nightclub alone. It had been a hectic evening, and I had hung around to assist with close-up chores. Behind the curved bar, Mónica hastily counted cash, while I arranged tables and chairs in the lobby. She completed her chores before I did, and I could feel her stare raise hairs on my back.

I folded the last chair near the bar, and turned toward idle Mónica. She maintained her fixated ogle, and subsequently placed her elbows on the counter before deliberately leaning forward. Her light blue blouse was cut low, and I could see the upper curvatures of her breasts. Mónica was a very attractive woman.

"Thanks for helping," she whispered sexily.

I stood breathless and speechless, gawking at her stunning body.

She dipped her manicured fingers through her chestnut brown hair, taunting me even more.

"Walter, it's late," she said. "Would you take me home?"

"Gladly, anytime," I said, tripping on a chair. "I'll go hail a cab."

Locating a taxi was effortless for the taxi drivers knew to expect often drunken late-night customers from the numerous downtown bars.

In the cab, Mónica raised goose bumps on my body wherever she ran her hands. She, of course, ran them where it mattered most.

"I wonder if the cab driver can see us?" I asked, as I noticed the him point his rear view mirror at us.

"What kind of aberrant behavior hasn't he seen unfold behind his cab?" she assured. "Does it matter?"

I nodded in agreement, thus heavenly pleasure persisted.

The entrance to Mónica's rather exclusive apartment building was manned by a most courteous concierge.

"*Buen dia*," he greeted, smiling and nodding at me like he knew something I didn't.

Nevertheless, we boarded the elevator to the eighth floor, which bore only two large apartments. Mónica's was particularly enormous. The bright living room was graced with floor-to-ceiling windows that opened onto a balcony overlooking the sprawling city. From her lavishly furnished balcony, I could see Buenos Aires' dimly lit harbor.

"Would you like a drink?" Mónica asked.

"I would rather have you," I replied, re-employing my now-perfected line.

She giggled sexily, held my hand and led me to the shower.

We made affectionate love from her steaming shower to her large bed with the lights on. Fifteen years older than I, Mónica's lovemaking experience certainly made a marked difference. She taught me patience, and how to please a woman. The ensuing blissful night shed ample meaning on the Argentine saying: "Old chickens make good soup."

Mónica insisted I keep our relationship a secret at the Zanzibar. She wished not to scare off a few high profile, heavy spending male customers that occasionally flirted with her. I wondered if one of them was with her the nights I wasn't. Did she teach them the same mature sex tricks?

However, when Mónica wanted me, she picked me up three blocks from the bar.

Normando Zúñiga, a soft-spoken, generous and wealthy farmer, waltzed into Zanzibar one rainy evening. A lavish spender, Zúñiga was a successful tobacco farmer from Salta, a scenic medium-sized colonial city in northern Argentina close to Bolivia.

I quickly composed a sketch of him.

"Do you like the country?" he asked, as he examined the well-drawn portrait.

"Yes," I replied emphatically, reminiscing many vacations at my father's rural hometown Hollerath in Germany's poor Eifel region.

"Well, why don't you come to Salta and stay with me," Zúñiga said, handing me a wad of money. "We could use hardworking guys like you on the farm."

A new venture was brewing. I could feel the excitement pounding my young heart.

While I was certain Mónica wasn't madly in love with me, I wasn't sure how she would react to my sudden departure.

"Women do not like being rejected," *Mutti* had once told me.

The next day, I hurried past the smiling concierge to Mónica's apartment, rehearsing my departure speech.

After we made passionate love, I placed my hand on her soft stomach, marveling at the marked difference between her supple skin and my rough hide. She looked endearing and gorgeous with her long brown hair tangled on the white pillow.

"What is it?" she asked, sitting up.

"Well," I hesitated. "Ah... You know Normando Zúñiga was in the bar yesterday, right?"

"Yes, and he was very impressed with you," she said, smiling. "He liked the picture you drew of him. Why?"

"Well, he asked me to go to Salta with him," I said, cringing.

She tilted her head, studying my disillusioned face with her brown eyes.

"Will you go?"

Silence.

"Yes, I think so."

"It's a great idea," she advised, standing up. "He's a good man and you should see more of Argentina than just Buenos Aires."

While content with her lack of surprise, I wished she'd been a little more regretful at the prospect of my departure. Alas, men, like women, also detest being rejected, I thought.

"We'll miss you here, Walter," Mónica said, as if reading my mind. "But when you get bored in Salta, there's always a place for you at Zanzibar. You know that."

Then she batted her signature seductive wink at me.

"And there's always a place for you here too," she said, as she patted the bed.

Salta, here I come.

Welcome to Salta

Put all good eggs in one basket, and then watch that basket. - Andrew Carnegie.

The next day, I packed the lightest of my belongings, and boarded a train at Retiro Station to Salta, a northern Argentine agricultural town.

The lengthy, picturesque journey to Salta weaved through metropolitan Córdoba, arid sparse settlement Santiago del Estero and college town Tucumán. The stiffening summer heat was exceedingly intolerable for the train lacked air conditioning. The orange sun burned luciferously, parching my sensitive lips. As we crossed the Santiago del Estero desert, fine, salty sand occasionally coated my skin, petrifying it to a painful crisp. The desert was cruel in its welcoming effects.

The winding trip between Buenos Aires and Córdoba was most colorful and adventurous. The conflicting sight of sluggish cattle grazing innocently against a distant backdrop of smoking industrial factories denoted Argentina's gradual transformation from pastoral to industrial society.

Home to the Quechua Indians, Santiago del Estero was a scenic small town world-famous for tourism. We passed through uneventfully. Most passengers offloaded at Tucumán, home of *Universidad Nacional de Tucumán*, and approximately 150 miles from Salta.

Upon arriving in Salta, I boarded a rickety bus to Normando's finca (farm) in Osma, a hamlet consisting of a handful of scattered farms.

I arrived at the entrance to Normando's tobacco finca with a small handbag and high hopes. From the bus, I could see his 50,000-acre stretch of land, protected by mountains, and partitioned in scattered 10-acre plots, perhaps to ameliorate the irrevocable ruinous damage of a locust attack.

A medium-sized farmhouse fronted the seemingly endless stretch of land and hills. I clambered off the bus in front of the fenced single-story farmhouse characterized by multiple arch entrances. Behind the angelically white farmhouse lay several dingy shacks, where presumably farm laborers resided. An electricity generator hummed as I rapped on the ebony door.

"Welcome to Osma, Walter," Normando said, as he hastily ushered me in. "I'm glad you made it all the way here."

"Yes, I'm glad I made it," I joked. "The sand almost blew me away."

Normando was married to an introvert Margo, who dragged into the impeccably neat living room as I waltzed in. Short, slim and unsophisticated, Margo was neither attractive nor ugly. I immediately imagined Normando, an extrovert womanizer, take advantage of Margo's insecurity. Her sullen eyes told the sordid story. Divorce was not a popular option in Argentina.

Soon Margo introduced me to my new residence, a small guest room furnished with a wiry bunk bed, a dusty study desk and a gaudy painting of Jesus Christ stretching out his arms to humanity, motioning for an embrace.

"Well, we sure could use an extra tough guy around," Normando said, handing my bag to an idle maid. "I've lost 50 laborers to Perón."

President of Argentina from 1946 to 1955, Juan Domingo Perón was an avid ultra-nationalistic "friend of the poor." He was solely responsible for a series of radical changes in the nation's left-wing politics and social services that led to the mass exodus of rural laborers to Argentina's large cities in search of riches.

"Damn Perón has left us with no laborers to work with. They're all in Buenos looking for gold on the street," Normando barked, glancing at his near-blank employee roster over dinner. "Would you mind joining me to the mountains on an employee hunt tomorrow morning?"

While peaceful and void of nosy policemen, Osma village presented its unique challenges. I was the only gringo in town. Awkward and conspicuous out in the open country, even my swagger amused many. The way I rode a horse or handled a hatchet often set off curious stares and jocular whispers. However, Normando's relentless hospitality soon abated the locals' suspicion of my gringo ways.

Normando's straightforward, business-like approach explained his wealth.

"Be ready in 10 minutes," he yelled into each shack at 6 a.m. the next morning. "We have work to do around here."

Ten minutes later, six men saddled with Normando and me, heading to the dense mountains to scour for scarce *peones* (laborers). As we traversed the mountains, we came upon one sparse village after another, deserted by city-bound Indians.

Perón had outlawed the derogative term "*Cabecitas Negras* (Black Heads)," used for decades to describe indigenous Argentine Indians because of their pitch-black hair. So Perón had changed the lingo to "*Hermanos del Interior* (Brothers from the Interior)." The Peronist administration's increased appreciation, albeit symbolically, of Argentina's scanty Indian population sparked newfound economic hope for the long-oppressed Indians. No longer was laborious farm work acceptable for Indian men.

My horse-riding training in Germany certainly came in handy as we trotted more than 10 miles across rough, undulating terrain. At the age of 12, I worked at a riding academy in Düsseldorf cleaning stalls and shoveling hay to earn a little money. Occasionally, the stable master permitted me to ride with his students, all members of wealthy families. The teenagers were always neatly clad in formal horse-riding attire, which I undoubtedly could not afford.

One day, a new instructor arrived.

"Walter, why don't you just come in your pajamas?" he asked rudely, frowning at my tattered attire.

Red with embarrassment, I never returned to the academy. I imagined the poor *peones*, struggling to earn a modest living, were also ostracized.

I savored the panoramic view of sparse vegetation on the roadsides as we climbed higher. It took us approximately two hours to encounter the first small settlement. Normando negotiated with the village leaders while I admired the small huts. The frolicking and previously gamboling children scampered indoors when they saw me. Pale white men like me were a rarity.

Normando's negotiations proved fruitful, concluding with the employment of 10 laborers who promised to arrive at the farm in a week.

As a thank you gift, one of the grateful new employees built a campfire. A relatively bizarre cooking method ensued. The Indians stuck slabs of fresh beef on long branches, and cast the grotesquely large shish kebab directly on the red-hot coal. The flames flared, and soon the pleasant aroma of roasting meat attracted villagers and stray mangy dogs.

One of the Indians shared his knife with me, so I mimicked the villagers as they cut strips of meat from smoking sticks.

"Look at the gringo," one of the Indians whispered, teasing my novice kebab-eating.

The beef was delicious. I was the laughing stock.

Our ride down the mountains seemed rougher than the one up to the village. My buttocks suffered immensely. Throughout the trip, the men taunted me for being the awkward gringo, incognizant of Gaucho life. It behooved me to admit difficulty riding a horse. Unfortunately, the ride got bumpier as we rode.

Perhaps sensing my discomfort, Normando proceeded to tell an anti-Perón joke, further substantiating his animosity toward the administration.

"Perón was once speaking to a crowd of Argentine people," Normando began, giggling mischievously. "After the speech, he asked the crowd 'Are you all Peronists?' 'Yes! Yes! Yes!' screamed the crowd. And 'No!' yelled one lone dissenter."

As if accustomed to Normando's joke-telling, the other men trotted closer, smiling animatedly. Soon, they were all ears.

"Surprised, Perón asked the lone dissenter, 'If you're not a Peronist, then what are you?' The man responded, 'I'm a Communist.' 'How come you're a Communist?' the President asked."

My horse-riding pain had since diminished.

"The man replied: 'My father is a communist, so is my mother, grandmother and my grandfather.' Then, Perón asked, 'If your mother was a whore and your father was a son-of-a-bitch, then what would you be? The man replied, 'Oh, in that case, I would be a Peronist.'"

The thunderous laughter that ensued Normando's political joke nearly threw me off my horse. In a facetious way, I began to dislike Perón.

When we finally arrived at Normando's finca, it took me an excruciating hour to peel my pants off the sweaty saddle. My khaki pants were glued to the raw red flesh of my buttocks. Sitting was a challenge for two weeks.

I was the laughing stock anyway.

Siesta on the finca was an absolute must. All activities ceased, even the dogs didn't bark between 1 p.m. and 3 p.m.

Working with *peones*, I learned tobacco-planting rules and practices. One *peon* transported young seedlings from the central nursery to each 10-acre field. Another *peon* dug holes, while his accomplice grounded the seedlings. A muscular burly *peon* was always responsible for regulating irrigation, channeling water from a nearby well along ridges to keep tobacco roots moist. The experienced *peones* worked in rhythm, planting, patting, and watering tender plants.

The work was enjoyable.

One day, emboldened by my rapid mastery of tobacco culture, I envisioned owning and cultivating my own plot of land.

I approached Normando.

"You want land, gringo?" he mused.

"Yes," I replied, expecting certain rejection.

"What do you plan to do with the land?"

"Grow tobacco, of course," I said enthusiastically.

I was fascinated with tobacco farming. I loved watching the small plants grow tall and green, valuable only when dried and brown. But I wondered if Normando had registered my passion for he was a man of few commentary.

"Of course, but what will I do?" he said, sounding disappointed. "I need you to work for me."

"I'll work your fields all day, but in the evenings and during siesta, I'll work for myself," I replied.

"You think you can do that much work in this heat?"

"Absolutely, all I need is the land."

"You can have the land, Walter," he said to my utmost delight.

Normando Zúñiga and wife in front of their farmhouse.

Thus, I came to own a 10-acre partition of land. I took no siestas. While other men snoozed, I toiled laboriously in the sunny fields along with the gigantic horse flies and skinny dogs. I braced the wooden handles, squeezing them firmly as the plough rocked and jostled ahead of me. The plough handle's rough, wooden grain smoothened to a glassy finish under my course palms, which soon darkened, stained unremittingly with sweaty dirt.

Young and brimming with exuberance, I luxuriated in the scorching sun, reveling the cool, dark soil caressing my bare feet.

Normando's finca quickly became my peaceful heaven. Until all hell broke loose.

The Tobacco Rancher

When you are in Rome, live in the Roman style. -
St Ambrose (340-397).

It was a hazy humid afternoon. An eerie silence pervaded the finca for it was siesta time. I clambered atop Normando's monstrous tractor preparing the soil for planting. Armed with enormous rugged tires, the tractor, unbeknownst to me, was parked in wrong gear. As I turned the ignition, the tractor lurched forward. I quickly lost control.

Soon the careening vehicle threw me to the ground like a bucking bronco. The blue, green and purple colors of the rainbow adorned my suffering tailbone for weeks afterwards.

"Walter, you should go see a doctor," Normando advised.

The only problem: The closest hospital was in Salta, a two-hour drive from Osma. Rather than expend time pursuing a doctor, I attended to my tobacco farming, albeit painfully. Nevertheless, witnessing my field's bloom sped the healing process.

I recently consulted my doctor in Austin, Texas in June of 2001 for a hip replacement.

"Doctor, why does my left hip look perfect, while the other is bone to bone?' I asked, peering at a disturbing X-ray slide prior to my surgery.

"You know, that's rather unusual," he replied. "Have you ever had a bad fall?"

"Yes," I said, smiling reminiscently.

My injury made work on the finca more exigent. Soon I had ten beautiful acres of leafy valuable tobacco. The injury vanished. Eager to earn extra money, a few *peones* agreed to work for me after regular hours.

A foreign trade policy shift in Perón's administration aided my sudden aggressiveness. The marked emigration of *peones* from rural to urban Argentina halved the local tobacco industry's productivity. To ameliorate their losses, local tobacco producers hiked prices, which in turn crippled their ability to compete with foreign companies, many of which were quite willing to sell tobacco products to Argentines at very low prices. To ensure stability for Argentina's ailing tobacco industry, President Perón had ordered a halt on all tobacco imports. The price of domestic tobacco skyrocketed.

I sensed imminent wealth.

"You know, Normando, I think I love Perón now," I once joked over breakfast as I stared at my lush fields. We were a few weeks from harvest season.

"My dear friend, your love is a little premature, I think," Normando replied "You still have a very long way before the money. Plus, Perón may not be president tomorrow."

Normando was right. In an era of rampant and commonplace coups d'état, it was considered unwise business to wholly rely upon Argentina's fickle economy.

While conducting business strategies over breakfast one morning, Normando and I watched *peon* children play near my plot.

Clad in their modest tattered clothing, the kids occasionally caught a lizard or a snake, which they would trap in a ring of rocks before cruelly watching the beast slither around helplessly. In complexion, some of the children looked white, but they all bore characteristic Indian high cheekbones.

Normando employed Native Indians as *peones* and *capataces* (mixed breed of Spaniards and Indians) as foremen. While Normando was friendly and generous, his discriminatory hiring methods were reflective of a crippling brand of dejure racism rampant and widely accepted in 1940's Argentina.

I was also guilty of such discriminatory practices, albeit subconsciously.

Upon reaching six to eight inches in height, the tobacco plants proceeded to crowd each other, the larger plants smothering and annihilating the smaller ones in the most Darwinian manner. So I supervised the thinning of rows for transplanting. Out of habit, I divided the light-skinned workers from the dark-skinned ones. The latter stacked mud and rocks to divert water supply, while the former had the near effortless task of relocating plants.

To fake non-favoritism, Normando would often share meals with *gauchos*, *capataces* and *peones*. I occasionally joined the men, eating slices of roasted beef off hot spits. The hot meat seared our tongues as the grease dripped down our chins, painful eating at its best.

Eating together was our only camaraderie for everyone dispersed according to race soon afterwards. The racial division didn't bother Normando as long as everyone worked hard. However, as in all societies, the finca inflicted the burdening pain of existence upon the lower-class, oppressed Indians.

Oftentimes I heard Indian women crying softly as they worked through the rows of tobacco plants plucking harvestable leaves. Pouting while competent, the men labored in, what appeared to me, an efficient rage.

As an oppressed concentration camp detainee, I sympathized with the lowly Indians, but with a grain of salt. Like Normando, greed and a burning desire for wealth had partly blinded me to the unjust racism and oppression inflicted upon the colored laborers.

Unbeknownst to me, God's wrath was near.

One drizzly Tuesday morning, a scrawny brown dog from the *capataz* camp had maimed and disemboweled a *peon* baby girl. The bestial crime had occurred near a hardscrabble creek that meandered through two halves of Normando's expansive farm. The small creek was irrevocably cursed with hard-packed earth, where Indian women knelt scrubbing dingy clothes while innocent children played, skipping rocks on water.

Laboring through high tobacco rows, I spotted the mangy dog presumably soon after committing murder, weaving furtively through my lot. It skirted the finca in a low trot, its muzzle and forelegs stained red. The sight of an emaciated dog drenched in blood seemed suspicious, but I ignored it, theorizing that the dog had killed a rabbit or some other small rodent.

Two hours later, panic struck. Screaming frenziedly and sodden with blood, a *peon* woman sprinted into camp as we retreated for siesta, cradling the mutilated body of her one-year-old daughter wrapped in red swaddling clothes.

The camp froze as we lowered our tools and heads in reverent silence. Soon the *peones* laggardly emerged from tobacco rows, converging on the mourning woman. The rest of us stood dumbfounded, leaning against our tools for strength. As the overwhelming heat of the orange sun flared, we stared into the shimmering gray haze of dust billowing around the *peon* woman.

Normando approached the huddled assembly, but was promptly shunned. The group dragged into the *peon* woman's shack and slammed the wooden rickety door shut. Doors were rarely locked on the finca.

The culpable dog Lobo (wolf) belonged to Gilberto Ramos, a stout, thirty-something-year-old *capataz* man, whose fleshy face was grooved with deep folds that seemingly connected his sunken eyes to his jowls. Gilberto resided with four other *capataz* men in a room adjacent to mine - I could hear him sighing and shifting uncomfortably in his bed at night.

For days, begrudging, silent whispers and grumbling plagued Gilberto wherever he walked. Gawking with accusing eyes, the *peones* would occasionally fall silent when Gilberto passed.

"Why do they hate him so much?" I asked Normando, as we strolled to my plot one misty afternoon. "It wasn't his fault."

"It is an old sourness between them," Normando explained. "Two years ago, the *peones* caught him with one of their women."

One afternoon, some of the men plotted to murder Lobo. Sensing imminent danger, the savvy dog cowered in bushes beyond the finca's shacks. I later caught glimpses of Lobo while working in the fields. Its skin had tightened around its ribs, and the bloodstains had darkened to a black mark. The canine made long, brave cognizance strides across a plateau overlooking the creek. He'd halt, look down at Gilberto, but, sensing the saliency of animosity in the humid summer air, he'd retreat into the parched grass.

"Gilberto, call your dog," the Indian men yelled.

He never did.

One day, during siesta, I wandered up the muddy lip of the finca's plateau to scout my tobacco plot. There, I found Gilberto Ramos feeding bacon to his skeletal dog.

"It was going to starve to death," Gilberto said, whimpering sympathetically.

Lobo's dry tongue whipped between Gilberto's fingers, lapping up the glistening bacon grease. Patches of loamy dirt clung to the dog where human blood had soaked its fur before drying. The short, sticky hair bunched together in scales across its chest.

"It's better that it starve," I advised. "Having killed once, it's a very dangerous animal."

"Do you know about the woman?"

"Normando gave me a hint, but go ahead."

A few years ago, Gilberto had fallen in love with one of the *peones*' young daughters, Juanita. Adorned with long black hair and broad cheekbones, Juanita was pretty, despite the loss of an incisor in a horse-riding fall.

"I always thought the defect in her smile made her even that more striking," Gilberto said, smiling reminiscently with tears swelling in his eyes. "I loved her very much."

Juanita had resided in a shack with her parents and seven brothers.

"I tried to find excuses to talk to her," Gilberto said, stroking the dog's mane.

However, the racial structure in which work was divided amongst laborers meant Gilberto, a light-skinned *capataz*, had few reasons to fraternize with Juanita, a dark-skinned *peon*. When he joined the dark-skinned *peones* voluntarily, the Indians had shunned him for they distrusted his courtship interest in Juanita, and understandably so.

"Her family went great lengths to prevent her from seeing me," Gilberto said. "I had no choice but to run away with her."

Apparently, one morning, Juanita's father had paid Normando a rude visit, informing him of her missing status. In turn, Normando had hunted Gilberto down for answers, but discovered that he too had vanished the night Juanita absconded. No sooner had Normando commenced investigations into the matter, did Gilberto and Juanita return to the camp one afternoon quite unexpectedly. The two lovers had simply spent the night outdoors, since privacy was virtually impossible on the finca.

Juanita's family was furious. Gilberto ignored them.

"She is my woman now and they can't do anything to me or to her," Gilberto had yelled to Normando, who subsequently absolved himself of the conflict.

Ever since the "abduction," bad blood had coursed amongst the camp workers.

"The *peones* plotted to teach me a lesson, but knew better than to start any trouble on Normando's plantation," Gilberto explained. "I live in fear now. Believe me, it's a most cruel punishment for loving. Tell me, Señor Walter, what kind of life do we live in when love is a crime?"

I replied with silence.

It was not long before Juanita had begun to recoil into a hard shell, like a turtle shying away from hostile socialization. One day, she was gone. Her prior solitude had delayed her parents' cognition that she had gone amiss. Juanita's family had simply assumed she had eloped with Gilberto, and he had rightfully assumed she was with her family.

Juanita took everything with her, except her dog Lobo.

"Heartbroken and lost, I searched distant horizons and high heavens for Juanita, but to no avail," Gilberto explained. "Here at home, I was treated like a criminal, a beastly rapist of some sort. I have committed no sin, but the sin of love."

Heaving absolute responsibility on the innocent laborer, Juanita's family had floated a rumor that their 18-year-old daughter had discovered she was pregnant, and subsequently committed suicide out of shame. Normando, the finca's sole arbitrator, had ruled that Juanita simply ran away for she departed with all her belongings. Thus, the case ended or so it seemed.

Gilberto stared at me as the dog licked his fingers.

"This was her dog," he said, pushing the dog's skinny ears back with one hand and ogling into its glossy eyes. "Why did you do such a stupid thing? Huh, why?"

The dog whined as if expressing remorse.

"She left the dog?" I asked.

"Yes, it is the only thing she left me," Gilberto said.

He dipped his hand into the reservoir, and splashed water onto the dog's scruffy, bloody coat, and then begun scrubbing with his stubby fingers. The bloodied water dripping from the dog met the dusty floor, forming dirty beads.

Late that night, I could not sleep. I popped my eyes open, waiting for my pupils to adjust to the pitch darkness of my bedroom. A temporary draft of cool air suddenly brushed against the hairs on my exposed forearm. I sprang from my pillow, scanning the dark the best I could with sleep-filled eyes. As my vision cleared, I noticed moving shadows dancing against my wall.

It was a man - I could make out his muscular silhouette.

"Who's there?" I yelled.

The man froze. I approached the door stealthily, and he begun retreating. In the moonlit dark, I could discern the glint of steel in his hand.

I opened the door. He was gone.

The next day, I paid Normando a panic visit.

"There was a *peon* outside my room last night," I yelled, pacing Normando's large study.

"Was she pretty?" he sneered.

"I think he was looking for Gilberto's room," I complained. "He had a gun; I could have been shot."

"The workers know not to cause trouble here," Normando replied, his voice quivering with an unusual amount of concern.

Normando had impressed me many times before with his true mastery of keeping calm, even in the face of clear and present danger. His quivering was thus anomalous and quite telling.

"I authorize you to take care of this matter as you deem fit."

At dusk, I climbed the dead trunk of a tree above the plateau and patiently waited, hugging Normando's Remington across my chest. I was determined to kill Lobo, the source of virulent animosity on the finca.

At midnight, the dog scampered out of the bushes to the pond for a sip. My first shot zipped through the water. Vulnerable, Lobo ran up the hill in full view. I threw the bolt open and cracked another shot off. This time, I hit the dog in the flank, losing my balance from the rifle's turbulent recoil. I fell from the tree.

After collecting myself, I noticed Lobo pulling away from me with its front legs. The camp lights blinked on as residents emerged from huts and shacks, tuning in to the action. I chambered another round and shot Lobo behind the ear, emptying his skull on the dirt.

The *peones* sprinted toward me in the dark. When they witnessed the dead dog and the smoking rifle, they stopped and formed a circle around me. In the fall, I had twisted my wrist so I clutched the painful limb to my stomach.

"Walter, are you alright?" Normando asked, as I handed him the rifle.

"Where is Gilberto?" I asked, scanning the crowd for the burly *capataz*. He was absent.

"Come home with me, Walter, and we'll wrap your hand," Normando said, hooking his weighty arm around my shoulder.

The silent, encircling crowd gave way for Normando as he guided me away.

Lo and behold, between the divided lines of men, stood a distraught Gilberto, staring at the dead dog.

"I have nothing now," he said, blinking tears down his cheeks.

I cried to sleep that night.

The eyeball is not exactly round like a gracious marble, as one might envision it to be. It is elongated, like an American football, and, in the intense heat of cooking, it dimples and develops bumpy bubbles of flesh where stringy connections once wired the eyeball to the brain. Cooked sheep eyeballs are a primo Native Indian delicacy.

As recompense for a laborious day of morale-depleting work, the Indians courteously invited me to join in their bizarre gastronomy. In Native Indian culture, rejecting such an invitation was considered an enormous insult.

Cringing in disgust, I arrived at a small open-air shack where a dozen men gathered that warm evening, plucking bloody eyeballs from sheep carcasses.

"*Bienvenido*, Walter," Pancho greeted fervidly. "Forgive my presumptions but we're surprised you showed up after all."

Of all the laborers, Pancho seemed the most literate, so I often engaged him in protracted, and, often heated, World War II discussions. His stunning breadth of knowledge impressed me.

"I'm always willing to try different foods," I lied. "Where's my eyeball?"

"The men are preparing them right now," he replied, guffawing. "But if you're so hungry you can have mine instead!"

Pancho and I sat at a large wooden table surrounded by mismatched chairs. Scrawny mutts scampered around, waiting patiently for scraps. A portable radio blared Argentine folk music in the background.

I observed the cooks cast the seasoned eyeballs on a smoking grill, fashioned out of old metal barrels. The foremen offered me a glass of red wine from Cafayate, a small town near Salta, popular for its wineries.

"So, Walter, tell us about your hometown," Pancho asked.

As always, I avoided divulging details of my detention in Nazi concentration camps. Anti-Semitic sentiment thrived in Argentina long after the war. Many Argentines associated Nazi concentration camp detention with being a Jew, which often led to isolation and aggressive prejudice.

Besides, an eyeball dinner was certainly not the time or place for dreary concentration camp tales. Our discussion grew increasingly colorful as the wine and beer took intoxicative effect.

A Native Indian woman served me a plate of savory empanadas, fried dough filled with meat, onion, olives and chilies. I was relieved to consume anything but the impending main course.

"Hey, Walter, your willingness to try new foods proves that you'd make a good poor man," Pancho joked, as the cooks stabbed the eyeballs with sticks testing their readiness. "Serve Walter first, okay?"

"I understand the cultural and economic imperative of eating every last bite of an animal," I replied. "I've eaten strange things before."

I nervously took a swig of wine as I noticed one of the cooks strutting towards me, the honored guest, with a wooden decorated plate garnished with a large eyeball. She sank the plate in front of me.

The cooked, distorted eyeball stared at me from the plate, fierce, grotesque and unblinking, bigger than a human eye. It saliently scoped its enveloping world in 360 degrees. Even in death, it was alive.

The cottony haze of alcohol, coupled with the fixated stare of the cooked eyeball, nauseated me. I felt like running from the world, but the ogling eyeball paralyzed me.

Mimicking my hosts, I sliced the enormous eye. A creamish paste squirted from the laceration. The white portion of the eyeball was boiled to a grayish hue, resembling the texture of a soft apple. I closed my eyes and ceased breathing as I mouthed a piece.

"I bet you don't eat such delicacies in Germany," Pancho assured.

He was right. As I shoved the slice of eyeball in my salty, nauseated mouth, I wished I were in Germany, anywhere but the claustrophobic thatched hut in which I was about to ingest an epicurean oddity.

Somehow, I surmounted the bravura to swallow the first slice. Surprisingly, the taste was remarkably scrumptious. I crunched into the juicy, spicy eyeball, which turned out to be an utter gastronomy. Of course, like virtually all Argentine cuisine, the overwhelming taste was a spicy sauce the eyeballs had been smothered in.

While I laggardly investigated the bizarre, yet delicious, cuisine, the Indian men dug into their portions with ample gusto.

"Well, we're glad that you're enjoying your eyeballs," Pancho joked.

The eyeball dinner solidified my relationship with the *capataces* and *peones*, so much so that their respect for me surged afterwards. However, after excusing myself from the party that night, I never ate sheep eye again.

Still, the Indian men insisted on initiating this sauerkraut-loving German into one more culinary adventure.

Not long after I wolfed down my first sheep eyeball, the natives drove a truck to the finca loaded with the ingredients for yet another unusual repast. As the truck whisked by me, I noticed two *peones* riding atop the truck restraining a large, gray-green enraged lizard eyeing the men warily.

The Indians insisted I join them for a dinner of roasted lizard.

So it came to be that I ate roasted lizard tail, while the Indians chronicled their near-death adventures capturing the unfortunate reptile. Seasoned and roasted on an open fire, the lizard meat tasted like barbecued chicken.

It was delicious.

Unlike the horrific post-experience that ensued my eyeball consumption, I slept well that night. No nightmares whatsoever after the bizarre menu.

I fell asleep that night wondering what my next adventure would be. Would it surpass becoming an Indian cuisine aficionado?

Race Improvement and Spider Wars

If you want to improve the herd, get a good bull. - Popular ranchers' saying.

Like a short-lived cool summer breeze, time passed since I first arrived on Normando's grand finca. Judging from the booming Peronist Argentine economy and the fervent progress on my farm, all was well.

My 10 acres of land was bursting with plants tall enough to conceal a man on horseback. Massalini Celasco, a renowned tobacco company, called one morning to purchase the adolescent tobacco, weeks shy of harvestation.

I received a 10,000-pesos advance to cover the impending harvest, wages and shipping. Emboldened by my sudden success, I paid my employees in one bulk sum.

Despite my good fortune, I felt empty and unaccomplished. Something was amiss: A woman.

"Would you like a glass of water," Margo asked softly over breakfast one morning as Normando and I routinely planned the day.

Like most Argentine wives, Margo was restricted to homemaking. I never really understood why she was unreasonably shy around Normando, like she was utterly terrified of him. Unemployed and childless, Margo busy-bodied around the house on some endless chore. She seldom spoke.

Her head bowed in humility, Margo served us bread and *dulce de leche* with a brusque smile. I shoved the sweet sandwich in my mouth, savoring the tack on my gums.

"I need a woman like that," I said, as Margo sauntered back to her home: The kitchen.

"You need any woman," Normando barked. "I've actually been thinking about sending you to see my friend José Hernandez."

"I need a woman, not a man," I said. "I'm not that desperate."

"Very funny."

"I know you mean well, Normando," I said. "Who is he? Does he have a daughter?"

"No, but he has more women than you can shake a stick at," Normando replied. "Plus, he wants white babies."

Don José Hernandez, a prominent Salta rancher and tobacco farmer, strongly believed in "improving" the race of his dark-skinned *peones*. He seized every opportunity to lure a gringo foreigner to his estate for what he called "breeding."

Latin American women prefer offspring with fair skin, blond hair and blue eyes. In direct contrast, Scandinavians and Germans are known to crave dark-haired, dark-skinned and brown-eyed children. The offspring of unions between gringos and native Latin American women are generally gorgeous.

White, blonde and blue-eyed, I was presumably a perfect candidate for such "whitening" practices.

Normando made one call, and Hernandez immediately invited me to his finca. Eager as a little boy is to work his new toy, I accepted his invitation. The word at Normando's finca had it that Hernandez also possessed the finest horses in the region. I also looked forward to reacquainting myself with equine life.

One Friday afternoon, I drove out to Hernandez' well-manicured plantation. The sprawling estate was bedecked with flowers, trees and a classic white ranch house.

"Well, gringo how do you do?" Hernandez asked, as he ushered me into the ranch house. "I'll show you around."

We toured the stables, populated with myriad well-groomed horses. Soon afterwards, Hernandez flaunted his expansive tobacco plantation and *galpones* (a barn-like facility wherein tobacco was dried).

Upon returning to the ranch house for dinner, Hernandez introduced me to Martina, an attractive *peon* lady in her thirties. I assumed her to be the rancher's wife.

"So, are you married?" Hernandez inquired at the dinner table.

"No," I replied, noticing that Martina was staring at me as if particularly interested in my response. "I'm single, but Normando tells me you have the prettiest damsels in town. Do they work here?"

Martina scurried away from the table and soon returned with a bottle of wine.

"Well, I guess you can say so," Hernandez whispered. "I'll introduce one soon."

While pouring me some wine, Martina flirted with her large brown eyes. I responded in kind, but with reasonable stealth. Was Martina Hernandez' wife or not?

The estate's diesel electricity generator rumbled to a halt at 8 p.m. Before the lights flickered out, Hernandez walked me to the guest room, adorned with a large bed, a wooden dresser and a half-naked Martina.

"Martina will take excellent care of you, be nice to her," he said, winking dubiously as he shut the door.

I was alone with Martina, clad in a porous nightgown that hugged her shapely body seductively. I could discern her erect nipples rubbing against the light night wear. As Martina strutted towards me, Hernandez' well-schemed setup became reasonably conspicuous. Equipped with an angelic smile, tan complexion and soul-searching, sparkling eyes, Martina was beautiful.

"Well, are you going to kiss me or are you just going to stand there?" she asked, erasing any doubt that she was to spend the night with me.

I enjoyed Martina's hospitality immensely.

I bounced to the breakfast table the next morning with a wide smile and an ebullient mood. Hernandez and Martina sat awaiting me.

"Did you have a good night?" Hernandez asked, giggling at the apparent success of his plot.

"I believe you know the answer to that, my dear friend," I replied.

After breakfast, Hernandez and I saddled two horses and rode up the hills. We returned for a large criollo lunch. During siesta, I retired to my room, where Martina was waiting, this time stark naked under the satin sheets.

I left Hernandez' finca late that afternoon wondering if my visit had produced any life consequences.

Normando once ordered that I procure a truckload of firewood from Orán, a Lebanese and Syrian settlement, heavily populated by immigrant Arabs rooted along brushy foothills of the Argentine-Bolivian border.

The finca was in dire need of firewood for Normando's *galpones*, small wooden houses in which farmers fire-dried tobacco leaves hanging from hooks in the ceiling above an open furnace.

As I drove into Orán, named after a city in northwestern Algeria, I wondered if I had fortuitously traversed some invisible international border. A gathering of Arab women flocked by me, clad claustrophobically in black scarves entwined around their shoulders and heads. I marveled at the outlandish clothing as the chattering women sauntered through the blistering heat.

I had been razor-shy for a week, the retribution for which was the uncomfortable accumulation of salty sweat on my mustache. The saline perspiration trickled into my mouth, inciting scrumptious thirst.

I stopped at what appeared to be the water supply for a nearby hamlet: A well, besieged by skinny, boisterous youth.

I weaved through the kids and began to draw water.

"You may cook with it, but don't drink it," one of the little boys warned.

"*Gracias*," I said, as I took a swig of the mysterious water.

After a short rest, I taxied into Orán, overtaking curious pedestrians on dusty, unpaved streets as they investigated my every move.

It was noon, but many of the staggering local men looked drunk. Apparently, instead of bad water, they drank beer or wine.

Orán was not as peaceful as it appeared superficially. I suspected dubiousness in the drunken countenances of the sweaty surreptitious men, clutching reflecting green beer bottles in the scorching sun. Schools of vociferous men gambled on ramshackled benches on balconies. Of course, their wives and daughters were predictably absent.

After glancing at Normando's illegibly hand-written directions for the thousandth time, I located my destination: A modest lumberyard perched at the end of a long dirt-road. I idled the truck, and slowly peeled myself from my seat.

"Five cords of wood, talk to Tarek," read Normando's instructions.

I rapped on the entrance. Tarek welcomed me in. I immediately recognized him from the bushy moustache Normando had described.

"You must be Walter, here for the firewood," he said. "Please, come in."

While Tarek, 35ish, tall and dark-haired, was rhapsodic and accommodating, an indiscernible and unsettling eeriness characterized his persona. Perhaps it was the suspect way his intimidating eyes danced and flirted, instantaneously estimating my physical and intellectual mettle.

"Let my men load the truck," Tarek urged. "You've been driving all day. Come with me and have a drink."

Tarek walked me into a waiting room bedecked with a circle of ranting men exchanging bets. At the center of the circle stood two tall jars each inhabiting a spider. The men tapped the jars with their long fingernails before passing them around, muttering to each other. Then the betting began.

Tarek shoved a small glass of grapa in my hands.

"Drink, it's good," he said. "Don't miss the spider war."

The drink was acidic and potent.

I joined the increasingly rabid spider battle crowd. On the smooth wooden floor, the arachnids circled each other tenuously, prancing sideways and hoisting their hairy forelegs like picadors anticipating the charge of a snarling bull. Despite the spiders' diminutive size, the colossal power in their sinewy legs could still be felt. The room clammed up to a near murderous quietude as we anticipated the sudden burst of violence: The rousing and tangling of topsy-turvy legs like Judo wrestlers thrashing each other about.

Finally, the attack! With awe-inspiring celerity, one spider lunged the first assault. Soon, like brawling little girls, the arachnids were scuttling across the floor and in-between the legs of dispersing, rambunctious spectators, who gleefully cleared extra space for continuous battle.

Surprisingly, the smaller spider maintained a marked advantage during the war, forcing the larger spider to cower from conflict.

"Many fathers have gambled and lost their daughters, land and crops here," Tarek said, pointing to a retreating, sobbing spectator, who had obviously lost his bet on the larger spider. "It's a saddening thing to watch."

"All this talk about spiders and gambling reminds me of a saying by John Dryden," I said.

"Who is he?"

"My uncle who lives next door!" I said sarcastically. "Who do you think he is?"

"Let me guess, some English writer?"

"No way!" I persisted. "Good. Now, can I get to the saying?"

"Sure," he said, pouting. "You have an attitude problem."

"Bets, at the first, were fool-traps, where the wise, like spiders, lay in ambush for the flies," I said, highlighting each utterance with a light thrust of my fist. "It's the only thing I remember from my English literature class."

"Good. I'm glad to hear that."

The circle of ranting spectators soon diffused. The smaller spider scampered about the floor clutching arachnid flesh in between its mandibles. It's deceased opponent was belly-up, lifelessly tranquil and fully disemboweled. One of the spectators tucked the victor back in its jar, where it presumably relished its bizarre meal. I wondered how many men lost their daughters and land that afternoon on a seemingly sure bet.

After the spider-wrestling bout, Tarek introduced me to a friend's daughter, Negra.

"Negra will soon travel to Salta to live with a relative," he said. "I wonder if you can assist her?"

"Certainly"

As we shook hands, I stared into Negra's pitch-black eyes, clearly the justification for her rather odd name, at least for an Arab lady. Negra was impressively beautiful in her tight, conservative dress. Her strong eyebrows and pendulous breasts teased me.

"I'd be delighted to help you in any way possible," I said, handing Negra my address in Osma.

I envisioned that our paths would eventually cross again.

With Negra on my mind, the trip back to Normando's finca was smooth as an infant's buttocks.

Little did I suspect imminent horror.

The Breathing Black Cloud

The block of granite, which is an obstacle in the pathway of the weak, becomes a stepping-stone in the pathway of the strong. - Thomas Carlyle.

Upon returning to Normando's finca with ample firewood supplies, the *galpónes* were set to work. The sweet aroma of adult tobacco drifted in swathing currents across the sprawling plantation. I remember occasionally idling in the fields to relish pockets of fragrance.

A relaxing week passed during which we did nothing but watch the tobacco plants grow that last little bit. The shiny green leaves seemed to gobble up abundant sunlight as if oblivious of their imminent demise. The scraping noise of *peones* sharpening their machetes aroused my yearning for long-awaited financial success.

One of Normando's flatbed trucks was stuck in a mechanic shop in Salta.

"If you go pick up my truck, I'll let you use it for your harvest," Normando offered.

As I came upon the mechanic shop, the truck's unpainted aluminum fender flashed at me like a signal mirror.

Across the mechanic shop stood a small café, in front of which a gaucho, squatting on the curb in tattered sack clothing, was weeping uncontrollably.

"Did she take your money?" I asked facetiously.

He pointed to the horizon.

"She left you? Went away?" I poked, ignoring the direction he was pointing in.

The dirgeful gaucho wobbled his head, and pointed again. This time, my eyes followed his callussed finger. In the distant horizon, an eerie and pulsating black cloud roared west toward Osma. I took a few steps to the fore and glommed at the animated black cloud blanketing the once blue skyline.

"*Langostas* (locusts)!" he yelled.

Mired in utter panic, I bummed an old army-like jeep from the café owner and sped towards Osma, trailing the enveloping massive cloud of locust that stretched approximately 100 kilometers of open terrain.

Driving with an open-top jeep, the locusts rained on me like living hail and hell. The dark brown pests splattered their grotesque innards on my windshield, impeding my line of sight.

I lost control and veered off the road. My jeep was irrevocably bound to slam into an outcropped boulder. A split second before a seemingly imminent accident, I regained control and swerved back onto the street. It was close. I switched the wipers on, washing away the opaque brown juice, while heaving breaths of utmost relief.

Some of the locust carcasses landed on the passenger's seat. One half-dead insect clung to the 40-kilometer pointer of my speedometer. Hurling down the dusty road at a break-neck speed of 100km per hour, I could care less about the suicidal insect.

As I scaled the hill overlooking Osma, I saw, to my relief, the locust cloud forge ahead of Normando's finca, presumably to another farm. My heartbeat calmed noticeably for my farm, on which I had labored to no end for months, seemed assuredly out of harm's way.

Assuming an end to my horror, I casually brushed the antennaed stragglers out of my vehicle.

As I pulled the last locust corpse out of my hair, a Junkers JU 52 whirled over me. It reminded me of the three-engine German planes that Hitler made available to Franco during Spain's Civil War, sprinkled paratroopers over Greece during World War II.

The plane recklessly dove into the black cloud and opened its belly, emptying hundreds of gallons of pesticide.

To my complete dismay, the black cloud circled away from the poison, and converged first upon my tiny tobacco plot. Even though I was miles away, I could feel the locust mandibles tearing away at my tobacco leaves.

Like a horror movie's damsel in distress, I fumbled nervously with the keys and stalled the jeep twice before speeding off to the finca. The night before, I had calculated bountiful profits from my harvest. Now I wondered how many leaves I could save.

The deadly race to Normando's finca was virtually pointless. Armed with flimsy sackcloth canvases, my men hopelessly raced to cover the tobacco plants. It was too late.

"Don't just stand there," Normando yelled. "Fight this damn vermin."

Emboldened by Normando's charge rhetoric, we immediately wrapped fabric around sticks and doused them with diesel. A strike of a match later, I had a flaming torch. Soon there were forty torches flashing through the storm. Clad in jackets pulled up over their heads, *peones* would occasionally whisk by me and then disappear, their firelight aura smothered by the compact and dark commotion of thieving insects.

As soon as my eyes adjusted to the darkness, a pulsating, stinging glow appeared in front of me. It was Gilberto Ramos staring soberly. Then he was gone. Losing my sight again augmented my hearing: The busy locust chewing my crops. Their ruinous teeth jigged like small busy machinery as the tobacco plants bowed under their weight.

After eons of thrashing around unsuccessfully, a vacuous clearing suddenly came upon me. At the unusual space, an intense rush of heat suddenly blasted me. Apparently, one of the *galpónes* had caught on fire.

Soon the ruinous flames jumped from the *galpón* to the canvasses and then, to my utter disappointment, the tobacco fields. Minutes later, a second *galpón* was ablaze.

In defeat, the torches congregated in one small portion of the expansive field. Mine soon joined them. When the locust clouds vanished, I was startled that it was still daylight.

I never farmed again.

After the locust devastation came emotional ruin. I secluded myself for days, mourning and growling at my misfortune. I often sat in the middle of my black, empty field and kicked at the rattling insect corpses. The plants had been lush and healthy; now they were reduced to scattered charred stalks. The tobacco leaves that would have earned me a million pesos were now in the greedy bellies of a million insects.

The once lush land was spiked with burnt tobacco stems, jutting skyward like weapons lost on a battlefield. In the scorching sun, I studied the subtle movements of the living insects - the stragglers and the wounded. I wished death upon each one of them.

During my lengthy stay at Normando's finca, I often dreamed of traveling to Germany with the ample proceeds of my tobacco plantation. I longed to purchase a new car and, perhaps, home for my parents. I envisioned bragging of my economic success to my old Düsseldorf friends. I even considered acquiring a small finca on which I would grow tobacco and raise horses. Now, my tobacco leaves were dead; so were my lofty dreams.

One afternoon, I sped recklessly into Salta, purchased a large bottle of grapa and sat at a corner table in Café Colón pouring myself repetitious drinks. Café Colón sat in Salta's main square, where businessmen, farmers, students and tourists often converged for coffee and connections.

Feeling lonely, I joined a group of *capataces* discussing politics at the table next to mine. At the center of the round table lay a small basket of coca leaves and a bowl of bicarbonate. The men wet the coca leaves with gin, dipped them in softening bicarbonate and lodged the small leaves in their cheeks. I joined in the bizarre, but perfectly legal Argentine pastime. Soon the alcohol and coca hit home, and I began narrating my travails, as a stowaway from Belgium to South America, to the increasingly fascinated men.

After discerning that I was German, one of the men handed me a German newspaper.

"I'm sure you would like to read a German newspaper," he said.

"Yes, I would."

It was the first German newspaper I had seen since my arrival in Argentina. The newspaper was published in Buenos Aires for the growing German-speaking population.

A small front-page article astonished me. The lead sentence read: "A German stowaway, who had been caught in Vitoria, Brazil, was turned over to authorities in Rio de Janeiro in order to be deported to Europe." The article regurgitated several other old back-stories.

As a stowaway, the first South American city I had arrived in was Vitoria, Brazil. It was January 14, 1949. The Captain had promised to accommodate me all the way to Montevideo, Uruguay. In return, he insisted that I remain quiet and undercover, while Brazilian port authorities scoured the ship.

"Don't trust the Captain, he is going to turn you over to the police," warned Lovey, a young black man from Curacao, whom I had befriended as a fellow trimmer on the ship.

Terrified of deportation, I had opted not to take any chances. As the ship slowly positioned itself in the Vitoria port, I had jumped off the deck. After swimming for approximately a hundred yards, a police boat had approached me. I was promptly apprehended.

"You'll be transported to Rio de Janeiro," barked a Brazilian interpreter in English. "From there, you will be shipped back to Europe."

The interpreter's name badge had read, "Hermann Schmitz."

"Being the son of German immigrants, you must help a young German, who has nothing to look for in Germany," I plead, employing a wise dose of psychology. "What would you do if I were your cousin? Why not just let me go? It would save you lots of problems and you would have helped a countryman."

Surprisingly, Herman was decidedly sympathetic to my cause.

"Let me discuss this with my superiors," he said. "I'm sure I can get you back on the S.S. Parkhaven."

Two days later, the Brazilian port authorities released me on the grounds that I would return only to the S.S. Parkhaven. I obliged, and on January 16, 1949, began the second phase of my stowaway trip to Montevideo, Uruguay.

After a lengthy stay in Argentina, it was extremely bizarre that the newspaper ran the aforementioned article. Apparently, the editor needed an outdated, but outlandish story to fill a space in the newspaper. I rejoiced that the article was untrue.

"What are you laughing at?" asked Jorge Santos, one of the *capataces*, as he handed me a nude picture of an attractive woman aiming her derrière at the camera. "Stop staring at the newspaper and look at this. You like her?"

"I don't know," I replied, as I gawked at the pornographic picture, reminiscent of Germany's booming porn industry. "Why look at this when I could be doing the real thing."

In post World War II Germany, pornography had suddenly emerged as one of the hottest lucrative businesses. It was not uncommon for young German peddlers to sell small gray photos to sex-starved Russian soldiers for right-of-passage from the British-controlled West Zone to the Russian-controlled East Zone during reconstruction. Pornography had become a healthy and near effortless side-business for smugglers.

In conservative, predominantly Catholic Salta, dirty magazines were harder to come by. The few that did circulate were deadly boring. The image of a ghostly plump model stretched across a sofa, with black mascara painted on each eye like dead holes, I imagined wrought adverse effects on the male sexual crave. The small black triangle, imagined more than seen, between the tightly folded legs was jocular at best.

I saw such boring magazine pictures occasionally, tucked away in the bibles of Salta farm hands.

Jorge offered the pornographic pictures to me for sale.

"She's a beautiful woman and she looks like you," he said, flashing the degrading picture at me as the other men guffawed.

Of course, Jorge was referring to the fact that the model was white, hinting at the importation of the photo from Europe.

One of the other *capataces* Luis snatched the photo the moment I tossed it on the table. I pulled out a small pad and, unbeknownst to the men, began to sketch pornography of my own.

"Her name is Monique," Luis read from a biography printed on the photo's flip side. "She is from France and lives in a village where she is courted all year by men from the towns around."

The boisterous giggling that ensued nearly deafened me.

"But she will have none of them because she's waiting for someone more blanco, mas gringo," Luis joked.

After a few moments of intense sketching, I held up a portrait of a young woman with pendulous breasts and widespread legs, revealing the deep creases of her vagina.

"This one is named Ramona, and she is courted all year by men from this entire area," I said, as the men guffawed in approval. "She makes love to each one of them as often as they desire."

The sketch represented the sort of vulgarity that aroused the repressed urges of the religious men amongst us. Ramona's sexy portrait was not necessarily fine art. 'Twas a ludicrous composite of many women I had known, but with exaggerated curves. Her face was an indiscrete oval, masked by long hair and adorned with a bovine jaw, implying catatonia. The eyes were dark and gray for I had erased them several times. Frustrated, I eventually drew her eyes closed, seeing and expressing naught.

Luis offered me ten pesos for the drawing. I subsequently received commissions for a dozen more from the horny *capataces*.

"It must be exactly the same," Miguelito insisted, pressing coins into my palm.

"It'll be a different one," I assured. "But I promise you will like her."

With these sketches circulating Salta, I later developed a reputation as the town's smut peddler, one with perverse sensibilities and boundless carnal knowledge.

Soon the men departed and I was left alone again. When my grapa bottle became impossible to hold steady enough for pouring into a glass, I sloshed the liquor on my fingers and slurped it from my wrist as the cold trickle disappeared up my sleeve.

"Easy on the grapa, Walter, or I may have to call the police," warned Luisa, the lone waitress in Café Colón that dreary afternoon, as she pranced from behind the bar to my seat.

Luisa's hair was streaked with gray; she was probably in her fifties.

"Go away!" I yelled.

Unruffled by my overt grumpiness, Luisa sat next to me, and poured herself a drink. In absolute drunken stupor, I only remember her stripping me of the bottle of grapa. I wrestled but she easily conquered, after which I lost all semblance of consciousness.

Heavy pounding awoke me the next morning. The thunderous sound, followed by sharp cranial pain, sounded and felt like a blacksmith hammering away on his own head. I blinked my eyes open only to acknowledge I was suffering from an intense migraine. The luciferous sun blasting through the window did not help matters much. Luisa's broad smile did. Eyes shut and snoozing peacefully next to me, she had an angelic aura about her (or maybe it was my migraine).

It was hot in the room and hotter lying next to Luisa, but I endured the discomfort. I shut my eyes and rested.

It was hard staying sane after the locust devastation, but I trusted that the sun always came out after the rain.

Nothing came of my brief acquaintance with Luisa. Still mourning the loss of my tobacco plantation, I was certainly in no mood to befriend anyone. A week after she hauled me from the Café Colón to her home, I geared myself up for new adventures. Luisa's weeklong hospitality was nice, but I had long overstayed my welcome.

"Well, if you must leave, I have a friend who works at a hotel in Santiago del Estero," Luisa said, as she walked me out of her home for the last time. "I'm sure he can find customers for you to draw."

Luisa handed me a sheet of paper with a name and address scribbled on it.

"Thank you for everything," I replied, kissing her goodbye. "I'll be sure to stop by the next time I'm in Salta."

A stone throw from Luisa's home laid a sprawling bus terminal, where I boarded a bus to the province of Santiago del Estero, clutching Luisa's contact information with dear life.

Save for the occasional nightmares of a swarm of black locust chewing off my arm, the trip was uneventful. As Luisa instructed, I arrived at Las Termas de Rio Hondo, a small town in Santiago del Estero province.

"Enrique at the Rio Hondo Hotel," read Luisa's note in legible handwriting.

"Can I speak to Enrique?" I asked the tall concierge, upon arriving at Rio Hondo Hotel.

"He's the maître d'hôtel. What might you want?"

"I'm his cousin from Salta."

The concierge walked me through a glass door into a large restaurant, bubbling over with guests shoving greasy steaks down their throats. I wondered how they could eat for the restaurant reeked sulphur.

"Please wait here while I call him," the concierge ordered.

Las Termas was famous for its thermal waters, in which thousands of the ailed bathed during the summer, hoping to be miraculously cured.

Enrique caught me gawking at the ailing, sulphur-reeking tourists chattering over lunch.

"Are you looking for me, young man?" he asked, tapping my shoulder lightly.

Caught off-guard, I snapped around to Enrique, clad in traditional maître d'hôtel attire. He was slim and appeared in his thirties.

"Luisa suggested that I meet you for work," I replied.

"Oh, this is about work, eh?" Enrique said, smiling generously as he ushered me toward the kitchen area hidden from the guests. "You look like you're from out of town. What's your story?"

"I used to own a tobacco plantation in Osma, close to Salta," I began, as flashbacks of locust razing my field sped through my mind. "But I lost it all to locust."

"Well, I'm the maître d'. If you're hungry, I can help. But, farming? Not my area of expertise at all," Enrique said, as we sat at a round table in the kitchen. "How can I help you, Walter?"

It felt like I knew Enrique for a lifetime, not five minutes. He seemed genuinely rich in his friendly and generous aura. My heart pounded thunderously as I sensed good fortune.

While Enrique was unable to secure me employment, he granted me the authority to solicit guests for as many portraits as I could.

"I'll inform the concierge that you are welcome to work at the hotel at any time," Enrique assured, to my utmost delight. "Don't tell anyone, but I'll get you a small room. Also, for your meals, just place it on my tab."

I suddenly felt like the artist-in-residence again. This time, my artistic status was not pivotal to securing liberty from a Buenos Aires police station. I was free, and my previously empty pocketbook grew larger.

Enrique invited me for dinner on the very last day of the tourism season, three weeks after I had first arrived in town.

The steak tasted unusually sweet. However, watching Enrique eat with enthusiasm, I figured the questionable meat had to be kosher.

Approximately five hours later, I suffered excruciating cramps, after which I defecated blood. Enrique was nowhere to be found the next day. I assumed he underwent a similar experience.

While short-lived, my meat poisoning experience was potent and disenchanting enough to warrant a change of location. I hitchhiked back to Salta. Had I been cognizant of the trouble awaiting me there, I would have remained at Hotel Rio Hondo.

Superwalter in Salta

The greatest obstacle to being heroic is the doubt whether one may not be going to prove oneself a fool. The truest heroism is to resist the doubt; and the profoundest wisdom to know when it ought to be resisted and when obeyed. - Nathaniel Hawthorne.

Two days later, upon arriving in Salta, I waltzed into Café Colón for morning coffee. Perched next to a large window, my broad view of Salta's vivacious main square was most refreshing and entertaining. Young men sauntered about fancying pretty girls as they happened by. Among the screaming ruckus of colonial-style buildings and bustling pedestrians slouched a shoeshine boy advertising his services from behind a small desk in front of an ornate white church.

"Come shine your shoes; only one peso!" he yelled.

There was more to the hollering adolescent than shoe shining. The giggling rascal was gawking at a small hand-held mirror he had affixed to the floor, cleverly peeking under the skirts of oblivious female passers-by.

"So, I see you kept your promise to check me up when you arrived in town," Luisa said, smiling as she placed a cup of espresso on my table. "How was Enrique?"

"He was great," I enthused, planting a kiss on Luisa's cheek. "He allowed me to sketch portraits of customers at the hotel for three weeks, but I figured it was time for a change."

"Well, it's not so much of a change to be here, but I'm glad you're back," Luisa whispered seductively, strutting back to the bar. "If you need a place to stay, please let me know."

"Thank you very much, you're an angel."

Swigging my first gulp of steaming espresso, I noticed a fracas across the street. It was a hulky policeman hitting a man with a club repetitiously.

I recognized the much smaller man. His name was Federico, an epileptic son of a wealthy Salta rancher. He was obviously undergoing one of his seizures, dressed impeccably in a suit and tie and jerking on the ground as the policeman clubbed him violently. Apparently, the officer assumed Federico was drunk.

I sprung from my seat to play super hero. As I sprinted towards them, Federico was crying aloud, flailing his arms animatedly.

"Leave him alone," I yelled. "The poor guy's sick!"

The emotionless policeman kept pounding Federico with his fists, until the epileptic curled on the ground in fetal-like position.

That's when I grabbed the officer, restraining him from the presumably wounded Federico. My interruption only infuriated the burly cop. He struck at me with his club.

Witnessing the unfair scuffle unfold regurgitated horrid memories of my countless run-ins with Nazi legal enforcement, emboldening me to wrest the club from the unjust man of the law.

I clubbed him until he too lay helpless on the curb, to the numerous bystanders' boisterous chants of approval.

Then I helped the still-shivering Federico to his feet?

"Now, officer, tell Federico how sorry you are," I demanded, as the cowering, bruised policeman struggled to his feet.

"I'm sorry," he muttered before scuttling away.

As soon as he gained considerable distance, the hobbling policeman swore vengeance.

"*Lo va a pagar duro,*" he yelled. "You'll pay for this."

While I wished the bully officer was joking, deep down I acknowledged he meant every word. As one could expect, an unwritten law in Argentina had it that if you assaulted a policeman, you could undoubtedly expect the punishing wrath of every officer in the city.

I needed to disappear.

After high-fiving Café Colón customers on my way back to my seat, I noticed a stack of local newspapers next to the bar.

"Local Salta pharmacist Maria Cristina d'Jallad hired onto the governor's staff," read one of the front-page headlines.

The newspaper was a gift from heaven for I had once met Maria. I rushed off to the address listed at the end of the article.

The daughter of Persian immigrants, Maria was once the leading pharmacist in town. During my brief stay with Luisa, strolling the bustling streets of downtown Salta became a favorite hobby. I did anything to escape Luisa's drab company. One evening, I ran into a homeless Native Indian boy sitting on a curb crying hysterically.

"Qué pasó?" I inquired, noticing that the little boy's knee was badly bruised and bleeding profusely.

He cried louder.

My heart heavy with compassion, I unhesitantly picked up the bawling boy, and hauled him to a nearby pharmacy. The petite, dark-skinned and pretty Maria rushed to the pharmacy's lobby as I stumbled in.

"Do you have any alcohol and band-aid?" I asked. "This boy is in a lot of pain."

"Are you his father?" Luisa asked, as she grabbed the little boy from my arms.

"No, I saw him crying on the street and I figured I'd help," I replied, as Maria hustled the eight-year-old behind a counter.

Thirty minutes later, she returned with a smiling, patched-up boy, clutching a bar of chocolate.

"You must be the nicest man in the world for helping a homeless kid you'd never met," Maria said, as the child hugged me firmly. "After much ado, I discerned his name is Carlito."

I thanked Maria fervently, and dropped Carlito off at a nearby orphanage. I often wonder how his life turned out. His bright wide eyes indicated intelligence. I wished the little starlet well. He is probably in his sixties now.

That is how I met Maria Cristina, whom I then sought to avail me from police trouble.

A distant relative of the governor, Maria had rapidly risen through the ranks of the state's health dept.

After scouring downtown Salta, I came upon her office building. Maria was predictably shocked to see me.

"Oh my, it's Walter the superhero!" Maria exclaimed, as she welcomed me into her large, gracious office, dominated with a gigantic portrait of the governor against a backdrop of downtown Salta. "What kid are you trying to save this time?"

"It's not a kid, this time it's a grown man," I joked.

I quickly narrated my tumultuous ordeal: From saving Federico to my subsequent dismal standing with the Salta Police Department.

"Perhaps you should consider wearing a mask because you really are a superhero," Maria said. "This time you saved Federico, a cousin of mine."

"Oh, he is?"

"Yes," she said. "I'll surely advise the police to leave you alone."

Armed with Maria's assurance of police immunity, I strolled to Salta's public swimming pool, blocks away from Maria's office. Immersing my bruised body in the cool, blue-green water was immensely relaxing, but yet felt uneasy.

Horror struck a few minutes later when I bobbed to the pool surface for air. The police had discovered my "hideaway." A dozen of them surrounded the pool, aiming their rifles at me.

One of the policemen was about to collar me when I dove under water and resurfaced on the opposite end of the pool. The clumsy policemen dashed to my location. Once again, I dove underwater and swam to the other side of the pool. We sustained this cat and mouse routine forever until I eventually surrendered, more out of extreme fatigue than cowardice.

"Stand back, let me get out," I yelled to the fuming officers, as I emerged from the pool.

They immediately handcuffed and hauled me to a reeking police station, a small older building near the square. Soon detained in a dirty, claustrophobic cell, I kissed my freedom goodbye for at least a month.

"See you in the interrogation room, you fucking idiot," one of the policemen snorted, not that I needed to be informed of the beating that was surely to follow my detention.

All of a sudden, like so many times in my life, fate intervened. The phone rang. It was a call from the governor's office; from my cell, I could hear the captain taking orders for my release.

Literally, five minutes later, the captain popped my cell open.

"You're free to go, but we'll get you sooner or later," he barked rudely, as he uncuffed me. "Watch your steps."

I once met Captain Bruno when I visited Salta to purchase horses from the Argentine cavalry for Normando.

One sweltering afternoon, while I downed a beer in Café Colón, Captain Bruno walked in. I immediately recognized his lanky, tall physique, very much equestrian characteristics. Captain Bruno's surreal reddish blond hair and distinctive fair skin hinted at Italian heritage.

He soon spotted and joined me at the table.

"You don't seem very happy," he immediately observed, as he firmly shook my hand. "Maybe this will cheer you up. Would you like to see two Germans screwing?"

Certain I was the only German in Salta, I sensed Captain Bruno, well known for his dry humor, was up to no good. I braced myself.

"Do you mean a man and a woman?"

"Yes," he said, pulling me aggressively from my seat. "A male and a female, real Germans."

"This had better be good," I warned.

I trailed Captain Bruno cautiously out of Café Colón into a nearby dark alley. After five minutes of floundering through putrid wastewater, I hesitated, weighed down with second thoughts about engaging in pervert voyeurism. Did I really want to peek through an open window to witness a man and woman engaging in fornication, with four white feet dangling from their bedcovers? What if I got shot?

"Come on," Captain Bruno yelled, waving me forward. "Don't chicken out on me now."

I slowly unlocked myself from my previously frozen stance. Captain Bruno suddenly stopped at a residential wooden fence. He approached the high threshold and poked his head through a hole, where a plank had decayed.

Like a mischievous adolescent boy peeking on a naked aunt, Captain Bruno began to giggle softly.

Soon I was standing sheepishly behind him, wondering if I had become the sorry victim of a bad joke.

"I have gone this far, I might as well go all the way," I thought, my heart throbbing with so much unbridled excitement I felt faint.

Lo and behold, there in the yard stood two German Dobermans mating aggressively, the male jockeying back and forth to maintain balance on sturdy hind feet as he toiled relentlessly, his tongue lolled out and drooling saliva in utmost excitement.

Captain Bruno and I enjoyed numerous rounds of infectious laughter as we walked back to Café Colón.

"Those are actually my dogs that I breed as a secret side business," he explained, as we walked back into Café Colón. "I thought you'd find that funny."

"Very funny, Captain," I replied. "Don't be surprised if I return the favor."

Over a cup of coffee, I soon divulged to Captain Bruno my devastating locust experience.

"So what are you planning to do now?" he asked, his voice laced with concern.

"Normando asked me to stay and I've had offers from other area farmers, but I don't want to go through that again," I whined.

Captain Bruno listened attentively with a smile glued to his face.

"Would you consider working for us as a language teacher?" he asked. "Many of our officers have children on base. They'd love for their kids to learn English."

"Will the children be boys and girls?" I asked, as I blushed with a fervid rush of excitement.

"Only boys, we don't mix them here."

"Captain, it sounds like we have a deal," I enthused, stretching for an animated handshake. "If you don't mind, I'll see you at the post tomorrow morning to discuss details."

Clad in my most impeccable attire, I arrived early the following morning.

"Walter, I want you to realize this job is temporary because some of the officers could be transferred anytime," Captain Bruno warned, shoving a stack of paperwork in front of me. "In other words, don't fall too much in love."

Captain Bruno's trivial warnings were like bullets darting above my head. I relished and looked forward to the impressive salary and the free room and board on the base.

"When do you want me to start?"

"Let me talk to the other officers first," Captain Bruno replied, grinning at my ebullient enthusiasm. "I'll give you an answer over coffee at 0800 tomorrow."

"Thank you for your vote of confidence."

I became a base employee the next morning. It was Friday, and I was to report to work on Monday.

"Then, I'll introduce you to your quarters," Captain Bruno assured. "I'll try to find you some books that may be of help."

"Would there be a chance to do some horseback riding while on base?"

"I'm sure we can work something out. See you on Monday."

I spent the entire weekend writing texts and syllabi for the rudimentary English classes. My students spoke no English, which meant an eerie return to the alphabet.

"German punctuality?" Captain Bruno observed as I sped into the office Monday morning.

I had arrived to work thirty minutes early.

My residence was a guest room, equipped with its own bathroom. Captain Bruno introduced me to other base officers, all of whom seemed excited to have me. The atmosphere was conducive.

"We'll put up a blackboard for you," one of the officers offered. "If you need anything, please write it on it."

The English lessons were scheduled from 2-4 p.m. Five officers constituted my adult classes programmed at 10 a.m. on Mondays, Wednesdays and Fridays.

As expected, my lessons with the kids were an astounding information exchange. They learnt just as much English from me as I learnt Spanish from them. The three adult classes brought even more fun-filled activity, often concluding with the officers inviting me for dinner, and me expressing my gratitude by drawing impressive portraits.

The parents seemed satisfied, and the youngsters loved me. I fully expected for Captain Bruno to extend my initial three-month contract.

After a few classes, the students spoke English reasonably well, albeit facetiously as they often struggled to express themselves with limited vocabulary.

"Hello, I call me Jorge," one of the kids said, translating literally, but awkwardly, from Spanish. "I have eight years."

I reveled in my academic activities, but sorely missed the country, the *peones*, the *capataces*, and the indescribable freedom of breezy life on Normando's finca.

A few weeks later, I scooped some dog feces from the street, and shoved it into a gift package, which I placed on Captain Bruno's desk.

"The German couple left this for you with many kind regards," read the accompanying note.

Captain Bruno was, understandably so, still fuming when I met him two days later in the city cafeteria.

"My mother told me to always be polite and return favors and gifts," I snorted, bribing Captain Bruno with a large mug of espresso.

We laughed at each other's silliness, and all was well.

The Bronco Rider of Salta

Great trials seem to be a necessary preparation for great duties.
- Edward Thomson.

Captain Bruno and I became the best of comrades, so much so that he hand-picked and invited me to Salta's colorful 9th of July, Independence Day ceremony.

After four years of unrest, Argentina effectively gained independence from Spain in 1816. Liberator extraordinaire Don Juan de San Martin, after whom virtually all memorabilia in Argentina is named, spearheaded the push for independence.

The slate of events included a cavalry procession, a rodeo and an equestrian contest. The small Salta arena was packed with enthusiastic, flag-waving Argentines. It was perhaps the most overt expression of patriotism I had ever witnessed since Germany's rabid celebration of Hitler's April 20th birthdays.

I sat next to Captain Bruno in the VIP bleachers, as the cavalry delegation, clad in colorful regalia, rode in utter elegance.

"Why aren't you part of the cavalry delegation?" I asked, standing in ovation like the rest of the spectators.

"My small house doesn't have the room for more trophies," he replied. "Besides, the younger officers should get the opportunity to shine."

The arena was spotted with high hurdles and artificial puddles of stagnant water. The stage was perfectly set for the 9th of July cavalry contest as the riders reigned their horses in preparation for what appeared to be a rather short but tumultuous and circuitous race. When the hurdle race began, Captain Bruno yelled chants of encouragement to the numerous competitors like a losing gambler.

After the cavalry competition, the festivities fell sinfully drab until a gaucho, bucking painfully atop a bronco, was ejected ten feet into the air, landing hard on the dusty ground. Boisterous applause soon followed.

"Is there someone in the audience that would like to try La Mama, a quick trip to the nearby hospital?" the announcer joked. "Let him come forward."

Nobody volunteered.

"Really, that doesn't seem to be so difficult," I whispered to Captain Bruno.

To my utmost shock and horror, Captain Bruno turned to the announcer and yelled, "We have a volunteer. *El alemán* will ride *La Mama*."

I had certainly not intended to imply that I wished to ride to my untimely death.

"Captain Bruno, how can you do this to me," I snapped.

"Don't let me down," Captain Bruno said, giggling.

My remonstrations were to no avail as two gleeful-looking gauchos on tenterhooks braced La Mama in preparation for my advance.

"*Arriba, vamos, viva Alemania*," the crowd teased.

My buttocks had barely touched La Mama's back when the wild horse hurled me to the ground, bucking vertically and horizontally.

"You bought much real estate," the announcer joked. "A special applause for the German!"

Despite losing miserably, the audience applauded vociferously. Fortunately, my bones were intact, and I departed the arena a popular man that day. As a result of my success that day, I dedicated myself to mastering the life-threatening Spanish tradition.

For bronco-riding training, Captain Bruno recommended Don Eduardo Gomez, a famous horse rancher resident near Salta. Eduardo possessed more than twenty untamed horses that needed to be broken.

I drove two hours to Eduardo's sprawling finca, dominated by a large white ranch house set against the backdrop of a hilly horizon. It was beautiful.

Eduardo was raking his front yard when I clambered out of my truck to approach him. He was a good-looking middle-aged man, impeccably dressed as a gaucho, with accordion-like shafted boots and bombachas. Draped over his torso was an elegant red poncho with black stripes, typical Salta colors. Under a white sombrero hid a weathered face graced with a well-trimmed black mustache. His slightly open poncho revealed a beautiful rastra, a silver belt buckle clasped with three silver chains on each side. Golden coins adorned his belt, an indication of wealth.

"It would be my pleasure to teach you the ways of the gaucho," he said, after a brief introduction. "You look like the type that could win at the nationals."

I took Eduardo's munificent compliments to heart, albeit superficially. He was, of course, referring to the popular Argentine National Championship of Horse Taming, of which I was mightily cognizant. Winning at the exigent national competition took years of mastery and expertise of gaucho life that I certainly could not boast.

"I'm not sure about winning the nationals, but thanks for your vote of confidence," I replied.

"I know a winner when I see one," he enthused. "Trust me."

Inspired by the rancher's words of encouragement, I practiced laboriously at Eduardo's corral every morning for three strenuous weeks. He coached me intensely as if deriving pleasure from my slow success.

One morning, Eduardo wrapped his muscular arm around my shoulders and yelled, "You are now a real gaucho!" His words brought much relief for my buttocks and palms had hardened like cement after three-weeks of riding and falling.

The National Championship of Horse Taming was scheduled for Córdoba (central Argentina) in four months. I had easily acquired gaucho skills and status. One overwhelming barrier remained. Only members of the exclusive *Agrupación de Gauchos Güemes*, a traditional gaucho organization named after Salta-born

Argentine independence hero General Martin Miguel de Guëmes, were permitted to participate. To become a member, one had to be an Argentine citizen and Salta native, a cumbersome criterion that clearly excluded me.

"I hate to disappoint you, Eduardo, but my gaucho competition days in Salta might well be over," I explained, packing my belongings.

"Wait. There has to be a way around their silly rules," Eduardo said. "You're a citizen, right?"

"No."

"Well, I didn't know you were not a citizen," Eduardo said, frowning in disappointment. "Anyway, establishing Argentine citizenship is not that hard, not anymore."

"What are you talking about?"

One of Perón's many liberal political endeavors, since my arrival in Salta, was a decree that permitted citizenship for all residents occupant in Argentina for at least four years.

Eduardo, Captain Bruno and Salta's Notary Public Julio Ortega all signed my naturalization application, swearing that they had known me for more than four years. I had known them for less than two.

Argentine law dictated that all naturalized citizens translate their names to Spanish versions. Thus, Walter ought to have been translated to Gualterio. However, the semi-illiterate Salta clerk converted my name to Walterio. His ludicrous blunder arguably made me the only Walterio in the universe, unless another dull clerk elsewhere made the same mistake. That was very unlikely.

Armed with an Argentine passport, I grew emboldened to visit American Consul Mr. Guerra to test my luck for a visa to the United States. I drove Eduardo's 1949 Chevy Convertible to Buenos Aires. On Corrientes Avenue, I popped the convertible roof, eyeing the local girls gawking at me in awe

On my way to the American Consulate, I zipped passed the Zanzibar, but I u-turned, quite unable to resist my goose bump-raising curiosity.

How was Mónica doing?

I pushed open the doors to the near-empty nightclub, and glanced around for Mónica's unmistakable hair and figure.

"It's nice to see you again," she whispered from behind me, scaring me enough to make me blush.

She hugged and kissed me nonchalantly like we had seen each other the night before. I quickly noticed why. Two angry-looking men stared rudely from the bar. I imagined they were Mónica's "special" customers.

"I'd like to see you tonight because I'm leaving in the morning," I whispered. "Shall I wait for you at the apartment house?"

My return to the Zanzibar was homely but short. The American Consulate was my primal goal. Would my changed citizenship status secure me an American visa?

"Si," Monica whispered in my ear on my out.

I walked to the American Consulate from the Zanzibar.

Mr. Guerra seemed suspiciously pleased to see me.

"Have you heard from Mr. Carroll?" he inquired.

"I've received a number of letters from him," I lied, sinking into a seat in Mr. Guerra's office. "He's still trying to get me that visa."

"I hope he succeeds."

"Mr. Guerra, I may not need any help from John Carroll. I'm now an Argentine citizen."

Suddenly, Mr. Guerra's jolly face morphed into one of indescribable woe. He looked down, wringing his hands. He appeared hesitant to be the hated messenger of some horrible news.

"I'm very sorry, Walter, but United States law makes it very clear that you have the citizenship of where you were born," he explained. "Thus, you're still a German and would still have to wait for a quota number to become available for a visa."

Utterly disappointed and enraged, I stormed out of Mr. Guerra's office.

"Take it easy, come back to see me," he yelled as I slammed the door.

At 2 a.m. the next morning, as consolation for my earlier misfortune, I drove to Monica's apartment. Five minutes later, a cab halted in front of the complex. Monica stepped out. She looked beautiful and my heart throbbed in eagerness to make love to her again. I caught a whiff of her unique scent as she strut towards me. My taste buds responded with a recognizance of her taste on my tongue.

With no "customers" around, we hugged and kissed intensely.

"Walter darling, I would like to take a bath, would you join me?"

The trip to erotic paradise soon began, and ended at 4 a.m. when I passed out in Monica's arms. She felt even better than before.

Over a breakfast of steak and eggs, I gisted Monica about my tumultuous life in Salta: My tobacco plantation and subsequent locust devastation.

"You seem to be born for adventures," she said.

I smiled.

"I know you must leave now but please come again," Monica said, her voice quivering and eyes swelling with tears, as I prepared to leave. "It's so nice to have you close."

"I missed you too, many times," I replied. "I promise to be back."

We embraced tenderly. I turned my back on Monica for the last time.

Apart from my sexual endeavors with Monica, my trip to Buenos Aires was a waste. However, while driving back to Salta, I braced myself for challenges ahead. How will I establish Salta citizenship in time for the championship?

After approximately an hour of brainstorming with Eduardo, which ranged from counterfeiting my birth certificate to changing my name to Walterio Gomez, Eduardo concocted the strategy of the century.

"You're an artist, right?" he inquired.

"Yes," I replied flatly. "But I doubt that'll save me this time."

"Why don't you do a portrait of General Guëmes and present it to the association," Eduardo said, slapping me on the shoulder. "That'll definitely get you in. Perhaps as an honorary member."

Eduardo procured a few pictures of the fully bearded General Guëmes, and I went to work, scribbling away through the night.

Just like Eduardo had predicted, the club accepted the portrait, depicting General Güemes standing upright in military garb, and subsequently inducted me as an honorary member, fully eligible to compete in the nationals.

"I'm very proud of you," Eduardo said, after the protracted induction ceremony. "I know you will win and I'll be there to watch you."

Two weeks later, Eduardo, his ranch *capataz* Felipe and I departed for the competition in a Ford truck. The first phase of the trip took us through Tucumán to Santiago del Estero.

We detoured temporarily into Santiago for breakfast and armed ourselves with empanadas for the rest of the trip. Eduardo and Felipe did the driving. "You need all your energy for the ride tomorrow," Eduardo advised when I offered to drive.

We culminated our 500-mile winding trip from Salta to Córdoba at exactly 5 p.m. I remember the time because I went to sleep without dinner that night. We lodged at a small hotel. Don Eduardo was fairly familiar with Córdoba for he had participated in the championship ten years ago.

Walter and the Governor of Salta, with Walter's portrait of the Governor

The next morning, I promptly registered for the competition at the stadium. The arena resembled a soccer field, with bleachers on both sides and a grandstand for distinguished guests, the announcer and judges. Vendors weaved through the bleachers hustling drinks and sweets.

The show began at 4 p.m. Applause heightened upon the governor's entrance. The competition commenced with an equestrian event and a display of Argentina's first batch of locally built cars.

To hasten Argentina's industrialization, Perón had partly banned car importation, authorizing instead the manufacture of Argentine automobiles in Córdoba. The cars never lasted. Perón was eventually forced to remove the embargo on the far superior foreign cars.

"Now, to introduce the young stallions!" the announcer said, as a horde of mustangs swarmed the pitch.

The broncos were unexpectedly small, not nearly as wild as Eduardo's.

"Perhaps transportation to the arena took some of the wild spirit away," I whispered to Eduardo.

"You better hope so."

I was the fifth rider to perform. I marveled at gauchos from Argentina's Pampas region riding with *alpargatas*, straw-soled slippers, instead of boots. The horses entered the arena through a large arch entrance. Following instructions, I clung onto the arch, spotted a horse and fell on its back.

I pounced on a brown bronco, and twisted his mane around my fingers. The animal bucked lightly despite my aggressive encouragement. Kicking my legs back and forth didn't help much either. I began to redden with embarrassment. The relatively gentle animal did not afford me enough action to impress the spectators.

My ride ended with me climbing down from the idle horse, scarred with a frown. My mood changed favorably when the announcer pronounced me bronze winner.

"Thank you very much Walterio, you have been a swell sport," the governor said, as he shook my hand and awarded me a red poncho.

My head bowed, I rejoined Eduardo.

"I know you're not happy, but you did very well and deserve third place," Eduardo said, trying unsuccessfully to encourage me. "I'm very proud of you."

This time, Eduardo's words proved barren and uninspiring for the trip back to Salta was dreary and uneventful.

"You did your share of work, I'll take care of the rest," Eduardo said, when I offered to cover some traveling expenses.

Eduardo was an all-around good man, one that would have made an excellent dad. I often saw in him many traits that my father could have used. Unfortunately, he was single with no children. It is a rather befuddling life phenomenon that men who deserve the joy of offspring never experience it, while those that do abuse it unremittingly.

We met with celebration and praise in Salta. I was the only one in our delegation that won a medal.

"*Viva el alemán!*" the welcome delegation yelled, as I rode into town.

And so it came to be that I became a respected gaucho in Salta, adorning my red and black poncho with utmost pride.

Senator Alberto Durán, who represented Salta in Buenos Aires, was present at the welcome ceremony. I came to know his sons, who also possessed large fincas near Salta. One of them owned a brand new Kaiser automobile, at a time when most Argentines drove old models.

One morning, the senator's young assistant came knocking on my door at the cavalry base.

"The senator would like to see you," he said.

"When?"

"He expects to see you at four this afternoon."

The senator's huge mansion in Salta was proximal to General Guëmes' awesome monument, depicting the Salta hero clad in gaucho attire and, of course, straddling a horse.

A uniformed servant ushered me beyond the mansion's heavily engraved oak door. The senator soon joined me in the gaudily furnished living room. He was an elegant looking aristocrat, with white hair and fair skin, definitely void of indigenous blood.

"I need somebody I can trust," he began, rather no-nonsense-like as we shook hands.

"Senator, the fact that you had me come to your house must mean that you trust me."

"Please sit down," he said. "I'm aware that you're quite the horseman, but do you think you could take a herd of steers across the Andes to the Chilean border?"

My blood sped through my veins, as I smelled adventure.

"I know I can."

"Let's have some coffee. Juan, get us two cups of coffee."

Standing by the living room entrance was Juan, the assistant that had knocked on my door earlier. No sooner had he departed than a properly dressed young maid served us coffee, sugar and cookies from a silver tray.

Without hesitation, we deliberated the number of cattle and helpers, which routes to take, provisions for the trek and my payment.

"Will there be any border control?" I asked.

"No. Everything has been arranged."

"How do I get back and how do the helpers return?"

"You'll get all the assistance you need on the Chilean border," he assured. "Either by bus or train, you and your helpers will get to Antofagasta. From there, you'll fly back to Salta."

"When do I need to be ready?"

"I want you to leave this weekend. Today is Monday. That'll give you four to five days to get everything ready. I want you to leave at dawn so you donh't call too much attention to the drive."

"Besides my clothes, what else must I bring along?"

"Nothing at all. All you need to worry about is the success of the trip."

I stopped to marvel a little at the mansion's undoubtedly painstaking and expensive décor. A life-size portrait of Senator Durán, bedecked in a suit and tie, graced the decorated wall above the menacing fireplace, which looked large and deep enough to fit three men.

"How about a beer, we should celebrate a little," Senator Durán said, interrupting my protracted stare.

"The brew master in Salta would be put in jail if he brewed such strange liquid in Germany," I joked, for I had never taken to the inferior local brew.

"I don't care much for the local brew either," he said. "We serve imported beer."

Juan was in charge of procuring provisions for the trip and rounding up helpers, all of whom worked on the senator's finca. The cattle were ranched at corrals near Salta.

"All the animals will be in one central area," Juan explained, after rejoining us momentarily to iron out a few details. "I'll pick you up from the base at 3 a.m. and take you to the senator's finca."

Juan knocked on my door at 2:55 a.m. Heart-throbbing excitement kept me awake all night. The helpers were alert and ready when we arrived at the finca.

"*El gaucho alemán*," several of the helpers mused, as I shook each one of their hands.

Apparently, they had heard of my rodeo championship exploits on the local radio.

Alas, my bronco-riding education in Salta paid off well for we virtually crossed the Chilean border on grueling horseback. We departed at dawn on Saturday, and drove the herd to San Antonio de los Cobres, a small mining town, to Salar de Arizaro, renowned for its salt mines, to Paso Socompa on the Chilean border.

To reach Paso Socompa, perched at a reasonable 3,858m (12,600 ft) altitude, we had to climb approximately 5,000m (16,400 ft) over terrain elevated by centuries of eruptions by the dormant Llullaillaco volcano, one of the highest elevations on the northwestern Andes (22,000 ft) and site of numerous human sacrifices during the height of the Inca empire.

Such daunting altitudes meant we would lose a few animals, a fact I had not discussed with Senator Durán. By the third morning, we had lost seven animals. The surviving animals had had enough by the seventh sudden death. They clamored around the fresh carcass, and turned their black, glassy eyes towards me, seemingly asking: "Well? What next?"

We started them off on the road again.

The scenery along the Andes was breathtakingly similar to images of the moon. With the exception of a blue sky, the scanty horizon bore a picturesque mixture of white and gray colors.

Walter Meyer, gaucho

In the evenings, we rounded up the steers and camped in our tents and sleeping bags. We occasionally grabbed something warm to eat at several small settlements along the dusty route to Paso Socompa. The meat was mostly vizcacha, a large hare indigenous to the mountains.

Other than the occasional steer keeling over to its untimely death, the ride was relatively straightforward, and we had little precipitation. Like Senator Durán promised, the Argentine border patrol let us pass into Chile without qualms. The undulating terrain and high altitudes prevented us from covering more than 20 km a day.

As we rose higher on the volcanic plains, blood began to trickle from my nose. Following the helpers' suggestions, I chewed coca leaves but to little avail.

"This coca only worsens my headache," I grumbled, spitting the leaves out of my mouth.

"Don Walter, if you want to live, chew on the coca leaves," the men joked.

The helpers seemed utterly comfortable with the high altitudes, which I found annoying for I was virtually drenched with blood. On several occasions, we ran into little native boys playing soccer as I struggled to keep my head from exploding.

"How in the world can they play soccer on such terrain?" I asked.

"They've grown bigger lungs and hearts," one of my helpers explained. "Even bigger than yours, alemán."

The helpers helped themselves to another round of boisterous laughter. I could not wait to surrender the steers to the party expecting us. Senator Durán arranged for Señor Mariategui, a middle-aged burly man, to meet us at a corral just south of Paso Socompa.

"Walter, you did very well," Mariátegui said, upon our arrival. "Thank you very much."

Mariátegui led us to a rail station, where we boarded a small train to Antofagasta, whereupon we were scheduled to fly back to Salta. On the way to Antofagasta, I ordered good Chilean beer for all.

We lost seven steers on the way. Beneath the early celebrations on the train, I wondered how Senator Durán would take the bad news.

"The altitude almost killed me," I explained to Senator Durán in his living room three days later. "I'm sorry, but we lost seven steers. I hope I can make it up to you somehow."

"Nonsense," he said, giggling. "I expected to lose at least 20."

Two weeks later, Senator Durán invited me to work for him in Salta, but I had since become obsessed with Perú, which was fast becoming one of Latin America's most stable countries. Two months after my bronco-riding bronze victory, I decided to investigate the conditions there, since the economic conditions in Argentina had begun to deteriorate.

When a local businessman requested that I drive one of his trucks to the Chilean border, I hesitated not.

Unlike my previous spontaneous departures, I felt little guilt leaving Salta. My academic endeavors on the base had culminated because the officers, whose children I was teaching, were transferred. Their replacements were childless.

"We'll miss you sorely," Captain Bruno mumbled, forcing back tears.

"Thank you for everything, including the German couple," I replied, as we burst out in boisterous laughter.

Surprisingly, I am still in contact with Captain Bruno.

Salta had become my surrogate home. So, before departing the beautiful Northern city, I accepted an invitation to attend a farewell party organized by friends on the base. It turned out to be one of my biggest mistakes, other than landing myself in a concentration camp in Nazi Germany.

Perón had placed an embargo on imported alcoholic beverages, which meant Argentines had to make do with distasteful local brew. The host served peanuts, chicharon, gin, coca leaves and bicarbonate, the usual party menu.

"*No te vayas a olvidar de Salta,*" Captain Bruno said, as the party came to an end.

I woke up that night vomiting fiercely, hobbled with excruciating abdominal pain. The Argentine gin had given me alcohol poisoning, a dreadful illness. I spent the next three weeks in sheer agony, many times doubting that I would survive.

As I chugged the truck out of town one morning, pale with malnourishment, and billowing piles of dust behind me, little did I know that more than twenty years would pass before my return to Salta.

Never again did I have another Argentinian alcoholic drink.

Mines, Mummies and Mary

All is acceptable until our giddy brains be satisfied; afterwards we let familiar things lie, and seek after new. - Martin Luther.

I had never driven such a humongous beast.

The Diamond C truck, an American surplus vehicle used in North Africa to load bombs during World War II, bumbled its way to my destination: The world's tallest sulfur mine, perched on the northeastern border of Chile and Argentina.

My task: To fetch an order of sulfur for Salta-native Horst Weiland. He drove another truck ahead of me.

"I'll drive a smaller truck ahead of you so I can prepare the mines for your arrival," said Weiland, son of German immigrants, prior to our departure from Salta.

After fifty miles of horrendously bumpy terrain, I pulled over and idled the truck to inspect my right palm. The rubber sheath covering the gearshift was nonexistent, and the exposed metal threads had transfigured my tender skin into numerous blisters in only two hours of driving. I tore off my shirt, tied it into a hard knot around the gearshift, and put the truck back in first gear.

The road out of Salta was just as exhilarating as it was a year ago. Winding unrelentlessly into the arresting Andes, the narrow strip of dirt looked undaunted by the ferocious snow-topped mountains. I remember the picturesque stretch of land graced with minor landmarks, unadulterated by the torturous hot weather. All seemed perfectly preserved by the high altitude and chapping dryness.

By afternoon, I reached San Antonio de los Cobres. Children ran alongside the truck as I chugged through the village. Some of the natives recognized me, flashing their dazzling crooked teeth. As they waved their arms animatedly, I noticed white bandages taped on their forearms. Apparently, a doctor had been around to inoculate them.

I screeched to a near murderous halt a few inches from two animal pedestrians impeding traffic. The muddied pigs rooted themselves on the road, unperturbed by repeated honking. I pulled over.

The stench of an open latrine filled the air as I clambered out of the truck. The animals stared me down rudely as I walked toward them, scowling and cursing. The pigs stood their ground as if threatening me.

"Shoo!"

The pigs' persistent, cold stare reminded me of a story villagers had once told me.

A priest had visited the village to teach. On his first day, he had squatted over a pit latrine to do his business. A pig came from behind, and bit off his dangling testicles.

Standing aback and guarding my crotch, I grabbed one idle piglet by the hind legs, and relocated it to the roadside. When I reached for the second, it squealed and raced to the high ground of a pile of roadside shale.

Eventually, I stumbled upon a decaying steer corpse. His unique cranial "X" brand made him reasonably decipherable. He was the first steer casualty during my first trip through the mountains. I immediately recalled his lugubrious resistance when one of the men had toiled unsuccessfully to guide him back into the traveling herd. He had begun to struggle to his death, oodles of blood oozing from every facial orifice as the altitude took its noxious toll.

As I drove past the carcass, imagery of the fly-infested pink flesh on his muzzle flashed across my mind. The steer had fallen on its knees, slid his face into the dirt and heaved its last sigh.

Other strewn, lifeless steers blotched the rest of the trip. Otherwise, the ride was beautiful. I had not thoroughly appreciated the sheer natural architecture of the Andes the first time. Above 10,000 feet, the hardscrabble terrain was nearly void of vegetation, only jagged buttes, violent, gray inselbergs and the occasional path of frozen runoff seeping along a shaded cliff face.

Blood splattered on my pants when I leaned forward for the ignition. The steady trickle was from my nose. The noxious altitudinal effects had overcome me quicker than before. I worked my jaw to prevent the flow of deafening liquid to my ears.

I spent two days in the mine's barracks, loading sulphur onto the truck, and toiling to rid myself of *puna*, the local term for altitudinal sickness. Even the trucks needed treatment. After sucking aggressively for scarce oxygen for so long, the carburetors got tired easily and needed adjusting. Weiland would leave the truck at the mine until summer.

I purchased necessary groceries at a commissary near the mine and boarded a train to Antofagasta, Chile.

Antofagasta had some 80,000 inhabitants, no skyscrapers, a lovely park and myriad wooden houses. Its main attraction was the city's picturesque clear beaches on the Pacific Ocean. The largest city of the Chilean Norte Grande region, Antofagasta was a product of the mining boom that hit the region in the 19th century.

Profitable nitrate mines of the last century brought many foreign settlers to the city. Chilean anthropologists theorized that the many Inca mummies erected on the open plains of the Atacama Desert were preserved by dry Norte Grande nitrate sand.

I checked into a small hotel in the *Barrio Histórico*, home to many historic Victorian buildings, including the clock tower of the Plaza Colón, an exact replica of Big Ben.

It was summertime in Chile, and I longed a dip in the several pristine beaches along Antofagasta's coastline.

"There is a nice beach not far away," the hotel manager instructed, as he showed me to my room.

Bedecked with gentle waves, white sand and clear blue water, the beach was simply beautiful.

From their boisterous mannerisms and unique slang talk, I could discern the volleyball players on the beach were Americans. I sunk into a beach chair, and watched the female side defeat the men.

"Hey, guy! Would you be in for a game of volleyball?" one of the men yelled. "We could use some energy here. Them women are kicking our asses."

"Sure," I replied, racing unhesitantly to the net. "You guys are a shame to mankind."

The women laughed.

"And you're the superhero that's here to save all mankind, right?" one of the women inquired facetiously.

"That's right!"

The male side won the remaining rounds of volleyball that afternoon. It was not because of my stellar performance for I was a poor player. The men had been down one man.

Employees of the Chile Exploration Company in Chuquicamata, (commonly known as Chuqui) the Americans seemed impressed that I had just crossed the Andes from Argentina. One Ralph Morgan seemed most helpful.

"We need an athletic director," said Morgan, as we strolled from the volleyball court back to the hotel. "You seem to be very athletic, why don't you come apply for the job?"

"I'm really trying to get to Perú, but I'll come by in a few days and look into the situation."

The Americans shook hands, and bade me well.

Upon reentering the hotel, a ritzy bar near the lobby made my mouth water for a glass of wine. I could not resist the temptation.

"Can I have a glass of Concha y Toro, please?" I asked, sitting on a stool next to a mustachioed young man.

"You know what they say about a man who knows his wines?" the young man said, smiling surreptitiously.

"He's a drunkard?" I joked.

Blonde and in his thirties, Adolfo had the bushiest of mustaches, which cast a cloud of untrustworthiness about him. However, he seemed genuinely enthused about transporting fresh fish from Antofagasta to Chuqui.

"Walter, to cut to the chase, I'm looking for a business partner," he offered, sucking on a cigar. "I don't know what it is, but you seem like the business type."

If only Adolfo was cognizant of the unsuccessful extent of my business escapades, I thought.

"I have developed lasting connections with fishermen operating on the Pacific," he said. "We can make a fortune."

"You know, I plan on getting a job in Chuqui," I said.

"I have to drive up there. Why don't you come with me?"

I traveled to Chuqui several times with Adolfo. On my first trip, we visited a restaurant to negotiate a fish sale. While Adolfo and the restaurant owner discussed prices and quantity, I helped myself to another glass of Concha y Toro.

Soon I was writhing on the bathroom floor, vomiting violently.

"You silly German," the restaurant owner joked. "Never drink in high altitude. Alcohol robs you of your oxygen supply."

On another trip, I tracked down Ralph Morgan, the American Chile Exploration Company employee, whom I had met playing beach volleyball.

Morgan eventually showed me the indoor pool, the bowling alley and other parts of the recreation section.

"Plus, the salary is not that bad," he added. "Like I said, the last time, we would love to have you."

I accepted a contract for one year.

My off-time travails in the area included a trip to the largest open-pit copper mines in the world, in Tocopilla and Calama, where I sat next to mummies in the Atacama Desert. The mummyfied statues were part of the Inca Empire, which stretched from Southern Colombia through Perú, and Bolivia to the east.

The air in the Atacama Desert and environs was so arid that men stashed Camels in refrigerators and women did the same with their stockings. Everyone had a chap stick.

I had a nicely furnished, but small, one-room apartment. The swimming pool, bowling alley and the volleyball court became my territories. I gave swimming lessons, participated in numerous bowling tournaments and volleyball games. I became well known in no time.

One day, a gorgeous lady strutted sexily to the pool. Armed with a rather erotically appetizing countenance, she had dark hair, big eyes and a sexy Texas drawl.

"Could you arrange private lessons, I'd be happy to pay extra," she said.

"Why don't you join everyone else," I replied, meaning the exact opposite.

"Well, I'd rather have individual lessons, if you don't mind."

Of course, I didn't mind at all, and I welcomed the additional money. The individual lessons led to romantic involvement, which seemed inevitable for our bodies were constantly so close and touching.

Despite being married, Mary brought needed romance to the dry and rather boring atmosphere of Northern Chile. As a Texan, she craved an outing to the desert. So, one afternoon, I volunteered to drive her into the heart of the Atacama.

Mary was clad in a tight red dress and a straw hat when we drove off into the scorching horizon. Throughout the trip, she posed for me like a model to a photographer. She was a silhouette in the sun, an utter beauty to watch.

We arrived at the desert, surrounded by dry, yellow grass bleached by sunlight. I touched her face. Her dry skin flushed with the light pressure of my thumb on her rosy cheek. She smiled at me through chapped lips. I stepped back to admire her. I had been shading her, blocking her sun. When I moved, the sun lit her up like a candle, and she squinted into the sun, shading her eyes with her slim arm. While doing the most trivial things, she was still beautiful.

If one is not rapidly sunburned or dehydrated, the desert is rather comfortable. Sweat rises to the surface of the skin and evaporates immediately, acting as an effective coolant. In the desert, Inca mummies sat with their legs upright at a 90 degree angle, and arms folded on their laps, staring into the distant sunrise. Their shadows circled around laggardly as the sun completed its overhead travails. Flies mingled briefly on the patches of ancient black hair plastered to their gray scalps. While desolate and arid, the desert was surprisingly bubbling with activity.

While Mary admired the terrain, I scurried to the side of a scrawny bush to pee. An Inca mummy squatted near me, its legs pulled to its chest and mouth agape, revealing a set of hollow black teeth. Mary did not notice our quiet chaperone.

"Do you like it?" she inquired from the hood of the car.

"It's very nice," I replied, assuming she was referring to her new hat.

"It was very expensive," she said, tossing the hat, "It's amazing, my husband thinks he can make me happy by simply buying me expensive stuff."

"What's so wrong with that?"

"It's a lazy approach to things," she explained. "For instance, the last time he took me on a trip like this was duirng our honeymoon. Now, all he does is return from 12-hour work days with an expensive, hat or shawl. That's an indication that he loves his work more, and wishes to simply buy me like everything else he owns. I detest the fact that he deems my love so cheap."

I caressed Mary's distraught face lightly. She smiled.

"You're so sweet," she said, pecking my hand.

Mary was my first American girlfriend, my first American adventure. While I was admitted to the U.S. Army hospital in Düsseldorf after the war, the GIs had shown off their pinup girls, passing them around delicately from cot to cot. The girls were undeniably pretty, frozen in the pirouettes of over-the-shoulder glances, coy smiles and sexy winks. Mary was a similar shapely, affable woman, rosy cheeks and all - a hidden promise.

The sun was orange now and descending. Shadows played out on Mary's face - her nose and eyelashes cast shades across the apples of her cheeks and the bony orbit around her eye. I ran my hand through her hair - it crackled with static electricity. So did our first kiss.

We sped back to town, hunting for the right spot to make love. I couldn't take Mary to my place, a little room attached to the swim club. Fortunately, I had keys to Enrique's vacation house on the outskirts of town, wherein we had partied often.

"Turn here," I said, pointing out of the window as Mary swung the car down the straight road to the small, unimpressive house.

We hid the car behind the house, where it couldn't be spotted from the road. It was her husband's spanking-new sedan, a brown Plymouth, which had accumilated a thin layer of dust in a day of driving.

I drew an "I" on the car's dusty hood, and looked at Mary.

"I'll tell him I had to borrow the car for the afternoon, and I went ..."

"Driving through the desert alone," I said, completing her sentence.

She nodded, smiling. Nothing mattered, but the explosive sexual attraction between us. Her eyes read that she was ready. I knew I was.

I popped open the back door. It was a nice place, decorated with colorful rugs, a few paintings and a reasonable collection of Chilean wines.

"Want a drink?" I asked.

"Gin and tonic."

I fixed Mary her drink and poured myself a small glass of red wine. She sipped her gin, while conducting a walking tour of the living room. My eyes followed her every move. Soon she returned to me and placed her hand on my chest. Her fingers were wet from the condensation on the glass, and I could feel the cold water through my shirt.

"I reckon we skip the childsplay and get to business," she said. "Where's the bedroom?"

We cut the lights in the bedroom, a residue of orange sunlight illuminating the room from the large sunroof overhead. Mary undressed me, tossing my clothing on a nearby mahogany rocking chair. We touched, kissed and made love, her rich black hair covering my face. She occasionally moved her head to kiss my neck, during which I noticed the early evening stars dotting the blue sky.

Then, I spotted something move beyond the sunroof. A man knelt on the roof, watching us grind away.

I immediately pushed Mary away and hustled to my feet. Sensing he had been caught, the man scrambled across the tiles, the sound of his feet slipping on the roof echoing through the bedroom. I threw my pants on. My destination: The car, as fast as possible.

While Mary whimpered in absolute confusion, I raced out of the room, assuming her husband had caught us.

"He'll literally kill me," I muttered.

I scampered out to the backyard, only to witness a man climbing down the rain gutter. He was dark-skinned, very much unlike Mary's white husband. I spun him around. It was Enrique.

At that moment, I wished I had a camera. The pitiful look on Enrique's face was a confusing cross between a forced smile and a childish grimace.

"I'm really sorry," he said, trying to be apologetic, innocent and cutely mischievous all at once, but the conglomerate expression was impish - a hyena's unconvincing grin.

Mary pulled on her shoes and smoothened her skirt as she stepped through the door. Her head was low - either in guilt or in embarrassment. Upon realizing that the man was not her husband, she froze, and burst out in laughter.

Life in the desert had been exciting. Once again, however, my blood boiled for new endeavors.

The Smuggler of Time

Man's crimes are his worst enemies, following him like shadows, till they drive his steps into the pit that he dug. - Creon.

I was bored. I needed money. Bolivia had no duties on imported merchandise. Swiss watches were less expensive there, so were fine English textiles.

One misty Friday afternoon, I took a leave of absence from my athletic director job in Chiquicamata, Chile and boarded a train from Antofagasta to Cochabamba, Bolivia to meddle in the illegal trafficking of Swiss watches from Bolivia to Chile.

Named after independence fighter Simón Bolivar, Bolivia broke away from Spanish rule in 1825; much of its subsequent history has consisted of a series of nearly 200 coups and counter-coups. Long one of the poorest and least developed Latin American countries, Bolivia was not exactly a bastion of booming capitalism, but Cochabamba was.

Founded in 1842 by Spanish colonists in the Kjocha-Pampa valley, the town had a thriving agriculture-based economy. Its climate: Warm sunny days and cool nights, made the metropolis a popular tourist attraction. The city lay in a fertile valley at 2,558 meters above sea level, surrounded by the Tunari hill, the Alalay lagoon and the San Sebastian hill. It was beautiful.

Almost every celebrity in Bolivia had a home in Cochabamba, including Simon Patiño, one of the nation's three famous tin barons. Construction on his sprawling Cochabamba estate, which is today an art museum and cultural center, began in 1915 and culminated in 1927!

Of underprivileged *mestizo* background, Patiño went from a lowly mining apprentice in Bolivia's Potosi tin mines to owning fifty percent of the national production, and controlling the European refining of Bolivian tin by 1924. Ironically, Patiño lived permanently abroad by the early 1920s and almost never resided in his grand Cochabamba home. The other leading tin-mining entrepreneurs, Carlos Aramayo and Mauricio Hochschild, remained primarily in Bolivia.

All three tin barons literally owned and controlled the diminutive country, including determining the policies of the Liberal Party administration, the success of which coincided with the tin boom in the early 1900's. Thus, the government assisted the industry and indirectly fattened Patiño's pockets by lightly taxing the nation's mining interests.

Upon arriving in Cochabamba, I scoured for the leading jewelry store near the famous Cathedral, located in the *Plaza 14 de Septiembre*. The cathedral, built in 1571, housed original frescos and paintings.

From The Cathedral, I could see El Cristo de la Concordia, an immense statue of Jesus Christ, which stood higher than the more famous Cristo de Corcovado in Rio de Janeiro, Brazil. Looking at Jesus stretching out his arms for a perpetual embrace afforded me ample confidence that I was in the right hands.

The jewelry store was tucked amongst a packed row of small shacks lining a major street in downtown Cochabamba, making it immensely difficult to find. I approached the storeowner, a man in his forties.

"Anything I can help you with my dear gringo," the storeowner said, in a heavy German accent. "My name is David Goldberg."

"You speak German?" I asked, suspending my mission temporarily. "My name is Walter."

"Yes," he replied. "I migrated from Leipzig in '38."

While I was certain David was not overtly advertising his Jewish heritage, migrating from Leipzig in the 1930's was loaded information. In 1938, Adolf Hitler delivered the infamous ultimatum that Jews exit Germany or face noxious consequences. Unfortunately, very few Jews managed to secure asylum in the many anti-semitic nations of the world, and millions of Jews were subsequently gassed to death.

David was one of the lucky.

He and I conversed lightly in German, my way of winning a sizeable discount on the watches. I purchased 150 for a third of the original retail price.

Mr. Goldberg was cognizant and quite supportive of my surreptitious plans to smuggle the watches across the border. My strategy was quite crafty. I took the armbands off the wristwatches, tied them together with strings and fastened the watches to my right leg.

"Do you know where I can purchase plaster of Paris?" I asked, uncoiling my right trouser leg over the strapped watches.

David immediately caught my idea.

"Hey, I know a quack veterinarian that would be more than willing to make you look as invalid as you like," David offered, giggling.

He handed me directions to the clinic. I took off.

Shortly thereafter, I resembled a man with a broken right leg. For an extra charge, the veterinarian gave me a pair of crutches. My story was that I had fallen off a horse. Word eventually got around that some German tourist suffered an accident.

The last train leaving Cochabamba to Arica, Chile was a private railroad car, consisting of only two cabins. The ride required a special VIP travelers permit.

I walked into the pristine, high-class ticket office at the train station, setting off what felt like a million stares. The ticket attendant gawked at me suspiciously as I limped to her desk.

"Where is your permit?" she snapped, before I had the chance to explain myself.

"I don't have one, but ..."

"Sir, please stand aside," she barked, as the on-site policeman tugged me away from the queue.

The tall policeman, gigantic by Bolivian standards, dragged me to a holding room.

"Wait here and don't move," he said.

The thudding of my heart felt much louder than the sudden noise of the officer slamming the door behind him. I was worried but unsurprisingly not scared. The punishment for smuggling was a fine and a loss of my cargo at worst.

The policeman returned to the holding room, snagged the telephone from a doorway stand and handed me the headpiece.

"It's the station manager," he said.

"I really need to get to Chile soon," I explained. "I have a broken leg."

"*Como pasó?*"

"I fell from a horse," I lied.

Clutching crutches that made me seem most invalid, I was permitted onto the train. The trip was rather agonizing for the corners of the watches wedged unrelentlessly into my skin. Faking a limp was quite uncalled for - the pain was as real as the morning sun.

Upon arriving in Arica, I checked into a small train stop hotel, where I ridded myself of the uncomfortable plaster of Paris.

Later on that afternoon, one of the passengers approached me in the hotel lobby. He batted his eyes repetitively in disbelief.

"I couldn't stand the pain any longer," I explained, shaking his flaccid hand. "It feels much better like that."

I limped passed the man to the exits. He certainly had doubts for, when I spun around, he was still ogling me.

At the Arica airport, I purchased a ticket to Antofagasta. Unbeknownst to me, there was a luggage check at the terminal. Stern customs officers ripped ethnic chic out of a whimpering lady's luggage at the terminal to my flight. Nervous, I swigged gulps of my saliva. The watches were loosely scattered at the bottom of my handbag.

Eventually, I was next in line.

"Flight 1-0-0-4 to Antofagasta will leave in approximately five minutes," a lady announced on the public announcement system. "All aboard please!"

The customs inspector smiled. I sensed luck was on my side. He lightly rummaged through the top of my luggage.

"Okay," he said, zipping my bag. "You may leave."

Sweating profusely, I grabbed my suitcase and boarded the plane. It was a close call.

In Antofagasta, I boarded a small bus to Chuqicamata. My laggard return to entrepreneurship was encouraging thus far, but I knew better than to count my chickens before they hatched. Swiss watches were popular in Chile, though, and I subconsciously braced myself for good profit.

As fortune would have it, the word got out about town that Walter Meyer was peddling black market watches. Soon the local carabineros were cognizant of my illegal escapades.

Snoozing peacefully one cool night, two policemen stormed my poolside residence and arrested me.

"Can I speak to a lawyer?" I insisted, as they shoved me into a patrol car. "How long will you detain me?"

"For as long as it takes before the judge will see you," one of the officers replied. "That may take two days to two months."

The first night, the men handcuffed me to a bunk bed in a dingy windowless cell. By the next evening, I had spurned amity with the on-guard policeman, Officer Gutierrez, who was not too intelligent.

"I bet I can shoot more accurately than you," I said, as the officer proceeded to cuff me to the bunk railing for the night.

"Oh, you think?"

Quite shockingly, our discussion actually prompted the policeman to do the unbelievable.

"Yes," I said. "If I win, you don't handcuff me tonight."

"Okay," he said, smiling.

I followed Officer Gutierez to the station's underground shooting range. He shot at a paper human target and hit the thigh.

"It's your turn," he said, handing me his revolver.

I shot the target right in the center of the forehead.

Then I braced the weapon to my chest, and faced Officer Gutierrez. His frown immediately morphed into a scowl. An eerie silence pervaded the shooting range for what seemed like an eon, as we gawked at each other.

He began to shiver, and I could almost smell fear underneath his cheap cologne.

Since I had no intention to employ the gun in any other way than to prove my point, I handed the revolver to the officer. Realizing how foolish he was, he grabbed it from my hand. Officer Gutierrez kept his word, though, and I spent the night uncuffed.

On the third day, he escorted me to the nearby Customs Office, where I paid a heavy fine for my release. After spending two nights in a claustrophobic decrepit cell, my potent yearning for freedom gave me a headache.

To my sheer dismay, the clerk dilatorily typed my release form with a single finger on an antiquated Gutenberg-like typewriter, while Officer Gutierrez giggled in the background. My trip to Bolivia was all for naught. The watches were confiscated and likely later served as gifts for some unworthy custom officials.

Once I paid the fine, I was free to go.

A few days later, the police were on my trail again.

I was sipping charily on a cup of espresso at a local restaurant when they stormed in.

"You are under arrest," one of the men yelled, like I needed the sound magnification.

I was bundled to the station without explanation.

Apparently, there were some violent skirmishes between Chilean and Argentine authorities along the border. The Argentine Consul in Antofagasta, whom I knew quite well, had been expelled from the country. Traveling with an Argentine passport and a previous history of social contact with the Argentine Consul made me a prime suspect.

Soon Officer Gutierrez transported me from the police station to Antofagasta's dormitory-style prison.

"Well, we meet again!" I enthused, as Officer Gutierrez arm-hauled me toward the disheveled prison entrance that somehow reminded me of cowboy movies. "I suppose you can tell me why I'm being detained?"

"*No sé nada*,"(I know nothing) he said, pressing his index finger to his lips.

Apparently, Officer Gutierrez had grown a brain cell since the last time we met.

He dragged me to a large, bedraggled jail, jam-packed with emaciated prisoners. The unconventional prison had no individual cells, showers or toilets. Just one large collective space, within which 25 prisoners slept, ate and defecated. The wall of stench nearly knocked me out as I stumbled in.

"Welcome to the Palace Hotel," one of the prisoners gagged.

The men laughed hysterically. I had apparently become part of an inside joke.

"My name is Unger," the handsome prisoner continued, offering his hand for a handshake.

Considering the amount of feces scattered about the cell, I hesitated momentarily to shake his hand.

"Hello, my name is Walter."

An Anglo-Chilean, Unger was one of Chile's best tennis players before catching a 10-year sentence for killing his wife and her lover. He had allegedly tied and shoved the inopportune couple into their Volkswagen Beetle, and pushed the automobile off a cliff into the Pacific.

Unger became my tennis coach. While obviously devoid of a court, the concrete prison courtyard served us well. Instead of a net, we strung ropes between two lampposts.

Tennis quickly became my only pristine solace for the prison was simply unbearable. Since there were no toilets, I learnt to make bombas like the rest of the prisoners. I squatted, did my business on some newspaper, folded it properly and tossed the "bomb" out of the cell's only tiny window.

The prison authorities provided no meals. The onus was on each prisoner to arrange his gastronomy. Many inmates had nearby families who brought food and drinks. Others had money and made arrangements with restaurants. I received portions from my coach, who seemed well-provided.

After approximately three weeks, an obese warden with a staff stormed into our cell. It was a Saturday morning, the only day we were permitted to sleep in.

"Where is Walterio?" he yelled.

"Yes sir," I replied, staggering to my feet. "Do I get to leave now?"

"No. You're being transferred to Santiago," he said. "Pack your things. Lets go!"

"Can you tell me why I'm being detained?"

"No sir," he yelled, raising both hands up in denial.

I was beginning to foresee deeper trouble. Perhaps I was being detained for being an Argentine spy?

Accompanied by a prison guard, I boarded the *Reina del Pacifico*, an old passenger ship, to Valparaiso, a Chilean port city. I was imprisoned in a small collective cell in the ship's hull, along with several other impecunious prisoners. It didn't take long before three passengers got seasick, spewing half-digested morsel of the meat sandwiches we had just been served.

I was once a sailor and veteran of many storms. Yet seasickness still seemed disgustingly horrible. Even when the stomach is vacuous, one continues to vomit painfully. I was half dead when we arrived in Valparaiso.

The guard was unusually nice for he did not cuff me. Perhaps there was some special consideration for "political prisoners," I thought. We boarded a bus to Santiago, where I was checked into the local prison until further notice.

Once again, the Santiago prison guards were oblivious of my crime.

Truth be told, I was exultant to be granted a cell of my own. For the oddest of reasons, my abode was never locked, affording me the priceless opportunity to mingle with other prisoners.

An old decrepit apartment building - characterized by frontal balconies for each flat - stood, quite conveniently for us, behind the prison's porous fence. So, we prisoners often communicated with its residents. There were two gorgeous sisters with whom a couple of buddies and I particularly flirted. One was a bashful brunette, the other a flirtatious sexy blonde, who flashed her model-like, round breasts at us twice.

"Here's the deal," I began, to a conspicuously aroused bunch of inmates after her second flash. "Whoever gets out first gets to screw the prettier blonde one. Agreed?"

The guys nodded concurringly, so we had a little impish bet going. It was our only practical way of remaining reasonably sane within prison walls.

After a week of imprisonment in Santiago, a mild-mannered Warden Jimenez walked into my cell, whilst I lay on my bunk perusing a novel. Hardened by my previous disappointment, I braced myself for the worst of news, perhaps a sentencing.

"Walterio, you are free to go," he said apologetically, as I remained frozen on my bunk. "I hope these days have not brought you too many inconveniences. We tried to treat you well. *Que le vaya bien.*"(Be good)

I packed my belongings, and exited the prison complex with Warden Jimenez.

"So, why was I detained?" I inquired for seemingly the millionth time.

"Sorry, Walterio, but I only follow orders."

I often wonder how many proxy wrongdoers in the blighted history of man have employed the same ignominious line to circumvent the responsibility of perpetrating heinous deeds.

However, I accepted the warden's superficial apologies. As usual, yet another venture lay ahead of me: The pretty girls across the street. Grimacing at the challenge, I pushed my way through the weighty prison doors.

Sweet freedom hung in the air.

Literally, ten minutes after my unexpected release, I was clambering up the stairs in the nearby apartment building to the ladies' flat.

The blonde opened the door when I knocked.

"Buenos dias," she said, in a coarse, sexy accent, ushering me in from the balcony as if we had known each other for decades.

By then, a few boisterous inmates had assembled near the prison fence to witness me claim my "prize bride."

"Walterio, Walterio, Walterio," they yelled.

Feeling emboldened by my sudden hero status, I waved at the men before shutting the apartment door behind me. The small flat was indicative of poor Chile: Shoddy furniture, a large framed portrait of The Holy Mary and a ponderous bible.

"My name is Gringa," she said, as I immediately hugged her firmly. The name fitted her well for she bore blond hair and fair skin that appropriately complimented her dizzying beauty.

Thirty minutes later, I was reveling in orgasmic ménage à trois with Gringa and her sister Monica, who was obviously not so bashful after all.

The next day, I bade the sisters goodbye, and boarded a bus to the scenic southern outskirts of Santiago, Chile, scattered with nostalgic villages established by German immigrants.

Back in Santiago, I toured the Carrera Hotel, popular for its rooftop swimming pool and a fashionable camaraderie point for jet setters. Strapped for cash, I entered an underwater swimming contest and won, establishing a new underwater record in the Carrera pool. My prize: A trophy and 200 Chilean pesos.

A French movie director had witnessed my brazen swimming escapades. He approached me as I walked away from the stage, clutching my prize.

"I have never seen as fine a diver as you," he said, motioning for a handshake. "My name is François."

"I'm Walter."

François was a paunchy giant of a man, bear-like and intimidating, but for his gracious smile, which implied otherwise.

François was in Chile to film "*Sangre Negra*," a story about a black male housekeeper Julio, who stubbornly protects the secrets of one of the daughters of the household Irma (an alcoholic teenager, who often comes home drunk) from her parents.

"It would be impossible to make such a film in the United States because of the racial undertones," François explained, as we ordered poolside lunch.

Irma's father eventually grows suspicious of her whereabouts. One night, he decides to scour the mansion for Irma, who had just returned home drunk. Hiding behind a curtain, Julio places his hand over Irma's mouth to keep her quiet, whilst her father passes by.

Accidentally, Julio constricts Irma's breathing. She dies. Realizing the consequences of his deadly error, Julio stuffs the dead body in the house's incinerator. A reporter discovers the crime.

"Can you be the reporter?" François inquired. "I could use a character with some intense energy."

"Of course," I replied. "I've always wanted to be an actor, but I have little ..."

"Training?"

"Yes."

"Don't worry about that. There is a screen test at the studio later today. I'm sure you'll do just fine."

My screen test was rather rudimentary. I simply walked arm-in-arm atop a lighted stage with a young lady and took a few steps.

"What a lovely evening," I mimed to the actress. "Look at the bright moon."

"That's perfect," François yelled, clapping vivaciously. "I told you this was easy."

Apparently, the talent test was a triumph. As I walked off stage to the gigantic director, my youthful heart beat happily with excitement at the prospect of finally realizing my acting dreams.

"Hollywood, here I come," I whispered to myself.

"Walter, that was awesome," François said, shaking my hand, stiff with the gushing blood of soaring confidence. "However, we won't start shooting until next month. But, you can consider yourself hired, my friend."

François delivered his heartbreaking words with punchy preciseness as if reading the premature celebrations off my face. His fraught words denoted another sudden culmination to my Hollywood aspirations.

My restive, youthful exuberant soul could definitely not wait that long.

The Bloody Train Ride to Bolivia

Tom's no more, and so no more of Tom. -
George Byron (1788-1824).

I had vanished from work for eons, but magically managed to sneak my way back into the Chiqui poolside office uneventfully, or so I thought. As I wiped three months of dust off my desk my first morning back, the director in charge of personnel, Robert, stormed into my office unannounced.

I figured it was explanation time.

"Walter, you're going to Bolivia," the manager barked, pinching his nose from the billowing dust.

"Bolivia?"

Having just barely returned unscathed from a tumultuous trip there, Bolivia was the last place on earth to which I wished to journey. Worst yet, it was now 1952 and the country was increasingly becoming dangerous territory for Americans and gringos in general. Since my last visit there, a bloody anti-American revolution (The Bolivian National Revolution 1952-64) had developed, leading to mass imprisonments, persecutions and even killings.

The controversy began on October 31, 1952, when Bolivian President Paz Estenssoro's socialist-leaning administration nationalized the three big tin companies, leaving the medium-sized mines untouched. Estenssoro also expropriated the lands upon which the mines depended for tin.

British and American investors had become immensely interested in the tin mines in their early stages, and by the time

Estenssoro expropriated the mines in 1952, a considerable amount of U.S. and British capital was invested in them.

The U.S. government refused to recognize or patronize tin from the *Corporación Minera de Bolivia* (COMIBOL), the new state firm under which two-thirds of the control of the newly expropriated tin mining companies was placed.

Thus, since Bolivia literally depended on tin exportation for its livelihood, the nationalization of the mines had an immediate negative effect on the Bolivian economy, hence the abrasive anti-American and anit-Western sentiment.

Without U.S. tin demand and financial support, the mines under COMIBOL produced at a loss due to the lack of technical expertise and capital to modernize the aging plants and nearly depleted deposits of low-grade ore. Low tin demand led to declining tin prices on the world market.

By 1953, under American pressure, the Bolivian government promised to compensate the owners of nationalized tin mines, and drew up a new petroleum code, which again allowed United States investments in the nation's oil!

Bolivia was simply no place for a gringo in 1952, but it behooved me to express these trepidations to Robert.

"You know the new guy Harry, right?" Robert asked, standing for fear of sitting anywhere in my dusty office.

"Yes."

American Harry Rembrandt, Chile Exploration Company's chief engineer had recently fled the company's Bolivia plant to join us in Chiqui. Fortunately, I had met Harry the night before at the bowling alley under my control. He seemed pleasant for a short, stout, bald man in his forties.

"Oh, good. Upon arriving here, Mr. Rembrandt suddenly realized he'd forgotten some company valuables in Cochabamba that we need returned urgently," Robert continued, his voice laced with a little sarcasm. "Of course, he doesn't speak a word of Spanish and would not last a day on his own."

"So you want me to go with him to retrieve the belongings?"

"Yes, and your train leaves tomorrow at seven."

"I guess I don't have a choice in the matter."

"No, I'm sorry Walter," Robert said, spinning around to the door. "And, oh, what is this place, some kind of indoor desert?"

I giggled at Robert's arid humor as he shut the door.

Truth be told, the trip's inherent danger augmented its adventurous appeal, which got me so riled up, I could feel heated blood pounding my jugular.

"The stories about overt anti-Western attitudes are probably exaggerated," I lied to myself.

Besides, telling the director that I was scared would have made me look like a sissy. I certainly was not.

So, early the next morning, one of the company drivers drove us to Antofagasta, the northern Chilean city. It took us less than an hour to reach the bustling railroad station. There had been hardly any traffic on the city's main dual-lane highway.

No sooner had we offloaded our luggage at the railroad station did Harry rush off to the restroom. When he returned, his face was red with frustration.

"You won't fucking believe what just happened in there?" he began, as we hurriedly dragged our luggage to the train's embarkation point. "I couldn't flush the goddamned toilet or wash my hands."

"Why?"

"Because there was no water or toilet paper," he yelled. "The other men used toilet paper from a big waste can in the damn restroom. Can you fucking believe that?"

By this time, I was laughing hysterically and teary-eyed, almost unable to keep my footing.

"What's so goddamned funny?" Harry barked.

"Look Harry, water is very scarce in Antofagasta," I said, in a consoling voice. "It's the same all over the city, not only at the station."

Harry shook his baldhead in disbelief. We were about 20 feet from our train.

"Look at it this way," I said, guffawing. "The high salaries paid to Americans like you come at the absence of luxuries like toilet paper."

"Fuck you!" Harry replied.

"Hey, remind me not to ever shake your hand."

For an international route, the train was relatively small, with only five cars, the last of which was a dining car. Despite the plethora of passengers transporting porous baskets of grains and other food items, the train was exceptionally clean.

Harry had complained of hunger so, after stashing our luggage, we dashed for the dining car, which was somewhat of a collection item. Equipped with a small kitchen, it was painted red with black stripes and bore a sunroof.

"The train will leave in about five minutes in accordance with the schedule," the announcer belted over the public announcement system.

Harry and I sat next to the kitchen and ordered good Chilean beer and munchies. We departed on time and were soon weaving through the Andes foothills. The arid Andean landscape eventually transformed into plush green vegetation, with myriad eucalyptus trees brushing against the sides of the speeding train.

The dining car was empty, except for a tall muscular man in a blue shirt, necktie and coat. He was sitting next to the glass sliding door that separated the dining car from the rest of the small train. The burly man occasionally peered over his magazine at us.

"Is there anything else I can get for you?" the Chilean attendant asked, working Harry and me for a robust tip.

"No, thanks," I responded, catching the mustachioed man sneaking another glance.

"Well, just to let you know, we are thirty minutes away from our destination."

"Thanks," Harry said, breaking his silence. He seemed the bashful type.

We played endless gin rummy rounds, and had a rather superficial conversation. I pried Harry for information about his country, his family and background, but he didn't seem interested in getting into personal matters. I did find out he was from Louisiana, like John Carroll.

"You're not still keeping malice with me about the toilet tissue thing, are you?" I asked, after the last game.

"No, not really," he replied, still pouting.

"Okay, I'll shake your hand now to make it up to you."

"Damn you, Walter."

Near the end of the journey, Harry departed the dining car to fetch our luggage. I stayed behind to give the waiter a generous tip.

"I really don't like Bolivians, so I'll tell you this," he said, cleaning up our round table. "Be very careful."

"Thank you, but I assure you we'll see you again on our way home."

I rose from my table and strode toward the demarcating glass sliding door, to join Harry.

Suddenly, the blue-shirted man sprung from his seat, swearing loudly.

"*Malditos gringos, chupa sangre, hijos de puta…!*" (damn' gringos, blood suckers, sons of whores) he yelled.

The man's monstrous body blocked the glass doors, the only exit point. Trapped, I rushed back to the kitchen and waited, hoping that he would leave the dining car before me.

"Hey, you can jump through the kitchen door," the waiter yelled. "It leads to the rails."

However, the train was still moving, albeit slowly for we were upon the train station. The man staggered toward me. He was obviously drunk, and I wasn't particularly in the mood for a fight.

"Don't worry, waiter," I whispered. "I'll wait for him to leave or pass out from drinking."

I clenched my fist when the man inched toward me and swore again.

"I'll show you how to respect a Bolivian police officer!" he barked.

Unbeknownst to me, the drunken man was a police officer. He must have been off-duty for he was clad in civilian attire. Since I had not shown any lack of respect, I stood my ground quietly.

My silence only further infuriated him. As he charged towards me, he grabbed crystal vases from the train's windowsills, and hurled them at me. The flowers had adorned the pleasant dining car. Now the space was fast becoming a pillaged battlefield.

He grabbed the next vase, and I ducked to the right as it crashed on the wall. Luckily, he was too drunk to be a good shot, but he kept trying, reaching for each vase as he passed the windows.

By the time he got near me, the floor was littered with broken glass and damp flowers.

Suddenly, the glass sliding door creaked open. A woman peeked in.

"Tomás!" she yelled, clutching a flashing object.

The man stumbled back to the glass door. He snatched a penknife from the woman, who immediately disappeared.

"*Gracias.*"

Our battle had not gone unnoticed by other passengers. A horde of onlookers, now including Harry, stared from beyond the glass doors, too scared to intervene. As Tomás stumbled back towards me, I noticed Harry crack the glass door.

"Get out!" he yelled, before shutting the door behind him for the police officer turned around and threatened him too.

"I'll kill you too," Tomás yelled.

For some inexplicable reason, I waited. Somehow, I wanted to keep the upper hand. My dismal experience with police officers and prison guards in numerous countries emboldened me to fight to prove my innocence.

I had barely seen the woman that handed Tomás the knife, but I figured she was his wife or girlfriend. She disappeared immediately, as if confident that her man would finish me off soon. Of course, being a police officer would certainly have cleared him of any punishment for murdering an unwanted gringo in a hostile Bolivia.

I was scared and emboldened at the same time, but I braced myself for a long fight.

In excellent physical condition, I had taken a few courses in self-defense. This was not my first fight. The man swung the knife at my head. I ducked slightly, but the razor sharp blade severed a lock of my hair. I watched as the strands hit the deck.

"You are dead, you gringo bastard!" Tomás yelled, his vocabulary becoming increasingly abrasive. His face, contorted by extreme, obviously, misdirected rage, was as bloody red as a beetroot.

He swung at me again. This time, I ducked, and immediately kicked him hard under the chin with cowboy boots that a Texan friend in Chuqui had given me as a birthday gift.

The behemoth policeman stood, bewildered momentarily, as the knife fell out of his hand, clattering on the floor. Seconds later, he fell, knocking his head on the edge of a dining table before collapsing atop the broken glass. He didn't move.

I placed my ears on his chest, and felt for his jugular pulse. Nothing! I had killed a Bolivian police officer in a country where I was already hated for being a gringo.

The glass door slid open and Tomás' woman stormed in, screaming uncontrollably.

The Chilean waiter grabbed my arm and pulled me away from the carnage, jolting me out of my shock.

"Get lost," the waiter yelled. "Run!"

I sprinted through the glass sliding doors, out of the train and disappeared into the thicket of train station passengers. I figured Harry would fetch our luggage. Weaving through the crowd, away from the train, my most daunting challenge was getting out of Bolivia alive.

Sirens soon filled the air and policemen and medics swarmed the train station.

"Where is the gringo? Which way did he go?" I heard some officers demand form passers-by. They pointed them in my direction.

I turned a corner, and, lo and behold, there were several idle taxis waiting for arriving passengers. I waved one down. The chasing police officers turned the same corner. They saw me clamber into the cab.

"Stop! Stop!" they yelled.

"Taxi driver, I'm in a big hurry," I plead. "Please drive quickly to the Cathedral!"

"Yes sir," the taxi driver enthused, not noticing the police officers giving a hopeless foot-chase behind us.

The chasing officers were long disengaged from their patrol cars. I escaped.

The Cathedral was near a posh upper-class suburb of Cochabamba, and home to Bob, a well-connected former Chile Exploration Company executive, with whom Harry and I were scheduled to reside.

I halted the cab about two blocks away from Bob's home, and walked the rest of the way. I had met Bob, a tall and charming American, during my last visit to Bolivia. Best pals with virtually everyone important in Cochabamba, including the police chief, Bob was the unofficial protector of all local gringos and Westerners. He was quick to donate money, cigarettes and liquor to guarantee gringo protection.

He was my only hope.

Bob was at home. I met him toying with his miniature train system installed in his monstrous garage. Bob's fenced home had a Feng-Shui touch to it that set it apart from the other mansions in the estate.

"Walter, how dare you interrupt my fooling around here," he joked, embracing me. "I got a call from Robert in Chiqui to be expecting you guys. Where is Rembrandt?"

"I have no clue," I said, sighing. "And I'm in deep trouble."

Over lunch, I narrated the horror story. Bob simply smiled.

"Is that it?" he inquired, giggling lightly.

"Yes."

"If that's it, then everything should work out well," he said, deliberately spilling some wine on the tablecloth. "If I don't do that, the maid will never wash the damn tablecloth."

I was impressed with Bob's smooth and light-hearted approach to my case. He reminded me of those laid-back Western stars who never show much emotion.

"Stay in the house and don't answer the phone," he ordered, leaving the dining table. "I'll be back very soon. And don't worry about Harry, I'll find him."

Upon Bob's departure, I chatted with the Quechua housemaid, who seemed impressed when I said, "The tablecloth is stained," in her language. A Quechua native on Normando's ranch had taught me a little Quechoa, the Inca language, which was most eloquent and advanced in its form.

"I suppose I have to wash it now," she said.

I sat in one of Bob's comfortable parlor armchairs and dozed off.

Bob returned a few hours later with a smile on his face.

"You are very lucky, my man," he said. "The police chief never liked the guy on the train, anyway. He was not surprised that Tomás' end was the bottle. He'll have a *salvo conducto* (safe conduct) ready in a couple of days, after which you can get the heck outa here."

"Oh, thank God."

"You don't need to get religious now. I talked to Harry. He's willing to contribute some money to pay off the chief."

"So, I guess I'm trapped here until the salvo whatever is done."

"Yep, stick around here. There is a lot to read. If you get hungry, there's stuff in the icebox, and the bar should have something that you like. I'll be gone for the rest of the evening. You may use the guestroom."

I was speechless, but utterly relieved.

Bob left again, soon after delivering the good news. I was alone until he tugged my shoulder the next morning.

"I thought you had breakfast ready," he joked.

"You didn't tell me when you would be back," I replied, dabbing the sleep from my eyes and rising from the couch.

Bob fixed some coffee. The Quechua maid prepared breakfast.

"So, are you married?" I asked over breakfast.

Silence. Bob wasn't the talkative type. I assumed his position as "gringo protector" put him in a somewhat secretive position.

"I see you're not very talkative," I said. "Kind of like Harry?"

"Yeah, talking about Harry," Bob said, seizing the cheap opportunity to change the topic of discussion. "He didn't want to come to the house because he's scared. He has elected to ride in a different railcar back home."

"Doesn't want anyone to think he's associated with me, huh?"

"Nope, I don't think so," Bob said. "And, quite frankly, I don't blame the guy. Who would wanna hang around a murderer?"

I giggled, assuming Bob was kidding. But he kept a scary, straight face.

"Psyche!" he yelled, bursting out in laughter. "I got you there."

I didn't get the joke. An American thing, I guessed. Bob left again.

He returned later that afternoon with another big smile on his handsome face.

"Here's your passport to freedom," he snapped, handing me a priceless salvo conducto. "This will get you back to Chile, I guarantee. Now, let's fix some dinner and enjoy our little victory."

"How in the world did you secure these?"

"Mostly because the police officer was very disliked," he replied. "But, next time, Walter, take it easy, don't kill. Okay?"

Of course he was being sarcastic again.

"It's really funny, Americans get together with money and merchandise to save you, and you're a damned German," he said. "I guess all gringos have to stick together, right?"

I nodded.

"You wanna hear something else funny?" I asked, mimicking Bob's American accent.

"What?"

"I really didn't kill the man, he fell."

Bob and I shed a few tears over the dry joke, after which we toured his miniature train system. The faux railroad came replete with bridges, tunnels, railroad-side cars and trucks. Bob simply pushed a button, and it took off. I had difficulty understanding how a grownup man could become so fanatic about what I deemed children's entertainment.

I had trouble sleeping that night. The trip back to Chile was on my mind.

The next morning, Bob drove me to the railroad station, frequently waving to taxi drivers and pedestrians along the way.

"Thank you," I said, clambering out of his jeep at the station.

"What are friends for, right?" he replied, shaking my hand vigorously. "Hey, Walter, here."

Bob handed me a piece of scribbled-on paper.

"His name is Cesar Estenssoro, nephew of the Bolivian President," he said. "Give him a call, sometime. He needs you and you need him"

I never saw Bob again.

This time, I avoided the dining car. I didn't see Harry. He was surely in one of the cars, hiding from me, Walter, the menace.

Time flew by. Soon we were traversing the lush vegetation of Bolivia's green valley. Again, we disappeared into the barren Andean region.

We stopped at a train station for water. Two customs officials climbed aboard.

"*Pasaportes, por favor,*" (Passports, please) one of the men barked. "*Algo para declarar?*" (Anything to declare?)

My heart pounded for I had nothing to declare. I showed my salvo conducto. The officer inspected it closely. He whispered a few words to his partner, and gawked at me, frowning so hard, his face creased like a rotten apple.

Four, five, six and seven minutes passed on the clock above the train's main entrance.

Then, the officers walked towards me. I stood still, frightened like I had just seen a ghost.

"*Buen viaje,*" (Have a nice trip) he said, suddenly returning my salvo conducto.

My heartbeat returned to normal.

At the train station in Antofagasta, I scoured for Harry. Finally, he climbed out of the last car with a scowl.

"I hope I never have to take another trip with you," he said, tossing my luggage at me.

"Go to hell, you no-good chicken," I yelled.

There was nothing to look forward to in Chiqui. I yanked out of my pocket, and stared at the piece of paper with Cesar Estenssoro's La Paz, Bolivia address.

A nearby train heading to La Paz tooted its horns appealingly. I quit my athletic director job *in absentia*, and boarded.

My Last Days in Bolivia

A pilgrimage is an admirable remedy for over-fastidiousness and sickly refinement. - Henry Tuckerman (1813-1871).

Cesar Estenssoro was an ultra-influential Bolivian Air Force officer.

Flanked by an intimidating six-man entourage, he was storming out of his La Paz office when I approached him.

"To what do I owe this rare honor?" he said, after learning that I had been recommended by Bob.

"So, Captain Estenssoro, any employment for an adventurous gringo?" I asked.

"Please, Walter, call me Cesar," he replied, waving off his uniformed bodyguards. "You see, I'm a big fan of Bob and I do have a proposition for you."

"What would that be?"

"Have you ever been to the Beni region?"

"No."

"We're flying a B-17 there tomorrow to load some beef," he said. "The glints in your eyes tell me you're in?"

I was. The scenic Beni region was a rancher's paradise, blessed with lush vegetation and grazing cattle. For beef traders like Cesar, however, it was insufferable hell for there were no roads to El Beni. Hence, the need for planes.

The cattle was slaughtered on ranches in the Beni, and the beef loaded onto the plane and flown back to La Paz, where the meat was promptly shipped to the many local markets. Landing on small airstrips to and fro took guts and expertise.

"How in the world do you do that?" I asked, returning from our tenth trip.

"Skill," Cesar replied. "You don't have to worry any more. This is our last haul."

"What?"

"Don't worry. I have a great opportunity for you."

Cesar's business idea was rather clever.

"You simply drive cattle overland from Bolivia to Brazil."

"Okay, how do you make money from that?"

The Bolivian government disseminated cattle exporting permits to well-tested businessmen under the pretext that all cash procured from sales would be exchanged at the *Bolivian Banco Central* (Federal Bank) at the government-sanctioned exchange rate.

"You're only permitted to report cash earned from the sale of cattle that you declared before leaving La Paz," Cesar said, parking the plane in its small hangar.

"I still don't understand how you make money."

"You export more cattle than the initial permit allows," he whispered. "Then you exchange the money received for the amount of cattle on the permit at the *Banco Central*."

"Then I exchange the rest of the money on the black market?"

"Yes sir."

Of course, the difference between the Bolivian Peso-Brazilian Cruzeiro exchange rates at the Banco Central and on the black market was enormous. I often needed a gargantuan bag to collect the pesos.

With Cesar's connections, I secured a permit for 200 heads of steer and purchased 400 cattle. I hit the road to Brazil with eight Cesar-recommended Bolivian *vaqueros* (cowboys), familiar with our destination: *Principe de Beira*, a bustling trading town perched on the northern Bolivian-Brazilian border.

We crossed the snake-like Mamore River, Bolivia's main waterway, and traveled north along Mamore's lip to Exaltación, our first debarkation point. For a small, predominantly fishing and ranching town, Exaltación was teeming with energy, so the *vaqueros* insisted we camp out for three days.

We did, and many sluttish Exaltación women frequented our camp as a result.

Three days later, we arrived in San Joaquín on the Machupo River. From there, only 150 km separated us from our destination. We had not lost a single animal.

Our trip coincided with the region's unbearable dry season, and it was literally hot as hell. Lakes had shrunk to muddy puddles, surrounded by iguana, heaped upon each other like mountains of firewood. The native children picked small iguanas up by their tails, swung them around until they squealed, and threw the frazzled lizards back in the puddle. As the children fully expected, the mother iguanas got aggressive and lunged attacks. In defense, the giggling boys hid behind trees, dodging left or right depending on the iguana's snappy moves.

In lush terrain, we rested and allowed the cattle, horses and mules to graze.

"If we keep stopping like this, we'll never make it to Principe de Beira," one of the *vaqueros* objected, as we watched the animals grazing on a green hillside.

"I'm intent on not losing a head," I replied. "And, one day doesn't make any difference."

Our journey was monotonous. We encountered very few Indians. They had headed north to hunt. We spent most nights huddled in collapsible tents. I often caught the *vaqueros* procuring sexual satisfaction from ugly, shriveled-up native women in villages along our trek. Roads were non-existent. Well-to-do ranchers, most of whom learned to fly by trial and error, traveled via small aircraft. Flight instructors simply did not exist.

The locals at the confluence border town of Principe de Beira, where the Blanco, Itonamas and Machupo rivers met, greeted us like Santa Clauses. Beef on the Brazilian side was scarce and buyers literally threw money at me - transaction was sheer pleasure. One businessman purchased the entire herd.

We boarded a small airplane back to La Paz. Cesar was pleased to see me.

The prettiest girls in Bolivia lived in the Santa Cruz de la Sierra province. So I bade Cesar farewell and headed there. However, Santa Cruz, the capital city, was otherwise unimpressive, a large town with unpaved streets. I had envisioned it bigger, and more advanced.

I explored the possibility of heading a cattle drive from Santa Cruz, south to Corumbá, Brazil. A second trek to northern Brazil would have been a hopeless venture for the rainy season had begun.

I quickly made friends with some Americans in Santa Cruz performing geodetic surveys in the area. The group was verifying mountains, valleys and rivers for map-making purposes. Since there was little to do in desolate Santa Cruz, the Americans hosted flamboyant weekly parties, filling courtyards and gardens within their rented estates with booze and attractive local women.

I had difficulty recruiting cowboys for the grapevine had it that headhunting Indians rode rampant along my preferred route. The rumors weren't baseless. One needn't travel far before locals offered for sale grotesque, shrunken heads with distorted features and stringy hair. One of the Americans took me flying. We located the headhunters' settlement, but it was vacuous. The Indians had headed north to hunt, leaving us safe passage.

Thus, 11 *vaqueros* agreed to ride with me, so long as I paid them three times the going price. But two backed out before we ever saddled up, and I dismissed two others upon learning they were drunks. One more changed his mind before we reached the first town.

The Americans decided to throw a goodbye party for me.

"Well, we figured we'd see the last of you," one of the Americans joked, presupposing headhunter woes.

Seven of us departed Santa Cruz at dawn the next morning, straddling our belongings onto twelve horses and four donkeys. I rode at the front of the herd, with two men flanking each side and two at the rear, the half-breed heifers and steers corralled between us.

There were fewer men than I thought we needed to control a herd of 380 cattle, but we trodded on nevertheless. Borrowing a solution I'd seen other ranchers resort to, I had a bunch of thick branches cut and cleaned. Fastened to the animals' necks, the yokes prevented the cattle from breaking loose.

The improvised yokes proved to be a necessity. No sooner had we departed did one more *vaquero* change his mind about attempting the trek. I couldn't blame the man. We had more than 400 miles to cover, plodding through arid land before venturing into swampy, undulating terrain inhabited by caimans and other wild creatures.

Despite the variations in topography, grazing grass was ample. We moved slowly, to excite the animals not. Our caravan crept along a deserted railroad that wound from Santa Cruz to Corumbá, Brazil. We came upon and passed the first village Cotoca with much fanfare and *vaquero* protests. The idea was to keep my helpers: some natives, some *mestizos* and others pure Indians, away from local women and booze. Only when we needed provisions did we enter towns. Even then, I allowed only two men.

We decided not to exceed 25 miles of travel a day. Some days, we didn't make it that far because of the tiring terrain. In the late afternoon, we gathered the cattle in a circle, with men stationed at equal distances around the herd. A *vaquero* by the name of Coqui was our cook. Clownish, he wore clothes a few sizes too big, and long hair stuffed under a well-worn straw hat. Dinner consisted mostly of rice and canned goods. We were packed with bottled water for men, and the animals drank from the many creeks and rivers we traversed.

It took us several weeks to reach El Cerro, located near Laguna Concepción. We rested there for several days. To the south was a wide-open prairie that extended into the Bañados de Izozog, several square miles of swampland.

"Please be careful and come back soon," I warned, as the men trotted off into town.

"Yes, Don Walter, we're not going anywhere," Coqui said. "Remember, we don't get paid until we reach Corumbá."

"You're right."

"And, if you know what's good for you, gringo," Coqui warned. "You'll stay here and not venture into town."

Coqui was right. Gringos were certainly not popular in these parts of the country. We left El Cerro for the small town of Taperas. In a month's time, we were only halfway to our destination. My helpers seemed a little uneasy, so I allowed them more visitation time in the town. After four days in Taperas, it was time to leave. The cowboys were all in place.

"One of the steers won't get up," Coqui yelled, as we saddled for our trip.

The animal was unable to stand, perhaps bitten by a snake. We left it behind, but the next day another steer keeled over in its tracks.

"We keep going until we reach Roboré," I ordered to the grumbling men.

Roboré was a week away, but things only got more difficult. Many steep gradients lay ahead of us. Worst, instead of nutritious vegetation, we encountered swampy terrain. We lost yet another steer.

"Okay, enough is enough, we quit," Coqui barked, halting our procession. "Do you men agree?"

The other *vaqueros* nodded. I felt trapped and desperate, like a deer caught in headlights.

"That's fine, you can go back home," I replied smiling. "I haven't paid you yet."

The men grumbled and cursed, but followed me. How cruel and steadfast a leash money is on the reasoning of men, I thought.

Our trip ended quite abruptly and unexpectedly in Roboré. The largest stretches of deepening swampland made it most impossible to persist.

"I'll buy the herd from you," a local businessman offered, at Roboré's chaotic open-air market.

Although his offer was markedly less than what we expected to earn in Brazil, I accepted and abruptly culminated our trek, to the delight of the *vaqueros*, who remained in Roboré. The sale of our horses and donkeys, however, more than made up for my loss.

Three days later, the businessman flew me back to Santa Cruz. I was back in town before Christmas and, of course, shared my experience with American friends over many beers. Granted, I had not earned enormous profit, but at least I didn't lose any money.

Of course, my head was still intact.

During our celebrations, I met a lovely brunette by the name of Mary Juarez.

When I greeted her, "Merry Christmas," she corrected me.

"My name is Mary Juarez, not Mary Christmas."

The next month, I drove with a Bolivian rancher Roberto Delgadillo to the city of Potosí, Bolivia blessed with hilly tin-rich lands.

"Potosi's streets are literally paved with gold," he joked. "Or tin, to be more exact, and I'm sure you'll find many lucrative opportunities for successful business."

The dry joke was too obviously rehearsed and rehashed to be funny, like he had told it a million times, although I hoped that he was correct about good deals to be made.

The initially promising trip morphed into a rather unpleasant adventure.

It was 1953, and Potosí was a political hot spot. Americans were accused of organizing and financing Bolivia's grassroots counter-revolution to President Estenssoro's socialist-leaning government. Anybody with blond hair and a pale face was assumed an American or Jew and persecuted.

"Be careful gringo," Roberto warned, as he dropped me off in downtown Potosí.

"I have a government permit to bear arms," I said.

"How?"

"My cattle drives took me through Indian land," I replied, shutting the door to his 1945 Ford. "There's little to worry about."

On my birthday, policemen burst into my hotel room, foraging for arms. They did not have to rummage long. My guns were confiscated, so were 16 pounds of gold that I had gradually accumulated in the Beni region from Tipuani Gold Mine workers in exchange for merchandise I had brought from La Paz. The fact that several boxes of streptomycin (which I had promised to a Maryknoll Hospital in the Beni Region) were in my possession didn't help matters much either. The officers carted me away to a miserable jail, where I spent the next six weeks.

Walter, standing, fifth from the left. Signed dedication reads:

Don Walter M, With the sincere heart of all his imprisoned friends, we dedicate our sincere memories to their distinguished companion who was able to survive the sufferings and joys in algid moments of this land of Potosi.... Potosi, 10 July 53.

To win my freedom, I paid heavy fines for trafficking gold that was not purchased legally from the *Banco de Fomento*, and possessing drugs without a permit. It was a rather fleet digression from being a millionaire (in Bolivia) to being poor. Fortunately, I had some money stashed in a bank account.

"You may leave but you can't leave town," a policeman warned, after 6 weeks in jail at the prison's crummy checkout desk. "Sorry, I can't give you your passport."

A few days later, I was on my way to the Argentine Consulate in La Paz, where I received another passport.

"You know this random seizure is quite unfair," the consul said, handing me the passport. "I know the Bolivian vice president very well. I'm sure he can help you recover your belongings."

The consul handed me a letter of introduction addressed to Bolivia's vice president. Armed with the invaluable recommendation and a new passport, I walked to his downtown office, secured with uncomfortable controls and security procedures.

"Sir, I'm afraid you have to leave," the vice president's secretary barked rudely.

"It's a very important matter, I need to see the Vice President in person," I insisted.

"Okay, take a seat," she said disappearing behind a glass door that served as a mirror to me, but beyond which I was certainly being observed.

"You can go in now," she said, ten minutes later.

Behind the huge office desk hung a large Bolivian flag. The vice president did not appear too friendly.

"Si, señor?" he snapped.

"I wish to recuperate my seized gold," I said, explaining my condition.

He barely listened to my narration, shuffling through a stack of papers.

"Do you have any proof that the gold and the drugs were taken away from you?" he asked sarcastically.

My response was loaded with annoyance.

"Your police servants do not give receipts," I yelled. "They simply steal!"

He gave me 24 hours to exit the country.

I hot-footed it out the vice president's office with a reddened, enraged face. While traversing downtown La Paz in search of a train station, I conveniently ran into George, one of the Americans I had met in Santa Cruz. Apparently, his Inter American Geodetic Survey was complete for he was clutching a travelers bag.

"Whoa, if it isn't Walter !" he enthused, hugging me like it was his last. "What are you doing in La Paz?"

"Trying to figure my way out of this country," I said, glancing at my watch. "I have 23 hours and twenty minutes."

"Another run-in with the law, huh?"

"Yep. Where are you going?"

We started the short promenade to the nearby tooting train station.

"I was on my way back to the States, but screw that," George said, his face lightening up like a chimney. "How about one last South American trip, huh, Walter?"

"What?"

We halted at the train station's ticket office.

"Can I help you?" the ticket master yelled.

"Give us a second, okay," George said. "Let's jump in my jeep and cross the goddamned Andes to Chile, Walter. Think about it, it'll be fun as hell."

With precisely the train fare amount ($5) lodged in my pocket and Bolivia's entire law enforcement hot on my trail, my reasoning said no, but my heart could barely resist.

"All right, George, you've got me."

We hit the road early the next morning.

George was a skinny thirty-five-year-old Oklahoman, who constantly had a cigarette clenched between his teeth. He could talk, laugh and curse with the cigarette still in place. We conversed little as we woved through the majestic, snow-capped Andean mountains, the arid wind whipping our chapped faces. In the valleys and along mountainsides, oftentimes tufts of thorny grass (grazing food for wild llamas and vicuñas) poked through our flip-top jeep. We occasionally sped passed terraced fields of potatoes and corn, billowing clouds of grainy dust on the plants' green leaves.

While picturesque, the scenery got agonizingly monotonous after countless hours behind the wheel. Our surroundings must have lulled George to sleep for he suddenly skidded off the trail, careening to the deadly edge of a 2,000-foot cliff.

The jeep's passenger side, where I sat petrified, tilted perilously over the cliff, jagged rocks jutting out of the sides of a seemingly bottomless valley. George jumped off expeditiously, shifting the jeep's weight my way. The automobile creaked loudly as it tilted and inched over the 2,000-foot drop.

"Don't move! Don't move! Don't move," George yelled.

"You goddamned cowardly American," I screamed. "You can say that because you've already saved yourself!"

"Let me get some help," he yelled, running off.

The doomed jeep continued its laggard, rocking procession off the cliff. I simply could not wait for George's feeble rescue effort. Slowly and painstakingly, I inched my weight to the driver's side. The jeep creaked terrifyingly, as I stretched my left leg.

To my horror, it started to roll off the cliff, slowly.

I closed my eyes and begun to pray.

"Holy Mary, Mother of God, who art in heaven," I prattled.

The gradual slide took an eternity, affording me enough time to remember the lines to The Lord's Prayer.

"Hallowed be thy... name."

A hand suddenly grabbed my arm, and yanked me out of the jeep. It was George, after all.

Soon after my rescue, we collapsed on the pebbly ground, heaving relieving breaths of life. It was the closest I had been to death for some time. Giggling like little boys, we soon peered down the abyss, marveling at our good fortune. Surprisingly, the jeep was still perched on the cliff, saved from the presumably perilous fall by a small bush jutting out of the cliff rock.

"You son of a bitch!" I screamed, only half-kidding, the echo of my voice permeating the valley. "You jumped off and left me there!"

"No goddamned point in us both dying!" George yelled, his language particularly profane in the heat of near-death.

We bear-hugged each other under the hot sun. There is a something truly awe-inspiring about sharing a near-death experience that bonds survivors inseparably.

"You know, Walter, the thought crossed my mind that I had no idea whom to contact if you didn't get out of this predicament alive," George said, unraveling the hug.

"Look at it this way," I replied, tears welling up around my eyelids. "I saved you the trouble of worrying too much about it."

Once again, I had cheated death.

No sooner had we hugged each other like newly weds did an Indian boy shepherd his llamas passed us. We quickly enlisted his help. The five tethered animals towed the jeep back onto the road. George handed the smiling native a generous tip, and we resumed our trip.

I drove.

Approximately 10 miles later, George yelled, "Stop the jeep, right now!" Frazzled and clueless of his motives, I did, and sat stoic in the car.

George grabbed a rifle, and disappeared into a nearby valley, where several vicuñas were grazing, peacefully. The echoes of three shots soon bounced off the surrounding snow-capped mountains like a puck careening off the borders of a Hockey rink.

"Hey, George, are you all right?" I yelled.

No response or sight of him. Just eerie silence.

"Yeah, I'm here!" he replied a few minutes later, dashing out of the small valley with three bleeding carcasses of the beautiful vicuñas, valued for their luxurious coat.

I was furious.

"Why in the hell did you have to do that?"

"Hey, calm down okay," he said, hurling the bloody animals onto the backseat. "The fine wool would be perfect on my seat covers back home in Stillwater. Think about it, when will I ever get this chance again?"

The damage was done. It would do no good to protest.

"Besides, what are you, some kinda animal conservationist?"

Two harrowing experiences later, and I was utterly eager to leave the Andes behind. However, life has a bizarre way of alternating and balancing between good and bad. What happened next brightened the darkness of our trip thus far.

An hour after George's brute murders, I stopped the car for a cigarette break. As my American partner snoozed in the jeep, I spotted a peasant Indian woman herding nine llamas down a grazing hill, a stone throw from our jeep. Each llama hoisted a mountainous load, but the woman was carrying an even heavier burden - she was very pregnant, her large belly protruding through layers of colorful skirts.

The woman wore two long dark braids tied with a colorful woolen ribbon. On her wealth of dark hair rested a cute black and round hat with a narrow brim, resembling a bowl. The Quechua Indians wore distinguishable hats as a way of identifying the village they came from.

Suddenly, the woman collapsed at the foot of the hill, moaning loudly. I tossed my cigarette, and approached her. Each time she opened her mouth, I caught a glimpse of several gold teeth, a mark of wealth amongst Quechua Indians. Having learned enough Quechua from the *peones* on Normando's finca in Osma, Argentina, I offered my assistance and asked, "*Imati munanki,*" (in Quechua, How can I help?), to no avail. She simply refused help. She expeditiously lay her poncho on the ground, and lifted up her skirt to deliver the infant herself.

Frozen with shock, I marveled at her bravery. However, God and the baby had made me a forced midwife. There was no time for nervousness - I dove in to help. The delivery process was brief. Despite the afternoon's coolness, the lady was sweating profusely, so I blotted her sweaty forehead with a handkerchief.

"Push! Push! Push," I urged, shortly thereafter.

She raised her teary face to the sky, and cried out in pain.

I cupped my hands underneath the baby's head as he emerged, and cut the umbilical cord with my pocketknife. Had I not been there to help, she would have bitten the cord off with her teeth. I had never delivered a baby before, but yet knew what to do. Male instincts, I guessed.

"Everything will be fine," I assured, as the woman reached for her bloody son.

Minutes later, the Quechua woman rose to her feet, and, to my utmost shock, washed the squalling infant in the icy water of a nearby creek. She subsequently wrapped the baby in the blood-stained poncho, and nursed him with her milk-heavy breasts.

"Are you okay?" I inquired, as she tucked her breast back under her blouse.

She nodded shyly, and strapped the baby to her back with the poncho. Then, the Quechua woman, the infant boy and the llamas resumed their trek. I watched in awe as her figure vanished in the hilly horizon.

Nothing has made as immense an emotional impression on me as witnessing that Indian baby's birth.

George woke up when I clambered back into the jeep.

"She ought to name that boy after you," he said, before lighting up another cigarette.

"Do you have children?" I asked.

"Hell no!"

I straddled the steering again. In a few hours, we arrived at the Chilean border.

Life in *La República del Perú*

The musician, the painter, the poet, are, in a larger sense, no greater artists than the man of commerce. - W. S. Maverick.

It was the summer of 1953. George and I arrived safely in Arica, "The City of Eternal Spring," located at the northern tip of Chile on the scenic shores of the Pacific Ocean.

The tourist-friendly enclave, sprawled at the foot of El Morro Hill, was the site of a major battle during the Peruvian War (1879-83). Many statues and monuments across the city spoke of myriad war heroes. Arica was an important trade center for products from the interior, thus Quechua and Aymara Indians still travel to the city hawking traditional handicrafts.

George fell in love with Arica, Chile and stayed. I continued to Tacna, Perú, another historically significant city.

Chilean companies once exploited, in the most unchecked manner, rich nitrate deposits in Bolivia's Atacama Desert Province, raping the lands and defying all laws of once pristine nature. In Feb. 1879, nationalist Bolivian President Hilarion Daza rescinded these contracts and nationalized the nitrate mines, a move that was frevently popular with Bolivians. Feeling cheated, Chile responded by occupying Bolivia's port of Antofagasta. The Pacific War ensued soon thereafter.

Chile demanded that neighbor Perú declare neutrality in the fervently acrimonious matter, but Perú, which had recently signed a trade alliance treaty with Bolivia in 1873, refused to do so. So it came to be that Perú, by proxy of its alliance with Bolivia, became a victim of Chile's pursuance of war.

By 1880, 12,000 Chilean troops had invaded and occupied Tacna, Perú and Arica, Bolivia. Four years later, the Treaty of Valparaiso restored peace among the warring nations. Chile returned Tacna to Perú in 1929, but withheld coastal Arica. Thus, Bolivia lost its only access to the coast.

Legend has it that Queen Victoria, upon learning that Bolivia had become landlocked, campaigned that the nation be erased off the map. Regaining access to the Pacific Ocean remains central to Bolivian foreign policy. Chileans and Peruvians are still uncongenial on the matter.

The famous Peruvian *frontera a frontera* (border to border) automobile race, stretching from the Peruvian-Ecuadorian border, to the Peruvian-Chilean border, had just culminated upon my arrival in Tacna, the southernmost city of Perú.

I had $5.00 in my pocket.

About a mile from the sleepy train station was a neon sign, burning luciferously in the hot, humid Latin American summer night: The Tourist Hotel. I made the ritzy lodge my first destination, plodding through puddles of stagnant precipitation.

The hotel manager, Hector Amaya, was a five-foot, obese Peruvian in his sixties, the sort of Latin macho that intimidated many, even though his generous smile implied otherwise.

"I'm a lone sojourning artist," I said at the bustling hotel entrance. "I wouldn't mind sleeping on the extra bed in your storage room for the night. I promise to be good."

Hector guffawed.

"Young man, come in," he said, endearingly. "We can work something out."

I spent the night thrashing around on a storage room bunk bed. The next day, I sat by the hotel pool, struggling to survive without food.

Hector approached me whilst I sprawled on a porch bench.

"I've been watching you sitting by the pool all day," he said. "You must be hungry?"

"I don't have any money, but I'd love to do your portrait in exchange for a meal."

In his private hotel quarters, Hector, his wife and a few guests posed as I drew one portrait after the other.

"You know, Walter, I'm so impressed with your workmanship," said Luis Avila, one of Hector's guests, as I handed him his portrait. "I have a proposition for you."

"Thank you sir. I'm all ears."

"You see, I have a son who needs mature guidance," he said. "I'm driving to Arequipa and would love for you to come with me to teach him a thing or two."

"Why me?"

"I don't know, Walter, because all Germans are mature and assertive?"

"Right."

Our trip to Arequipa, a large, clean city at the Andes foothills, took four hours. Upon arriving there, I met Mr. Avila's wife and his aforementioned son, Ricardo, who was preparing for a trip to Lima. Ricardo had ample money to invest in his older brother, Felix's fledgling Lima business. Neither had the entrepreneurial experience.

"Felix runs a store in Lima, selling Husquarna sewing machines," Luis explained. "The store is on the verge of bancruptcy. Ricardo has good intentions, but I'm afraid his money will go down the drain too."

"I think I can help," I said.

"I'm sure you'll straighten them out," Luis assured. "I simply don't know Lima enough to make much of a difference."

I resided with the Avila family for three days.

On the fourth day, Ricardo and I were off to Lima, a whopping 800-kilometer trip from Arequipa. The trip along the coast was painfully bland, monotonous and vegetationless, except for few fertile valleys that bore cotton and sugarcane plantations.

In Lima, I checked into an inexpensive hotel on *Avenida 28 de Julio*. We checked out Felix's large downtown store, which was rather sparse, merchandise stocked half-empty.

During one of my adventurous sightseeing trips through Lima, I came upon a fast-food joint "*Oh, Qué Bueno,*"(Goody-goody) which was a replica of many hamburger joints in the States. I investigated and discovered that an American, John P. Solomon, owned the business. Solomon's burger joint introduced the ice cream machine to Lima.

I proposed the ice cream idea to Ricardo, while he drove us back home in his antiquated Buick.

"Don't you think it'll be a good idea to fill the empty half of your store with an ice cream joint?"

"That, my friend, is the greatest idea I've ever heard," he enthused. "How soon can you start that? What do you need to get started?"

"Don't you think we should inform your brother first before we get too excited?"

"He has no choice. Remember, I'm the one with the money."

Ricardo and I discussed the idea with Felix, who signed on.

Felix accompanied me to an in-town sales representative to purchase an ice cream machine.

After much price negotiation ado, Felix tacked some receipts to a clipboard and handed them to me.

"Sign these," he said, almost ordering me.

"Whaaat?" I said, pessimistic of Felix's motives.

Signing the ownership documents meant all the equipment was technically and legally mine. The brothers had bad credit.

"Sir, your new ice cream machine will be available within 3 weeks," the receptionist said, snapping the signed receipts from my hand.

With the brothers' assistance, I rearranged the store and visited virtually all the local dairies. They all promised the availability of the necessary dairy mixtures.

Banishing the sewing machines to a peripheral status, "*El Gringo* Ice Cream" became an ice cream joint. I sold the ice cream cones as *Gringuito* for 50c, a *Gringo* for 1 sol, a *Gringazo* (little Gringo, Gringo, giant Gringo) for 1.50 sol.

The business opened with much fanfare, and the never-ending, serpentine lines of customers were simply overwhelming, oftentimes winding out of the restaurant and snaking along the sidewalk. Customer traffic was particarly attainable because the store was conveniently located in a bustling district, close to the main market. With catchy trademark products, "El Gringo" became a salient household name in no time. I painted appropriate order signs and posters to make product selection more convenient.

I reveled in good business fortune, albeit temporarily.

Three weeks later, traffic had slowed down at El Gringo, and I began to grow unceasingly impatient. One sweltering afternoon, a blonde, tall and slightly potbellied man sauntered into the store, manned by Ricardo and me. From behind the glass display of fruity ice cream aroma, I could still smell the American in him.

"Hello, my friend! Today, if you buy a thirst-quenching Gringuito, you get one free. How can I help you?" I rambled dryly and expeditiously seemingly for the thousandth time.

"Hi ... Walter my name is Herman," he said, after reading my name badge. "Tell you what, brother, I'll go ahead and get a whole gallon of Cherimoya-flavored ice cream."

"Sure, Herman," I enthused. "I hope you have the room in that suit for all the free Gringazos."

"Ah, don't worry about the free stuff," he replied, digging immediately into his ice cream tub as he turned around in departure.

The munificent American was our first client in four hours, so I felt compelled to engage him in amicable chatter.

"You sound American," I inquired.

"Yeah, I'm from Eureka, California," he said, spinning around. "Just in town operating a whaling business on the coast, north of Lima."

"Oh yes, I've heard of you men," Ricardo said, breaking his unusual silence. "You work with the famous German-Peruvian entrepreneur, Gildemeister, right?"

"Yeah, well, we don't necessarily work for him, we just use his facilities to hunt whales and sell the meat," Herman said, halting long enough to shove the last spoon of ice cream into his mouth. "It's fun."

"I see you don't waste much time. Would you like more?" I asked.

"No, but since you gentlemen are such good salesmen, let me interest you in something."

"What?"

"You'd make a killing here if you sold whale meat hamburgers," he said. "It's the finest of all meats."

Herman's savvy proposition landed him a random sale, and led to a small order of tasty blue whale meat. We promptly added Burgers to our menu. Spiced with onions and hot pepper, the meat made utterly delicious burgers. Patronization at El Gringo soared afterwards.

"What in the world are these Burgers made out of?" many a customer asked, to which our standard response was simply, "It's a secret."

Whale cuisine was illegal. To obscure our secret, we erected a canvas above El Gringo's patio, to keep nosy tenants above us out. The smoke was thick, but nobody complained. As an appeasement strategy, we often gave our neighbors Burgers and ice cream for free.

One day, after copious futile attempts, Herman talked me into a whale hunt. The voyage gradually morphed into an unforgettable event. At Huacho, a port near Lima, we clambered aboard Herman's old torpedo boat. We had barely sailed a mile into sea, when Herman spotted a hefty blue whale breath-fountain.

"Gentlemen and gentlemen!" Herman bellowed aristocratically from the ship's top deck to a boisterous group of American fishermen on the lower deck. "Get ready your goddamned harpoons, its whaling time, baby!"

In robotic response, the men roared barbarically like ancient European pirates, snapping long, bloodied harpoons from unsanitary racks on the ship's deck.

I watched the blue whale, oblivious to imminent danger, swim precariously close to the ship's beam.

Aware of the whale's close proximity, the fishermen suddenly fell mute as they slowly tiptoed to the beam, where they waited for Herman's final command.

Growing up in Germany, *Mutti* had deluged me with many a blue whale story and legend.

"It's the largest mammal in the world," she often said, pointing to the smiley-faced mother blue whale and her calf in the only animal picture-book we owned. "It can swallow twenty Mercedes Benz in one gulp."

However, nothing, not even *Mutti*'s fantasized exaggerations, really readied me for the sheer monstrosity of the blue whale in reality. I could discern the never-ending mass of its gargantuan body beneath the clear-blue water as it floated by the ship's beam.

"Now!" Herman yelled.

In a two-second flash, two men unleashed their harpoons onto the whale's back, immediately bloodying the previously pristine water. The animal moaned and shrieked vociferously as it thrashed uncontrollably in the ocean, unable to stray far for at the end of the harpoons were cables strapped to the ship. For a terrifying moment, it seemed the thrashing whale would yank the bobbing ship below water, as it hopelessly tugged to free itself of the flesh-ripping harpoons.

The resistance ended about twenty minutes later.

"Okay, fellas, you know what to do!" Herman barked, so undoubtedly charged by his work that his eyes lit up. "Let's haul this large motherfucker to shore."

As the groveling ship dragged the enormous whale towards the nearby port facilities, I saw a small calf hurriedly trailing his bludgeoned, dead mother. The sight was instantaneously evocative of the picture in the children's book *Mutti* often read to me as a child, except mother whale bore no smile, just the lugubrious scowl of death. Baby whale was certainly bound to die of malnutrition.

I never whaled again.

With Burgers on our menu, El Gringo was virtually a gold mine, but Ricardo grew long fingers that got lost in our cash register. His avariciousness, coupled with my never-ending guilt of marketing blue whale meat, led me to, yet again, consider moving on. However, overwhelmed by unbridled success, approaching the Avila brothers about my intention to quit was most difficult.

Whilst we closed down El Gringo one evening, a local congressman strolled into my bedraggled back-office with the proposition of a lifetime.

"Walter, I've watched intently as El Gringo has gone from scratch to its current promising status," he said, sucking on a cigar as he slowly swiveled in the office chair. "It's for this reason that I propose to purchase the establishment for an amount that you simply can't resist."

Struggling to conceal my excitement, I said, "How much?"

"Twenty thousand soles."

I faked a cough.

"That's a very generous offer, sir, and I would love to accept, but I need to talk to my partners first."

"There's no need to because I already did," he said. "You see, Walter, you don't have much of a choice."

Unbeknownst to me, Felix owed 20,000 soles to the Peruvian congressman. I felt cheated and used, but played along.

"I'll give you 20,000 soles, provided you sign a release form for the ice cream machine," he said, handing me a contract form. "The factory sales representative, who sold you the ice cream machine, said he wouldn't turn the machine over to me without you're written consent."

"Yes, that's correct. We bought it with credit, and still owe some money on it."

I snatched and signed the release form, which the congressman then tucked in his suit before any cash exchanged hands.

"And, ah, by the way," he said, dodging my eyes surreptitiously. "I only have ten thousand soles right now. I'll give you the remaining 10,000 soles later, if you don't mind."

I didn't trust him, but he was a congressman.

"Of course, I don't mind."

After instantly procuring 10,000 soles in cash, I accepted the congressman's word of honor for the balance payment in a week.

I am still waiting for the promised money.

For months, I hounded the politician's large house intermittently only to be rudely informed that he was suspiciously unavailable. About a year later, I spotted the conniving congressman in front of his house, climbing into his stretched automobile.

In the street, I stood in front of his moving vehicle and yelled, "For 10,000 soles, I want the world to know you're a son of a bitch!"

He almost ran over me.

Two months later, I invested the 10,000 soles into the importation and sale of world-famous Düsseldorf mustard. I grew up with the son of a mustard factory owner, with whom I entered a contract. Soon barrels of "Otto and Fritz" Düsseldorf mustard arrived in Lima, replete with a pump for conveniently filling up small jars. Of course, Peruvians had numerous German "Otto and Fritz" jokes, similar to American Polish jokes.

I operated the mustard business out of my small bedroom. Some grocers paid me immediately, others made me wait thirty days.

"Otto and Fritz, huh?" one shopkeeper observed, during one of my deliveries. "I know a famous joke."

"Believe me, I've heard it all, but go ahead."

"Otto returns home after a long day at work to find his wife, Frieda, having sex with another man?"

"Okay?"

"What does he do?"

"I don't know," I said. "Surprise me."

"He decides to sell the couch."

I laughed only out of the need to satisfy and sustain my clientele.

Popularity came instantly, and businessmen interested in importing other exotic German products soon sought me.

A banker friend of mine inquired about German coin-counting machines. I contacted my dad in Germany. He listed several manufacturers, many of which sent brochures and catalogues. Lima had many banks. Eventually, I sold 18 machines, procuring considerable commission. Another popularly sought imported item was the electric hand dryer, which tens of restaurants purchased for bathroom facilities.

Life was good in Perú.

My silver-gray Jaguar and classy Briar pipe augmented my popularity in Lima, particularly among the ladies. After numerous repairs, I sold the Jaguar and purchased a Volkswagen bug, which was the talk of the town at the time, that simply made me a magnet.

I dated Olivia, daughter of a Peruvian general, who later became head of a popular military junta. Olivia was tall, slim and soft-spoken, beautiful without trying. She was also one of the most doting women I've ever met. Olivia's family loved Germans, and treated me like a son.

One Saturday afternoon, the general and I sat by the poolside at his impressive Lima estate, chugging beer and deliberating world politics.

"How I wish that Hitler were never born," I said, after a lengthy Holocaust discussion.

"How I wish that you'll consider marrying my daughter," he replied, suddenly making eye contact.

The general's random wish was somewhat expected. He had been a little too nice after all. Nevertheless, had I married Olivia, it would have primarily been because of the generous general.

Unwilling to commit long-term, I severed my relationship with Olivia during dinner at a posh Lima restaurant.

"I'm not quite ready to become engaged," I explained.

"What?"

"But I assure you that I've never known a more beautiful and nicer young lady. I love your parents too, but I just need a little more time."

She slapped me twice. I deserved each one. A change of scene was imminent.

With some Swiss friends, I explored the hinterlands of Perú. We backpacked through the highlands to Cuzco, Macchu Pichu, Trujillo and Chimbote, through the Amazon jungle and to many clear beaches untainted by man. Perú was simply a paradise.

We once camped at one of Perú's most romantic beaches, replete with white sand, clear water, crabs and exotic shells. We erected tents along the beach and stayed for a week. An old farmer residing nearby produced pisco, the Peruvian national drink.

"I've learned the art of wine-making from my home country Italy," the old man claimed repetitively.

We doubted the old man's suspect claims, but purchased a whole *damajuana* (demijohn) of wine and a few bottles of pisco. Tipsyness became an on-camp staple. The bay was simply gorgeous. The gentle waves scurried to the shore, bringing with them exotic shells. I loved chasing down the scampering crabs.

My date for the backpacking expedition was Cucha, a gorgeous Peruvian Panagra Airlines stewardess, who fit quite well into our gringo clique.

Our last day on the beach, Cucha and I carved out some rare one-on-one time to sunbathe.

"What do you say we get naked, huh," I said, as we scampered out of our tents to the beach.

"Let's do it!"

To the chagrin of our fellow campers, we stripped, did a brief wiggly butt-dance and lay flat on the cool beach sand. The ensuing sunburn on my derrière lasted months.

Upon my return, I learned that Olivia had met a new candidate. This relieved me of much guilt.

A friend of mine, Miguel, who owned a fumigating business, lived in a small house in a lovely Lima suburb. Eager to return to his native Uruguay, Miguel convinced his landlord to lease the house to me.

The house sported an apple-shaped pool, devoid of a filtering system, which meant it had to be cleaned and refilled at least once a week. For companionship, I adopted two dogs and a goat. I named the ruminant Bambi. She accompanied me everywhere, until neighbors started complaining. People often tolerate dogs, but goats are seldom welcome guests, and justifiably so. Goats have a putrid pungent natural odor that most, except goat farmers, find rather offensive. In the neighborhood, Bambi tore down and ate all the climbing geraniums. It was simply amazing how high she could climb.

One day, I locked Bambi on top of the flat roof as punishment for ravaging a neighbor's garden.

"I'll make goat stew of her if she comes near my flowers again," the neighbor yelled, as Bambi scampered into my yard, clutching the incriminating flowers in her mouth.

I was sitting on the front porch reading when, suddenly, rain began to fall. But it never rained in Lima, and the "precipitation" stunk. Bambi was pissing on my head from above! Tempted to make her into stew myself, I opted to give her to a friend, who owned a small ranch outside Lima.

Two weeks later, at a bar, I met Walter "El Brujo" Ledgard, Perú's Berlin 1936 Olympics swimming champion. A winner of numerous masters' championships as an octogenarian, El Brujo literally swam to his grave in the late 1990s. Founder of a modern swimming academy, Ledgard courted me to become Assistant Coach for Perú's Olympic Swimming team.

Walter as swimming instructor

I had other plans. Exploiting my small house pool, I began offering swimming classes. No sooner did I begin to advertise did students swarm my home for lessons.

The newspaper in which I placed an ad took an interest in my swimming academy. Journalists wrote numerous articles about

Lima's children learning to swim, which brought in more business. My classes filled steadily, so did my bank account. Having read several newspaper articles, an elderly, well-dressed gentleman, Arturo Banderas, paid me a visit one Monday morning.

After gawking momentarily at the children in the pool, he asked, "Would you accept children with polio in your classes."

"Of course!"

It was not until the man departed that his odd curiosity made sense. Many Peruvians believed polio to be contagious. I expeditiously arranged special classes for the afflicted. Like before, word about my special classes got around town and, before long, there were two full classes for polio victims.

The polio classes were my favorite. Swimming was such a relief to the youngsters whose bodies felt free in the water, far from the everyday struggle of ambling on land.

I once read of a hydrotherapeutic rehabilitation resort in Warm Springs, Georgia where disabled U.S. President Franklin D. Roosevelt spent much time. In 1926, FDR had purchased the run-down resort, and over the next 20 years turned it into a unique, first-class rehab center, based on a unique philosophy of treatment - one where psychological recovery was prized as much as medical treatment.

Warm Springs was run by people with polio, for people with polio. In that spirit, FDR is still known as the father of the modern independent living movement, which puts people with disabilities in control of their own lives.

At the resort, patients were afforded therapeutic swimming, amongst other innovative treatments. Reading about the successful Warm Springs facility inspired me to found a similar resort in Latin America.

George Rudolf, a Swiss architect comrade of mine, commenced designing the facility, a family resort, replete with posh restaurants from which parents could observe their swimming children. A beauty salon, a bar and a gym were included to afford parents ample activity whilst the children underwent therapeutic swimming lessons.

Later, Arturo Banderas paid me another unexpected visit, this time enrolling his polio-afflicted granddaughter. Unlike most guardians, Arturo lingered behind, intently watching his little brave granddaughter float across the pool all day, the water gently ushering her legs forward. My fondest memory in Perú was the day - after three months of therapy - the pretty girl took several poolside steps toward her grandfather.

With tears tumbling down his cheeks, Arturo looked at me and whispered, "I'm at your mercy any time. Just let me know what I can do for you."

Arturo turned out to be owner of a reputable chain of Peruvian banks. One afternoon, George and I walked into his Lima office, project-financing proposition in hand.

Arturo was impressed with the partially underground structure.

"This is the most original idea I've ever seen," he enthused. "I'll back this up, just prepare a cost projection that I can present to my board for logistical reasons."

Financing for the center was secured. The land on which to build the center was another matter. Raising sufficient capital for relatively expensive Lima land became my next goal, a quite implausible task since the swimming academy did not bring in enough cash.

While shopping at a Lima store for swimming pool supplies, I ran into Mirna, a cordial friend of mine, who, along with her mother, ran Night and Day, the only nightclub in Lima that had a permit to stay open 24 hours. Mirna was Yugoslavian.

"Walter, I'm going to America," she said, before any initial greetings.

Mirna was not the prettiest of ladies, but I admired her for her persistently ebullient spirit. She simply lit up quite effortlessly, come rain or shine.

We chattered along the store's innovative dog food isle, satiated with Swiss grub made of an eerie combo of meat and carrots.

"How come you get to go to America?" I asked.

"I'm getting married to an American."

"What about your mother?"
"She's coming with me."
"Where will you live?"
"In Missouri, my fiancé is from there," she explained.
"And, what is going to happen to the club?" I asked.
"We're trying to sell the club. You know many people. Perhaps you can help us. We'll be happy to pay a commission."
"How much do you want?"
"Why don't you buy it? We'll give you a very special price."
The price Mirna offered was indeed utterly special.
"Let me think about it."
The fervently popular club could resell easily and rake in fortunes, which I envisioned using to purchase the strip of land.
"You must come to the wedding. It will be in two weeks."
"Okay."
Three weeks later, I was proud owner of a five-star Lima nightclub. On one of my many trips to the Night and Day, I met Amy, an English middle-aged broad, who signed on as my first bartender. She turned to be quite the drink-mixing expert.

Unfortunately, Amy had other areas of unpleasant expertise: hunting for a husband. I soon became one of her candidates. Plus, Amy often had health problems. I had to let her go.

George Rudolf redesigned and transformed bland Night and Day into *La Caricatura*, an urbanesque, post-modern club, replete with a large glass display case - mounted on the wall behind an arch-shaped bar - featuring caricatures of my most loyal customers.

The animated display case resembled a checkerboard, illuminating the surrounding bar. Otherwise, the club was pitch dark. The idea was to provide surreptitious safe haven for disloyal married men - unwilling recognition - as they partied with their girlfriends.

Unable to secure the right waitress, I ran the show myself, closing at 4 a.m. Then I would snag two hours of sleep, and rise early enough to administer my first swimming class. On too many occasions to count, the children's boisterous arrival served as my alarm clock.

One night, a drunken customer walked in with trouble written all over him.

He insisted on taking over as bartender. "Let me behind there or this bar will not run tonight," he barked.

"Why don't you leave and save yourself from getting hurt," I threatened.

His behavior only worsened. Soon my bar was near-empty. Enraged, I grabbed the smaller man by his shirt collar, and threw him out the door. He returned looking for a fight.

"I'm going to kill you," he screamed. "You damned foreigner."

I delivered two karate chops to his neck. That certainly did it. He stumbled quietly to the door and disappeared.

Later that night, my arm throbbed with excruciating pain. By the next day, it had turned a purplish blue. At the local clinic, I was informed that my arm was broken. Shifting gear, teaching swimming and running a club with my left hand was most impossible. I was left with no alternative but to sell *La Caricatura* prematurely. The sales was somewhat profitable, but painfully less than what I needed to procure the land for my hydrotherapeutic center.

About a month later, I opened my mailbox to discover a large, brown envelope from Dortmund, Germany. It was an invitation card from the German Swimming Federation, soliciting my participation at the grand inauguration of The Westphalia Hall, a government-commissioned, state-of-the-art athletic dome in Dortmund. It was a most fulfilling honor, finally an advantage of my days as a champion swimmer with the Hitler Youth Swimming Team.

I planned a trip to Germany via the United States to afford myself the golden opportunity to see John Carroll again. A few days later, the American Consulate in Lima awarded me a tourist visa to do just that.

The funds procured from selling *La Caricatura* became my traveling money. I often wonder the extent of societal change that the center could have afforded Lima and its citizenry had I completed it.

I departed Perú one week later.

My First Days in the U.S. of A.

The home of freedom, and the hope of the downtrodden and oppressed among the nations of the earth. - Daniel Webster.

Borne of sheer unexpectedness, my first odyssey to the United States transpired in the sultry autumn of 1954. Since flyer miles and www.cheapfare.com were non-existent in the fifties, cinching an inexpensive flight was downright daunting. I settled for a low-cost Honduran airline still operating D-C 3 planes. After a depressingly protracted stop in Panama, we landed in Miami, Florida.

"Walter, welcome to the U.S. of A.," the immigration officer enthused at the passenger entry counter. "You're going to California, eh?"

I found his curt salutation most startling. In most countries, it is grandly boorish to address novel acquaintances by their first names, at least until chummy rapport has been established. On initial introduction, last names, sir or madam are unquestionably preferred. In Germany, informal addressing is acceptable subsequent to a festive *Brüderschaft* ceremony, during which two friends indulge in a glass of champagne among family and friends. After chugging cold duck, the two declare casual friendship, and thus the commencement of first name usage.

Worst yet, the officer was strangely cognizant of my destination.

"The famous FBI has informed you of my arrival?" I replied brusquely.

"Any reason to be hunted by "Uncle Sam, Walter?"
"Who is Uncle Sam?"
The immigrant officer guffawed.
"I apologize for jumping to conclusions. Uncle Sam is the U.S. government."

August in Miami was literally hot as hell. The enfeebling humidity felt like being unceasingly trapped in some claustrophobic space. As my horrid fortune would have it, the monstrous Shriners' Convention was in town, bringing with it more than 900 Shrine business representatives. The Shrine was founded in 1872 by a group of 13 men belonging to the Masonic Order. Originally established to provide fellowship for its members, the Shrine grew to what many consider "The Worlds Greatest Philanthropy," consisting of broad network of specialized hospitals.

The best-known symbol of Shrinedom is the distinctive red fez, and Miami was flooded with them. The bustling streets of Miami were swarmed with photogenic parading Shriners, encumbering traffic flow. They pranced about in their religious regalia, donning the red fez proudly. Others marched in oriental, brass or drum bands.

Inquisitive residents lined the streets, cheering animatedly at the variety of parading mini-cars. Some Shriners drove the standard classic car style, while others cruised automobiles inspired by Volkswagen Beetles, racecars or semi-trailers. Several cars were modeled to resemble flying carpets. One group rode camel cars. Both pint-sized and full-sized motorcycles and scooters careened along the several routes. The most elaborate contraption was the 12-men bike.

I enjoyed the colorful show. It reminded me of the many utterly effervescent Gypsy circuses I witnessed as a child in pre-WW II Germany, until Adolf Hitler declared the powerless Bohemians impure, and thus enemy of the Reich. Unbeknownst to the historical layman, many Gypsies like Jews were annihilated during the Holocaust, all because of their so-called dissident heresy.

Hotel rooms seemed non-existent, until I stumbled upon a petite room at the decrepit Granlyn Hotel, a most unimpressive wooden structure serving mostly elderly patrons. The youngest occupant there could not have been younger than seventy-five.

I checked into my room, also known as the hotel's attic. It had neither air conditioning nor ventilation. So, to the hotel lobby I trotted to purchase, for the first time, a few bottles of ice-cold Coca Cola. I lined the chilled bottles under the thin bed sheets and rested my knees upon them. Two minutes later, I felt my body temperature nosedive. However, the relief was rather short-lived. Soon the bottles had fully absorbed my body heat, and I was again unbearably hot.

From my small hotel window, a store sign, "ROOT BEER," blinked enticingly. Root beer was certainly not part of my German or European lingo. I assumed it to be some brand of alcoholically charged beer that would surely be slumbering.

The unpleasant medicinal taste of the syrupy beverage still lingers on my tongue.

I was kicked out of the hotel room the next day.

"I'm sorry sir, but the room has been reserved for someone else," the rude receptionist barked from behind the front desk in the hotel lobby.

"Where can I go?"

He simply shrugged and pursued some other chore.

My destination was Dallas, Texas to meet Jody, a Braniff Airlines stewardess I had met in Lima. I had become mightily acquainted with many a stewardess for both Braniff and Panagra airlines were headquartered in Lima.

"Call me whenever you're in Dallas," Jody had once said, her high-pitched American accent still reverberating in my head.

So, the following morning, I boarded a plane to the "Big D."

Once in Dallas, I checked into the White Plaza Hotel recommended by a pleasant taxi driver. I called the Braniff Airlines office from the single-bed in my hotel room.

"Hello, Braniff Airlines?"

"Jody, the stewardess, please?"

"You mean white Jody or just Negro Jody?" she said, condescending in her utterance of the latter.

"White Jody, I guess," it was my first taste of politically incorrect racism, quite popular in Texas at the time.

"Well, Jody's outta town till tomorrow. I reckon you call back then."

"Okay. Will you give her my name and number?"

I hung up the phone, marveling at the hypocritical and unfortunate similarity between the United States, South America and Europe on race issues. America, land of freedom and equality, I often heard. But was it as free and equal for blacks? Certainly not, and the nauseous sight of mortifying black slums and news reports of white policemen clobbering and shooting peaceful, unarmed black Civil Rights Movement protesters in the South attested to Uncle Sam's solemn injustice and hypocrisy.

I had been in the United States only a day, but this jaw-dropping, surreal Nazi-like repression of a people seemed too glaring to be true. Both leaderships in Germany and America acted to control their own populations, each country with its own techniques - crude in Germany and more sophisticated in the United States - to make their rule secure. The only difference: The United States went to work - without overt swastikas, goose-stepping or advertised officially declared racism - surreptitiously suppressing a powerless race of people they deemed dissident and heretic.

Having not slept much in Miami, I slumbered on these innate thoughts, relying on the Braniff secretary to relay my message to Jody.

The phone rang at precisely mid-morning. It was Jody.

"Hey, would you like to travel to Oklahoma to visit my folks?" she offered.

"Yes. I guess so."

"Plus, if I were you, I'd move out of that expensive hotel. You can check in at the YMCA upon our return."

I was stunned to learn of my pricy hotel bill. Jody picked me up in a rather elegant Mercury Coupe. We drove four hours to her parents' small ranch house on the arid Texas-Oklahoma border. Jody's folks were nice to me, but I had immense difficulty understanding the slang-filled Oklahoma drawl. Jody's brawny and tall father Max was a blue-collar steel-plant worker. We enjoyed a festive lunch, followed by multiple sessions of horseshoe throwing.

"You throw mighty well, Waller," Max complimented.

"Thanks a lot. I think it has something to do with the lush grass."

"Yeah, that carpet grass sore's the prad of ma home," he replied grinning.

As a matter of fact, carpet grass was a salient landscaping fad in the Southwest at the time. Every other home and business was surrounded with it. I must admit; walking on it was sheer pleasure.

One of the men blazed barbecue, which I found quite delicious. Unfortunately, we had to leave the next morning.

"Y'all come back any tam now," Max offered.

We billowed turbid clouds of dust as we traversed arid terrain back to Dallas. I was reminded me of the dehydrated desert tang of Northern Chile. Nothing grasped my attention firmer than the whizzing eighteen-wheelers. I had never seen trucks that long. One of the drivers noticed my amazement. He waved his brawny arm and honked twice.

Just as we had planned, Jody dropped me off at the Dallas YMCA.

"I'll call you later," she said, before driving off.

Eager to rid myself of the coat of traveling dust, I snagged some soap, a towel and headed to the public shower facility, leaving my room unlocked and my suitcase wide open on the bed. It was not until the next morning that it struck me that someone had snuck in whilst I showered away obliviously. The money and Peruvian jewelry in my suitcase was gone. My finances were reduced to a twenty-dollar bill tucked into a hidden zipper pocket.

I called Jody the next day.

"Now I can't take the plane to Los Angeles," I whined.

"Walter, you can't panic. I'll arrange something, just stand by."

Jody picked me up at lunchtime. We drove to a large house owned by her friend Frank with whom she relayed my condition.

Judging by his grandiose manor, I envisaged some form of financial assistance from Frank.

"I'm really sorry, Walter," he said. "Don't hold it against all Americans."

"Don't worry about it," I said. "The thief was probably Russian."

Frank owned and operated an automobile transportation service.

"You know, we're always hiring men to drive cars to different parts of the country," he said, as we cleared up the dining table. "I pay good."

"What's available?"

"Well, right now, we have a Chevy Bel Air that needs relocation to Salt Lake City."

Frank's offer ended up being a needed prize. Upon arrival in "The Beehive State," the employment agreement detailed, I would receive another vehicle for transportation to Los Angeles. My salary for the trip: A mere $30.00. I had to pay for gas.

In two days, I procured an international drivers license. Jody and Frank insisted we make merry. So away we went partying at a local bar. As we clambered into Frank's sleek Cadillac after the bash, he asked, "Walter, have you ever watched an American football game?"

"No, I've never seen American football, but I've seen many football games in South America."

Frank laughed. "That's not real football, that's soccer. The best football is played here in Dallas in the Cotton Ball. We have an extra ticket, why don't you come with us?"

Our entourage included Frank, Jody and about seven of their acquaintances. I do not recall which teams played, but the game must have had superior significance for the Cotton Bowl stadium was jam-packed. Unbeknownst to me, tickets for such games were near unattainable.

American football did not make much sense to me. The refs kept halting play. During the frequent cessations, the fans shrieked, waving their arms vivaciously, while I sat there unaware of how to act. Stunning lasses in petite skirts induced the screaming. Except for the cute girls, I found the game boring.

"How did you like the game?" asked Frank afterward.

"I liked the dancing girls, but I don't understand why they kept stopping to have a conference every few minutes."

Everybody laughed.

After the game, we drove to one of the guys' house. Beer seemed to be the most popular beverage, although a few drank Coca-Cola with rum. The men sat around the television, awaiting another game.

"Well, Walter, tell us a little about South America," Frank asked.

"Sure. Argentina is ..."

"Hold on, Walter, the game is about to start. Can we talk about this later?"

"Yes."

The football game flickered on, and soon everybody's attention switched to the television. The men talked to the screen while they chugged beer and ate pizza. Jody had to leave during half-time.

"I have to leave, Walter, do you need a drive back to the YMCA?"

"Yes," I said, turning to the boisterous group of men. "Thanks guys for your time!"

Frank slipped an envelope into my hand, and whispered, "Have a safe trip. If you have any problems, my phone number is on the envelope. Keep in touch, send us a post card and remember, don't hold the theft at the YMCA against all Americans."

"Thank you for all your help," I said.

Then I left with Jody, who dropped me off at the YMCA.

"I'll pick you up tomorrow morning to take you to the car service place," she said.

"Promise?"

"Promise."

I planted a gentle kiss on her cheek before climbing out of the car. Jody blushed.

"Good night."

"Night."

Upon settling down in my room for the night, I slit the envelope. In it were two ten-dollar bills and a card with Frank's phone number. Thankful and moved by the kindness, my assessment of Americans began to ameliorate. I slept well.

Jody picked me up at 7 o'clock the next morning. On the way to the car service, we stopped for coffee and donuts. By the time we arrived at the auto place, it was still closed.

"Ah, shoot. What do we do?" she said as we idled in disbelief.

"Don't worry, I'll be okay. You can leave me here and go on to work. Thanks for all your help."

I hugged Jody.

She kissed me on my lips.

"I'll see you in Lima, have a safe trip."

A few hours later, I picked up the key for the Bel Air and signed some paperwork. Armed with a map Jody had given me, I commenced my trip to Salt Lake City, enjoying the comfy Bel Air along the way. The weather was pleasant, so grabbing hamburgers from roadside diners became a provisional habit. This was long before McDonald's cluttered the American landscape.

Autumn had stripped the trees of their leaves and the dry summer had left most of the countryside parched. The landscape was not eye-catching. It lacked the green lushness of many parts of South America. Several of the roads I traversed weaved through the poorer parts of rural Southwest America. Bedraggled shacks lined both sides of the road, while previously impressive structures were badly maintained and left to rot. But the rugged beauty of the American landscape revealed itself as I drove through the "Land of Enchantment," New Mexico. The blood-red hills reflected sunlight picturesquely against the gorgeous blue skies. The scenery was breathtaking. Nothing I had seen in Europe or South America could compare to the expansive, rugged terrain.

At eleven o'clock that night, while driving through Castle Rock near Denver, Colorado, a policeman stopped me. I parked on the right shoulder. The officer approached my car slowly, clutching a blinding flashlight.

"In a rush to get somewhere, son?" he asked.

"No sir, is there a problem, officer?"

"You were 10 miles above the speed limit. Plus, you crossed the yellow line. You wanna pay or you wanna see the judge?" he demanded.

I could not discern if the stocky policeman was legitimate or conspiring to frighten me out of my cash. Hobbled with limited funds, I decided to take my chances.

"I want to see the judge."

"Follow me."

The officer duck into his patrol car and pounced on the highway. Once I was positioned behind him, he turned on his flashing red lights and augmented his speed. I was confused. Had I attempted to keep up with the officer, I certainly would have been speeding. Unsure of his intentions, I maintained the speed limit and focused on the flashing lights. There were no other cars on the road to distract me.

The officer was clambering out his patrol car when I arrived at the jailhouse. He pointed me to a nearby visitors parking lot. He waited, hands on hips, spitting tobacco, until I disembarked the Bel Air.

"Follow me," he said, as he marched through the doors of a single-story brick building.

An elderly gentleman, dressed in faded uniform, sat at a desk by the door.

"Leave all your valuable items here with me, young fellow," he said.

I emptied my pockets unto the desk: My wallet, the car keys, some change, a bottle cap and a book of matches. He stashed it all into a plastic bag on which he scribbled "Walterio Meyer." Most of my possessions were in my luggage, locked in the car trunk.

"I hope my things would be safe and the car key won't be used to loot my belongings," I whispered to myself as the officer whisked me away.

There was no night judge on duty. The officer soon shoved a blanket into my arms.

"Your shoes and belt?" he ordered.

He soon led me to a dingy jail cell, empty but but for one man who sprung from sleep as I walked in.

"Howdy," he said.

"Hi."

He sprawled on the bottom bunk, so I climbed to the top, readying myself for sound sleep for the judge was not scheduled to arrive until sunrise. My cellmate mumbled a few words. Having spent many days behind bars before, I didn't mind him craving conversation with the new kid on the block, but I could hardly understand a word. I guessed from his garbled drawl that he was a drunken cowhand. He soon fell asleep, and within minutes I drifted off.

A different guard, Joe, stormed the cell the next morning. Sporting a generous smile and soft-spoken, Joe was unusually endearing for a prison guard. Similar to the officer the night before, he was in his fifties, and clad in shabby uniform. He hauled me across the street from the jailhouse to a diner for breakfast. The heavily accented cowboy was still snoring when we departed.

The eggs were runny, the bacon was dry and the coffee was bitter, but I was grateful for the free meal. Joe escorted me back to the jailhouse and locked me back up.

"I'll be back to get you later, when the judge has time to see you," Joe said.

The cowboy was gone! Perhaps he had seen the judge, while I ate breakfast. The hours elapsed at a snail's pace without the garrulous and incomprehensible cowboy. I dipped in and out of slumber for three hours, often waking up disoriented, unsure of my location.

At noon, Joe walked in and handed me a sandwich and a warm bottle of Coca-Cola.

"The judge will see you later this afternoon," he said.

"Thank you," I said. "Do you have anything around here to read?"

"Don't think so, but I'll check."

Joe returned with an old issue of Popular Mechanics. Some of the ads had been ripped out, but, at least, it kept my young mind busy. Three hours later, the guard revisited.

"Judge can't see you until the car is checked out. You'll have to stay another day."

Another guard escorted me to the roadside restaurant for dinner. He smoked and drank coffee while I gobbled my meal. We exchanged no words. Soon, I was trapped alone in the cell again. The lights went out at 9 p.m.

The next morning, Joe hustled me to the courtroom before breakfast. The judge sat behind a large, high desk as an orderly blared out the charges. The arresting highway trooper lounged in the back of the courtroom. Slouching non-challantly behind his desk, the judge seemed uninterested in the orderlies' words, as if bored by the everyday routine of his job.

Finally, I was permitted to speak.

"Mr. Judge," I began not knowing how to address an American judge. "This is my first trip to your country…"

Suddenly, the judge banged the gavel on his desk twice.

"Twenty-eight dollars, plus court costs," he barked.

Before I could utter another word, Joe tugged my arm, and walked me out. The case was obviously dismissed, but not in my favor. With court costs, I owed forty dollars.

"I don't have that much money," I explained to the guard.

Once again, Joe was sympathetic.

"Maybe we can work something out," he said.

"Please."

"For starters, that's a nice ring you have," he said, eyeing my gold pinkie ring. "Is it real gold?"

"Yes, it's from Perú."

"Would you be interested in selling it?"

"Perhaps."

Joe drove me to another restaurant, a fair distance from the jailhouse. We sauntered straight to a suit-wearing, leery gentleman seated at the rear end of the restaurant.

"Hey, man," Joe said, shaking hands with the man. "This young man has a ring to sell."

The man eyeballed the ring in the palm of his hand.

"Forty dollars," he said.

"The ring is hand crafted," I replied. "It's worth at least one hundred dollars."

"Forty dollars," he insisted.

"Alright, alright," I said. "Just give me the damned money."

I settled the fines in the courtroom, while wishing silently that the judge would die prematurely, and secured my car, checking first that my luggage was still in tact. It was.

I drove to a nearby gas station, which boasted one old pump operated manually. An attendant filled the glass tank, by proxy of which the petrol coursed into my gas tank.

"Have a nice trip and come back," he said, shoving the hose back in its cradle.

"Thank you."

I said good bye to Joe.

"Sorry about what happened, come again and have a good trip." He handed me a couple of sandwiches through the driver's side window and waved as I took off.

"Thanks, Joe." I yelled and waved at him.

With the rude intervention done with, I hit the road to Salt Lake City, the sight of Joe waving in the rearview mirror most relieving.

Two hours later, I was driving though dense woods, reminiscent of the Black Forest or Schwarzwald in Southwestern Germany. The Black Forest - known for its timber houses, many of which are 300 years old - is so named because of the beautiful mountain landscape with its dense population of dark pine trees; region of incomparably unspoiled nature, graced with its forests, mountains and meadows. Black Forest craftsmen are renowned worldwide for their cuckoo clocks, and the Christmas season is never complete without a nutcracker from the region. Castles, vineyards and orchards dot the hillsides.

No sooner had I psychologically exuviated my ghastly Castle Rock ordeal did horror strike yet again. A deer darted out from

Tomorrow Unfolds

the forest. I careened and screeched, but hit the animal anyway, smashing the right fender and light to smithereens before nosing to a halt two inches away from the rugged bark of a pine tree.

I popped out of the smoking, hissing automobile. The deer simply limped back into the forest. As cars and trucks whizzed by, I gawked at the sizeable dent on the right front fender.

Unable to assist the fleeing, but surely hobbled deer, I resumed my journey. My Castle Rock nightmare made me paranoid and ultra mindful of my speedometer. Thus, I was surprised when another police officer stopped me ten miles later.

As the unusually skinny officer approached my vehicle, I gripped the steering wheel nervously, using the inanimate object to steady my very animate emotions. He leaned into my window.

"Follow me," he barked, storming off afterwards.

I obeyed his orders, albeit begrudgingly. The police station was close by, and, after parking, I followed the austere man into the small station.

"Your drivers' license and car papers," he said, holding out his hand.

I handed him my bound paperwork, which he proceeded to inspect rather charily.

"Anything happen here lately that you'd like to report, young man?"

Naïvely, I narrated my entire Castle Rock ordeals, replete with imprisonment and freedom.

"Oh, we got us a jailbird," he said. "Why didn't you tell me about the deer." His voice was brusque and reproachful as if I had run over a small child instead of a wild deer.

"I didn't know that I had to tell you about an animal running out of the forest."

"Well, you do have to report it, and it will cost you," he said. "Not reporting an accident involving wildlife carries a fine of two hundred dollars."

The utterance of the words "two hundred dollars" raised my blood pressure. I only had $12 to my name. My acute abhorrence for police and uniformed men churned riotously inside of me. Another police officer walked into the room.

"What's he doing here?"

"Well, captain, this here fellow is a jailbird that didn't report a wildlife accident."

My face reddened with rage.

"I longed for years to come to America. Now I'm here for the first time. I had no idea that I needed to report accidents involving deer. I don't have any money. The money I had was stolen from me at the YMCA. I had to sell my ring to pay the fine in Castle Rock. If you want to put me in jail, then do so!"

The middle-aged captain's face was long by the time I concluded my emotional speech. He looked at his subordinates, and murmured in a most benevolent voice, "Let him go."

Soon I was back in the Bel Air, my transportation, hotel and dining room. The trip through Colorado was beautiful. I imagined the verdant forest and rolling mountains looked rather scenic in the winter.

I arrived at the Auto Auction lot in Salt Lake City at mid afternoon. The large car lot wrapped around the small, box-like office in front of which I parked. A burly man dragged out of the office, and walked around the car once, noticing the bent fender immediately.

"Eighteen dollars," he said, at the cashier desk in the office.

"What do you mean?" I asked.

The man handed me twelve dollars.

"The original payment for delivery was thirty dollars, and we are deducting eighteen dollars for the fender damage. That leaves a balance of twelve dollars."

"Do you have a car I can take to Los Angeles for you? That was Frank's promise."

"I'm sorry sir, but we don't have any cars heading to L.A. right now. Why don't you check back from time to time? Things around here always change."

"Where can I store my things?"

"You can keep them here for a few days," he offered.

I took him up on his offer. Somehow I had to make it to Los Angeles.

Tomorrow Unfolds

To pass time, I strolled through downtown Salt Lake City, wherein I came upon an inviting, Swiss-like house in front of which stood a sign that read, "Room for rent" in an impeccable front yard. Out of unbridled curiosity, I rang the bell. A kind, elderly lady stepped out.

"May I help you?" she asked.

"I saw your sign. I was so impressed by the neatness of your house, that I was wondering if you would rent a room for two days?"

"I appreciate the compliment," she said softly. "In turn, I'll let you have the room for five dollars a night, for as long as you want. What's your name?"

"Walter, and yours?"

"Mrs. Clarkson."

I paid $10 upfront, and Mrs. Clarkson handed me a key.

"Now, do an old tired lady a favor and not come in past eleven o'clock at night, will ya?" she said, as she ushered me to my room.

"Sure."

The bedroom, replete with a Mormon Bible, was as clean and neat as the rest of the house. After settling in, I ambled through downtown Salt Lake City; the people seemed proper and respectful. My next destination: The Joseph Smith Jr. Stationary Store, named after the 1820 founder of the Mormon Church, to purchase a drawing book, some pencils and an eraser.

"Who is Joseph Smith Jr.?" I asked the storeowner, as he stuffed my drawing materials in a paper bag.

He giggled.

"You're not from around heres, are you?"

"No, just traveling through here to L.A."

"He's founder of the Church of the Latter Day Saints, also known as the Mormon Church," he said, with a fair dose of sarcasm. "Personally, I think they're all a bunch of freaks."

He handed me the paper bag.

"Why? My landlady is one."

"They believe that in the spring of 1820, Joseph Smith Jr. retired to the woods near his home in Palmyra, New York, and offered a prayer to our Father in Heaven," the bookstore owner bellowed, his arms hoisted in a V, mimicking some Mormon historical text. "This prayer set into motion a series of events that brought forth The Church of Jesus Christ of Latter-day Saints. And, God bless us all."

"How come you named your store after their founder when you obviously don't like the church?"

"Because they fucking control everything here," he said, his creased face laced with a streak of frustration. "As you'll find out, being unMormon is not a thing of pride in good ol' Salt Lake."

"Thanks for the advice," I said, walking away. "I'll keep that in mind."

Equipped with my drawing utensils, I walked into a small coffee shop and sketched for a few dollars, enough to purchase a bus ticket to Los Angeles if necessary.

The next day, left my delightful little house.

"You remind me of my mother," I complimented Mrs. Clarkson as I walked out the door. "Thank you for your hospitality."

"You're welcome."

Upon returning to the Auto House, one of the mechanics introduced me to two customers heading to Los Angeles.

"Talk to them. They need a driver," he encouraged.

True enough, the two gentlemen agreed to give me a lift as long as I did the driving. I was more than happy to comply. Better yet, the Buick Sedan was spanking new, a sheer pleasure to steer. The two gentlemen, Lance and Justin, sat in the back, chatting and obviously pleased with their chauffeur.

The route was a piece of cake. We were ten miles away from Las Vegas, when we stopped at a service station for gas. While queuing in the isle, the gentlemen briefly fraternized with two ladies, who seemed like mother and daughter looking for some fun. One word led to a conversation, and soon my hosts had a word for me.

"Look, Walter, we decided to stay in Vegas," one of the men giggled, sticking his head in the driver's window. "You understand, right?"

"Yes, I do."

We drove to the nearby Las Vegas Grey Hound Station. Justin handed me an envelope.

"This ticket will take you to L.A. Have a good trip and thanks for being such a good sport."

"Thanks a bunch," I replied, winking at the ladies.

The bus station was inundated with enticing slot machines, but I fought off the urge successfully. I curled into my incommodious bus seat, and catnapped during most of the trip.

To Düsseldorf via the Golden State

Be it ever so humble, there is no place like home. - John Payne (1792-1852).

The first half of the humdrum bus-ride from Las Vegas to Los Angles boded little in the way of doozie adventures. Then, ten miles from L.A., a minor earthquake rattled me from my sound siesta. Trapped between trepidation and frazzling disillusion, I clung onto my throw pillow and curled into a human ball in my clammy seat.

The rest of the passengers remained stoic, apparently quite undisturbed by nature's ominous wrath. A bearded old man next to me shuffled daintily in his chair, then adjusted his half-rimmed glasses, and returned to perusing the L.A. Times.

Earthquakes were non-existent in Germany. We have wars instead.

"Ladies and gentlemen, we just experienced a light earthquake," the driver reported over the crackling PA system. "There's absolutely no reason to worry. Small earthquakes come a dime a dozen in these neck of the woods."

Twenty minutes later, the bus coursed into a besmirched, lifeless Greyhound Station. I immediately checked into the Golden State Hotel across the street, and holed myself up in a crammed room punching contacts' numbers. Of course, John Carroll was at the top of my list, his address - 16610 Chatsworth Street in Granada Hills - scribbled on a piece of paper he had handed me years before.

"You have to deposit some money before I can give you any more connections," the operator brusquely admonished after two dials.

I hung up in distress. Having grown up in a totalitarian country, the extortionist and opportunistic financial approach of breakneck capitalism made me uneasy, immediately disliking a country I had barely known.

I left my luggage at the hotel and boarded a bus to Granada Hills. Save for a few uncertain detours, John Carroll's grandiose mansion was quite easy to locate, sitting in the middle of a dashing horse rink. The wooden manor was appreciably flanked by a miniature caretaker's residence, leased by one Roger Brinkley, an exceptional horse trainer who doubled as estate manager, and his pretty teenage daughter Samantha.

I knocked on the guesthouse. A slim mustachioed man in his forties walked out, clad in a pair of blue jeans and a cheesy T-shirt that read, "What time is it? It's horse time!"

"Can I help you?" he asked.

"Sorry sir, but I'm here to see John Carroll," I said, choking back tears of laughter.

"He's not here, who are you?"

"My name is Walter Meyer," I said, stretching my arm for a handshake. "I'm a friend of his from South America."

"No shit. My mother migrated from Argentina and my dad from Bolivia. You from anywhere near those?"

"Yes shit," I replied clumsily. "I've lived in both Bolivia and Argentina."

Roger was teary-eyed in laughter, which must have caught his daughter's attention. She soon joined us on the porch. No words under God's sun can rightly describe the sheer magnitude of Samantha's beauty. Perfect comes close, but not quite. Clad in tight jeans shorts and a flimsy white T-shirt, she was tall, slim, abnormally unblemished and blessed with the world's greatest curves. I stared for an eternity, and rightfully so.

"Hi," she said sexily, acknowledging my admiration.

"Hi."

"Hey Samantha, Walter here was just telling me he's from Bolivia and Argentina. Ain't that cool?" Roger said.

"I guess."

"Ah, whatever. Anyhow Walter, I only manage the rink. Sadly, that means I don't get to know John's whereabouts. As you're probably aware, since you're his friend, John is not exactly the confiding type."

A Cadillac cruised in, parking in front of the shack. Samantha's face lightened up like a candle as a tall, handsome man stumbled out of the blue luxury car.

"Hey, John, how might you be doing today?" asked Roger.

"How many times have I told you, Roger, that 'how might you be doing' isn't good English," Mr. Derek joked, shaking Roger's hand vigorously. "Otherwise, I might be doing just fine."

The two men got a good laugh out of Mr. Derek's joke.

"Mr. Derek, this is Walter," Roger said. "Walter is looking for John Carroll. You don't happen to know where he is, do you?"

Mr. Derek shook my hand firmly, like it was a matter of life and death. He had the bluest of eyes and, I assumed, all the Hollywood ladies too.

"Hi, Walter, my name is John Derek, also know as Linda Evans' husband," he joked, punching me lightly in the midsection. "I know where John is. I'll take you there."

"Oh, thank you. Forgive my ignorance, but who is Linda Evans?"

John looked at Roger; they held a jocular stare momentarily, and then burst out in laughter.

"Do you watch any TV?" John asked.

"No. Not yet."

"When you start, you'll find out."

Son of Hollywood writer/director Lawson Harris and bit-actress Dolores Johnson, film actor, director and screenwriter John Derek made his first starring role as a death-row juvenile delinquent in Columbia's Knock on Any Door (1949), in which he was given more screen time than star Humphrey Bogart. Although Derek played supporting roles in such acclaimed films as The Ten Commandments, All the King's Men, and Exodus, he is best be remembered as the husband of beautiful actresses, including Ursula Andress, Linda Evans and later Bo Derek.

John wrapped his right arm around my shoulders amicably.

"Let's go."

John Derek dropped me off at another stunning mansion in Beverly Hills, where John Carroll and Lucille were squatting temporarily for some bizarre, discrete reason. The home owner Frank, a test pilot, had traveled to Europe, leaving the ostentatious estate in the couple's care. The white mansion looked like it had been yanked out of a book on medieval Roman architecture, replete with six grand columns and stained glass windows.

I knocked. Wearing khaki shorts, a Polo shirt and clutching a tall beer can, John Carroll creaked the door open.

"Well, well, well, Lucille," he yelled. "If it isn't long lost Walter Meyer from Argentina!"

John gave me a bear hug, literally.

"Lucille and I were just about to hit the road, but come on in."

The mansion looked even better inside, bedecked to the teeth with leather furniture. Lucille tossed a couple of mitts and rushed from the monstrous kitchen to hug me, planting a kiss on my cheek. Whatever she was cooking smelt scrumptious.

"Hi, Walter, you look marvelous," she greeted dramatically. "How are you?"

"Just fine. And, from your good looks, I guess you're okay," I replied.

Despite their hugs and kisses, John and Lucille had a superficial or phony attitude about them, which I soon discovered was quite typical of Hollywood. Even in real life, they acted. Charbon, a black poodle, lapped my trousers in faux admiration also. I wondered if he was an actor too.

"Well, Walter, I assume you need a place to stay," John said, hustling to the point. "You're more than welcome to stay at my ranch."

"Oh, you mean the wooden house in Granada Hills?"

"Yes. We'll move back there in a few days."

One of John's chauffeurs drove me back to "The Ranch," where I spent the rest of my three-week stay in California in the mansion's guestroom, unknowingly fraternizing with many a celebrity during numerous Hollywood-inspired bashes. I was present when a small-budget movie pilot was shot at John's house.

Quite the inhospitable duo, John and Lucille were almost never at "The Ranch," except whenever John's teenage daughter Julie, who probably resided permanently with his former love interest, was in town.

"Walter, you can eat whatever you want in the fridge," Lucille always offered upon departing the ranch house.

One morning, I decided to take Lucille up on her offer, and ravished a plate of stewed meat that had been sitting in the refrigerator. Two days later, the couple arrived at the mansion to prepare for one of their flamboyant parties.

"Walter, did you see the stewed meat in the refrigerator?" Lucille asked, inspecting the refrigerator, while I ate a bowl of cereal one morning.

"Yes, I ate it. And it was very delicious. Why?"

"It was Charbon's food. It was dog food, Walter!"

I smiled at Lucille, and started barking. She laughed.

In John Carroll's absence, Roger and I became the best of friends. We rode the rink daily, discussing everything under the sun about horses. Roger specialized, and was a multiple award-winner in cantering, the horse galloping slowly for hours without losing its gait.

Samantha turned out to also be an excellent rider, assisting Roger with the estate's everyday chores. John Derek swung by often to see her. He taught me "fast draw," but I was never able to beat him. The lovebirds would often ride together.

John Carroll owned a red convertible Buick. One day, he honked his way into the estate. I rode up to his flashy automobile.

"Jump in," he yelled. "I'll take you to Hollywood."

John might as well have been a racecar driver, the way he sped to Hollywood, defying every speed limit there was. On the outskirts of town, he sped through a stop sign and nearly knocked down an old lady carrying two huge bags of groceries.

"Shit!" John yelled as he pulled to the curb.

He put on his fake Hollywoodesque smile and walked up to the lady, who was, like most annoyed Americans, swearing profanities to high heavens. The brief dialogue and engagement that ensued typified Hollywood in a nutshell.

"I'm so sorry," John said, smiling and wrapping his arm around the lady's slouched shoulders.

"Can I have your autograph?" she said, returning his phony smile.

"Well sure, what's your name?"

"Betty."

John took out a dollar bill and scribbled on it.

"There you go, ma'am," he said, hugging the grinning lady, who seemed oblivious that her groceries were strewn about the street.

"Thank you."

"Yeah. Don't spend it!"

John jumped into the car, ready to speed off again.

"Won't you help her out with her stuff?"

"Nah. She's fine."

I popped out of the car, and recovered the groceries for the lady, stuffing every bit in the paper bags.

For some weird reason, she didn't ask me for an autograph, not even a simple "thank you."

I rejoined John in the car. We sped off.

"Just out of curiosity, what did you write on that dollar bill?"

"If you must know, 'To Betty with all my love.' Any problems, Mr. Good Samaritan?"

"No. Just wondering."

Surprisingly, considering John's break-neck speed, we arrived at our destination in one piece, another huge ranch house.

"Wait here," John admonished. "I'm going to see a friend. I'll be right back."

John returned an hour later, and we drove back to the ranch. As a result of John Carroll's unceasing absence, I didn't get to see much of California's hill country, well regarded in South America.

Neither John nor Colorado afforded me much reason to fall in love with U.S. of A., at least not at first sight.

Presumably, sheer guilt and pride forced John Carroll to arrange my transatlantic flight from New York to Germany. The onus was on me to quarterback my way from California to the "Big Apple," whereupon one of John's accomplices, a famous movie producer, was scheduled to rendezvous with me and pay for my ticket to Düsseldorf.

The DC-6 from Burbank to IDLEWILD International drifted slowly and uneventfully. Sitting quietly next to me was a heavily bearded middle-aged man, clad in black slacks, a white rimmed hat and a blue long-sleeved shirt tucked underneath black suspenders. Something about him reminded me of Germany, so I prodded.

"How are you sir?" I greeted. "My name is Walter."

The oddly dressed fellow turned away from perusing his Farming Magazine, and took his hat off chivalrously.

"Fine Walter, my name is William," he bellowed in an indecipherable accent. "Heading to the Big Apple?"

"Yes, but I'm really going to Germany. Are you from there by any chance?"

"Germany? No, I'm from Pennsylvania, but I do have German heritage."

"Anything recent?"

"Not really, I'm Amish."

"What's that?"

"We're a religious sect."

William smiled, reveling the opportunity to divulge his background.

"We live in mostly rural settlements in 21 or 22 states, I think, particularly in Lancaster County, Pennsylvania, where I'm from," he informed quite robotically, like he had articulated the same words two million times. "As a matter of fact, the oldest group of Amish, about 16 to 18,000 people, live in Lancaster County."

"So, how come you have an accent?"

"Well, Walter, most Amish are trilingual. We speak a dialect of German called Pennsylvania Dutch at home, use High German at our worship services and we learn English at school," William said. "We generally speak English when dealing with anyone who's not Amish, you know, like you."

"Forgive my abrasiveness, William, but most Americans are horrible dressers," I whispered. "I assume your modest attire speaks to your religion?"

"You're right."

"And?"

"Well, we Amish stress humility, family and separation from the world and corruptive civilization," he said. "In a nutshell."

"Ah, that's how come I sensed you were German!"

"What?"

The Amish have their roots in the Western European Mennonite community. Both were part of the early Anabaptist movement in Europe, which took place during the Reformation era.

The Anabaptists believed only adults who had confessed their faith should be baptized, and that they should remain detached from the larger society. Thousands of early Anabaptists were persecuted and put to death as heretics by both Catholics and Protestants.

Some fortunate Amish escaped the genocide, and fled to the desolate mountains of Switzerland and southern Germany. Therein began the Amish tradition of farming and worshipping in homes rather than in churches to avoid the then relentless arm of the law.

Old Order Amish groups drive horses and buggies rather than cars, do not have electricity in their homes, and send their children to private, one-room schoolhouses, William later divulged.

"Children attend only through the eighth grade. After that, they work on their family farm or business until they marry," he said. "We feel our children don't need more formal education."

"We learnt about you in school," I said. "One of the few days I was actually there."

"Oh, I see."

"So, how come you're on the plane?"

"I knew you'd ask that," he said, returning to his magazine. "I just attended a two-day farming conference in L.A. Just because we choose a simple life doesn't mean we're stupid, you know."

"I never thought so."

"If you don't mind, Walter, I'd like to return to my reading, thank you," William snapped.

Having learnt all that there was to learn about the Amish, I proceeded to gradually order everything on the menu, flirting with the gorgeous stewardesses in the process. One Amanda was particularly attractive, an eight-figure, pretty face and all.

"What else can I help you with, sir?" she asked rudely, discontent with my mischievous antics.

"The woman serving me," I joked. "You are something ...."

The plane suddenly spiraled out of control, sending Amanda tumbling down the isle. The lights blinked intermittently as the aircraft bumbled though violent turbulence. We were trapped in the center of a storm; I could see the black clouds swirling defiantly through my window.

Passengers screamed. William started to vomit, losing his hat in the process.

"Hello, this is Captain Lexington," the captain pronounced on the P.A. system. "This is a short-lived storm. Please remain in your seats and keep your seatbelts fastened. Thank you."

The plane stopped jostling in just as sudden a fashion as it had started. Five minutes later, William was crawling on the isle searching desperately for his lost hat, which, from the horrid look of his folded baldhead, he needed very much.

New York's Idlewild International Airport was upon us in no time. I was under the naïve impression that the film producer would procure my ticket as a generous gesture.

I was wrong. He paid for the ticket but I had to pay him back.

"This goes towards income tax deductions for later."

I stayed alert the entire journey from New York to Amsterdam, expecting the worst. However, the flight was nothing to write home about, including the half-hour connecting trip from Amsterdam to Düsseldorf.

The bulk of my exhilaration during the flight was in anticipation of seeing my parents for the first time in seven years. What do they look like? Will they be happy to see me? Do they love me more? Two million such questions raced through my mind as the aircraft hit the rugged landing strip in Düsseldorf.

I recovered my luggage expeditiously and paced the "Welcome Center" in anticipation. The Düsseldof airport looked mighty poles apart from the heavily fortified and guarded facility I remembered from the Nazi-controlled era. There were no long, ransacking queues, Swastikas or wailing Jewish families being whisked away violently by Gestapo soldiers, only a spattering of lightly armed British occupying forces. At the time the airport was also used as a truck depot.

Père and *Mutti* suddenly burst through the doors. My father had aged some, a few strokes of wrinkles now blotched his forehead and cheeks as he smiled. His brawniness and physical presence had markedly ebbed since his days as a brazen figure in occupied France, working as a liaison officer for about 750 iron and steel factories in the north. Clad in a long, maid-like, flowery dress and scampering behind *Père*, *Mutti* looked like she walked out of a picture taken 20 years ago, unchanged, still subservient to my overpowering dad and pleasant. I ran to engage them in a passionate hug.

"Oh, my God, you look so different," *Mutti* cried, cupping my face in between her still-fragile palms. "Your hair has darkened."

"You look more like a South American than a German now," *Père* said, slapping my shoulder, which was quite characteristic of him.

"Thank you," I replied. "I've missed you so much."

"And, you sound very American now," *Mutti* exclaimed, as we headed for the exits.

During WW II, more than 75 percent of Düsseldorf was leveled. By 1954, reconstruction was at its height, and the roads were annoyingly impeded with endless construction projects.

We boarded a cab, winding around road stops, and thus affording me the opportunity to reacquaint myself with the resuscitating "Garden City." Everything looked different, except the familiar sight of women, sticking their heads out of high windows with both elbows resting on crummy sills, gossiping with neighbors.

My parents still resided on the second floor of an apartment complex in southern Düsseldorf near the Rhine River, a major commercial shipping waterway linked by canals to other important European rivers.

Weaving through a number of scenic valleys, the Rhine River was literally a stone throw away, so I spent my evenings walking along its lip, reminiscing my childhood when I would spend hours skipping rocks on the glassy, lucid waterway.

I spent my first two evenings at home describing every minute detail of my perilous and climactic trans-atlantic adventure to South America, from my status as a suffering stowaway to being a singer and artist.

After recounting my adventures in Argentina at the dinner table one evening, my father asked: "From whom did you inherit so much gypsy blood?"

"I think I know the answer to this one," Mutti interrupted. "Walter is very different."

"What do you mean?" Père inquired, frowning and setting his forkful of potato aside.

"I wanted to make love in nature, away from the city and traffic," she began proudly. "I dragged your father into a beautiful forest. That's where you were conceived. That's why you're so different."

"Any other sex stories you want to share, Jettchen?" he asked, returning to his meal.

"It's okay Père, I've always wondered," I said. "Now I know."

The Westphalia Hall inauguration, to which I had been invited, was a week away.

While imprisoned in the Rockenberg prison - to keep my brain from rotting - I had attempted and excelled at a few "modern history" classes, the definition of which, according to the German penal system, was the history of Europe beginning with the rise of Hitler.

After a few classes, I found myself - despite my previous scholastic catastrophes - at the top of my class. Due to my superior performance, I was afforded the opportunity to work as an assistant to the prison's purchasing agent. An interesting array of freedoms ensued, ranging from purchasing groceries in town to inspecting off-limits administrative buildings, wherein I discovered an almost irresistible opportunity for escape. In one of the rooms, the sandstone forming the window frame had weathered, making one of the bars easy to remove.

The prison rules allowed us to receive and send one letter each month. Truth be told, I did not particularly miss my parents (I certainly didn't miss *Père*'s whippings), but I anticipated hearing from them; it was a needed break from the unbearable tedium. Letters were a luxury, and personal visits were even better.

I was expecting a visit from my father. My idea was to squeeze through the window and meet *Père*, who would then stash me away in France. I scribbled my surreptitious plan on a piece of paper, which I figured I'd slip *Père* during his visit. Horror struck a day before my father's visit; while I was trying to get out a key in the kitchen, the note fell out of my pocket. I hadn't noticed, but a nearby guard had seen me drop the note.

A few hours later, I was summoned to the warden's office. A guard ordered me to step inside a painted white circle in the center of the room. In front of me, sitting behind an abnormally large desk, abnormally far away, was Warden Zeugner. He looked like a spider, his tall, bony figure complimented by a pair of rimless glasses perched atop an aquiline nose.

"Twenty-eight days solitary confinement," he barked minutes after recounting my crimes. "Take him away!"

For twenty-eight straight days, I lived on a diminutive daily diet of seven ounces (or two slices) of bread and a jug of water in a small, dark room isolated from the rest of the prison. Actually, Warden Zeugner ordered me to the bunker thrice during my trouble-making stay in Rockenberg, each time for 28 days.

For many years, I had sworn revenge against "The Spider," who had inflicted much suffering on my young, impressionable soul.

He hadn't even afforded me the option of suicide for the cell had been stripped of everything that could have been used for such, which, in retrospect, was probably a good idea in my case.

Whilst in Los Angeles, John Carroll's only gift to me was a Colt 45 revolver in excellent condition. I planned to pay good ol' Warden Spider a surprise visit, during which the handgun would finally be of some use. As a result of being imprisoned literally under gunpoint in several Nazi concentration camps, I had come to regard guns with ample aversion. Three days after arriving in Düsseldorf - from a bedside study desk in my bedroom - I strategized the perfect assault.

First, I would drive to the little town of Rockenberg, near Frankfurt. I knew where Warden Zeugner lived, and I'd knock at the entrance. A fat housekeeper would probably crack the door. I would ask for Dr. Zeugner, and, without hesitation, storm into the house to confront the miserable bastard.

"Do you remember me?" I'd ask.

As he bunched his elderly face in difficulty recognizing me, I would persist, "Do you remember the young man whom you forced to stand in a circle in front of you, three times? And each time you ordered that he be taken to the special cell and remain there for 28 days?"

There still would be no sign of recognition.

"You must remember the young man who did a caricature of you in an atlas, depicting you as a spider?"

The catalyst for the third and near-death solitary confinement was a ludicrous charge of "destroying government property," to use Zeugner's terminology. Psychologically perturbed by prison conditions and post-solitary confinement stress, I sunk into deep depression, which excavated an eerie artistic yearning. From the near-bare library, I borrowed an old atlas, which boasted many blank pages for my drawings.

Since Warden Zeugner's caricatured image hung unceasingly in my head, he became the subject of my atlas collection of art. I drew "The Spider," replete with eight hairy limbs, and surrounded by several guards with exaggerated facial expressions that made them all appear comical and ludicrous.

The guard who discovered the grand collection of atlas artwork didn't find it funny at all.

"I had done this on the blank page of an atlas," I would yell, jabbing the revolver nozzle in his face. "You decided that I had destroyed state property and sent me back for another 28 days. Three times I was condemned to 28 days in the bunker!"

I imagined there would be some corporeal reaction indicating gradual reminiscence, upon which Zeugner would begin to quiver with fear. Perhaps his once cold, obdurate eyes would swell with pusillanimous crocodile tears. With the psychological upper hand, I would then proceed to speak unhurriedly, pronouncing every word lucidly.

"I thought of you many times and I resent that my mind should occupy itself with bastards like you," I planned to say.

I would then point my gun at his ugly face.

"Should I shoot him in the temple or through his rimless spectacles?" I contemplated.

What would his evil brain look like spattered on the carpet?

I informed neither *Père* nor *Mutti* of my revengeful intentions. I simply borrowed a friend's car and drove northwest to Frankfurt, from which I figured my way to Butzbach and then Rockenberg. While mildly incognizant of the warden's residence (I had never been there), I discovered it with considerable ease. It's quite staggering how accurate a determined mind can be, especially in the Machiavellian pursuit of evil ends.

I rapped rapidly and thunderously on the oak door like a Gestapo agent. Just like I had envisioned, a forty-something-year-old, obese housemaid cracked the door.

"*Ja bitte!*"(yes, please !) she greeted in as friendly a fashion as I had ever heard anyone say those words.

"I'm here to see Dr. Zeugner," I replied spryly, feeding off her enthusiasm. "He's expecting me. Can I come in?"

The loaded gun in my pocket poked my belly as I lurched forward to let myself in. My heart pounded hard on my rib cage like some surreal Herculean beast crashing it's way through an unwanted steel barricade. The sullen, evil riot inside of me, waited impatiently.

"I'm sorry, Dr. Zeugner moved to Hamburg a few months ago," she said, holding her ground in between the doorjamb.

"Where did he move to?" I asked, my voice quivering with disappointment.

"I don't have an address, but you should be able to find him through the prison authorities," she said. "He's retired."

"Okay, thank you very much," I replied, as she shut the door sonorously.

I sat on a bench near Warden Zeugner's former residence, staring at the Rockenberg Prison, where I had splurged perhaps the most dreadful year of my life.

In retrospect, the prison was quite an architectural masterpiece, fronted with a convent-like administrative building that housed, most notably, the Warden's office. A few hundred yards behind the administration building stood a prison complex shaped like a cross, the center of which was unceasingly manned by a gun-toting, attentive prison guard. Equidistant between the administrative building and the prison complex stood "The Kitchen," wherein the worst food in the world was prepared.

On the bench, I prayed for spiritual guidance, contemplating my degeneration from a small town goody two-shoes to a possible assassin. After two hours of meditation, I decided to forget Spider.

"One day, the bastard will get caught in his own web," I whispered to myself.

I have never regretted making the decision to live and let die for many beautiful things truly lay ahead.

Westfalenhalle indoor arena was considered symbolic from the very beginning, and thus it was built on the highest point in Dortmund in 1925. From the sprawling 48,270 square-foot complex, the breathtaking green Westphalia countryside could be seen, blessed with red, ferruginous soil. The domed, circular building, a protected architectural monument, has thrived on political, economical and artistic vibrancy ever since. Large German political parties, *Sozialdemokratische Partei Deutschlands*

(SPD) and *Christlich Demokratische Union* (CDU), once crowned their candidates for chancellorship in the *Westfalenhalle*.

Dortmund has always been effervescent with appreciation for sports. Thus, sporting events were included in the statutes of Westfalenhalle in its opening year: "The subject and aim of the company is to support and promote all sports...."

As with most historically significant monuments in Germany, the Westfalenhalle was sadly destroyed during WW II, the once gracious complex and natural terrain reduced to eyesore rubble. However, when the complex was reconstructed and reopened in February of 1952, the motto was, "The Olympics are calling," denoting German resilience.

Two years later, the Westfalenhalle swimming complex had undergone complete reconstruction. I was invited to the re-inauguration for my days as a Hitler Youth member and swimming champion.

In 1940, at the age of fourteen, I had been required to join the Hitler Youth (Hitler Jugend, HJ), just like every other health German boy of the right ethnic background. A pre-military organization, the Hitler Youth ran all sporting, social and recreational programs in particularly urban Nazi Germany. Hence, if you wanted to go to a party or play a sport, Hitler Youth was involved at some level. HJ spawned from the Boys Scouts, incorporating the discipline, patriotism and camaraderie of the scout program, but adding elements of indoctrination and training that had military applications. We were cute little kids in uniform - everyone loved us.

As a little rascal, the Hitler Youth was quite an odd experience for me. Everything was organized and regimented. The organization was split into five branches, each corresponding to a respective branch of the military. A strong swimmer, I naturally joined the navy branch.

Prior to the war, swimming competitions were organized between various private clubs. By 1940, everything was regulated by the Hitler Youth. So HJ Düsseldorf, section 6, of which I was a member, would compete against HJ Cologne, section 7 and identical units in other cities. A monstrous playoff series concluded with the *Reichsjugendmeisterschaft* (national youth championship), which had an indoor competition in Stuttgart and an outdoor meet in Breslau.

Eventually, the scope of the contest grew to encompass the rest of the newly seized German territory and became known as the European Youth Swimming and Diving Championship. I attended two of those, one in Milan and one in Vienna. I won several medals and was very popular.

Now it was 1954, and I stood to receive recognition and praise for symbolic victories I had secured as a radical teenager. The inauguration of the swimming complex was scheduled for a Saturday evening. I was still dateless by Saturday morning, pacing my parents' home for phone numbers of old Düsseldorf lady friends. I had never been so desperate for female companionship. *Mutti* seemed sympathetic. At first.

"So, *Mutti*, you're telling me there's nobody around that I can date for one night?"

"Walter, it's not my fault all your friends are already married," she replied, tears trickling down her cheeks. "You've been away for seven years, what do you expect?"

"You're crying," I said hugging her. "Why?"

"Walter, for one, you're not married," she said. "Plus, you're never around."

"Okay, *Mutti*, I'll keep those in mind. Now I need a date."

"Oh, how about Mary Schwartz?"

"No *Mutti*, she's a little too ugly for me. This is an inauguration, remember?"

"Okay, suit yourself!" *Mutti* snapped, leaving me to my woes in the kitchen.

It was then that the picture of beautiful, young Margarita del Campo flashed across my mind. Rita worked as a stewardess for a division of Panagra Airlines that frequented Germany. Prior to leaving Lima, I had given her my phone number in Düsseldorf.

"Call me if you're in town and I'll give you a tour of my country," I had promised when Rita came to visit *La Caricatura*.

I called Panagra's Berlin office. As my luck would have it, Rita was aboard the last leg of a flight to Düsseldorf, which was scheduled to land two hours before the inauguration. She obliged to accompany me for a few days, and I picked her up at the Düsseldorf airport.

The Westfalenhalle swimming complex inauguration ceremony was held in a large, heavily festooned conference hall, befitting a wedding. Colorful balloons, confetti and banners clung to the walls and ceilings like it was my fifth birthday. The hall was inundated with sport dignitaries, statesmen and celebrities, ranging from Germany's winningest Olympic swimming coach to the Mayor of Dortmund. With gorgeous Rita clinging to my left arm, I wove through the near impenetrable crowd, shaking as many hands as space and time would permit. Rita was certainly worth showing off.

"Walter, how do you say 'How do you do' in German," Rita asked, as we scoured for our labeled seat. "I'm sick and tired of saying 'mucho gusto' (enchanted) or 'How do you do' to people that can barely understand a word I'm saying. It makes me look like an insensitive idiot."

"Okay, which dignitary would you like to greet next?"

"Him, the national swimming coach," Rita replied, pointing at a man standing in the middle of a sea of humans. "He seems rather popular."

Immediately ahead of us, a line of admirers had promptly assembled to procure autographs from Olympic Coach Jupp Jumpertz, whom I quite disliked. At the tail end of my Hitler Youth career, I had joined the HJ water polo team virtually by error. The goalie had been called to join the *Kriegsmarine* (German Navy), and the water polo head coach, who was quite impressed with my multiple medal-winning HJ swimming performances, promptly invited me to fill the spot. He figured I could help resuscitate the fledgling water polo team, and perhaps I did for henceforth we competed quite well with other HJ units, securing a few medals.

The water polo team trained in the same Düsseldorf swimming facility as Coach Jumpertz' female national team. Jumpertz was allegedly a brute and womanizer. Even though he was never arrested, the grapevine had it that he had sexually abused his often under-aged female swimmers. He was tall, brawny and rather unattractive, the kind of man that certainly did not possess the tools to command sexual partners as beautiful as his swimmers without physical and psychological coercion.

I was 28 years old, but felt like an unruly teenager again as a mischievous gag coursed through my mind.

"Rita, after Jumpertz greets you, say, '*Du bist ein altes Arschloch*,'" I said, choking back my laughter.

"What does that mean?"

"It's the same thing as saying, 'I'm pleased to meet you.'"

"Thanks," she said, pecking me on the cheek. "I'll practice it for a while."

For a few minutes (to me, it seemed an eternity), Rita mimed and rehearsed the few words in her dulcet Peruvian accent. Soon she was ready to show off.

We approached Jumpertz just as he turned around to secure his seat. The line had since dissipated for the hall was finally settling down. Jumpertz immediately recognized me, his glassy, cold eyes holding my 6' frame intensely for a second before turning more permanently to Rita. I felt like socking Jumpertz for stripping my date of her clothes with his pervert eyes, but restrained, savoring the moment to come.

"Miss Margarita del Campo, I would like to present Mr. Jupp Jumpertz," I bellowed.

"It's nice to meet you, Ms. Campo," Jumpertz said.

He reached for Rita's hand and kissed it lightly like a gentleman that I was certain he was not.

"*Du bist ein altes Arschloch*," Rita replied, her hand still in Jumpertz's possession.

"What?" he snapped, tossing Rita's hand aside. "How dare you?"

Before dashing off in a huff, Jumpertz glanced at me. The flaring glint in his enraged eyes spoke volumes of his discontent with my dirty prank for "*Du bist ein altes Arschloch*," actually means, "You're an old asshole," in English.

I couldn't stop laughing. Rita was not so amused, and rightfully so. My incessant apologies didn't do much good either; she held it against me for many years.

"How inconsiderate of you to embarrass me this way," she cried, her voice quivering like a little girl. "You invite me here to treat me poorly?"

Rita's sonorous diatribe had quickly made us the center of attention, as virtually everyone in the banquet hall peered in for some dramatic action.

"I promise to keep this a secret," I replied, trying to mend things as best I could. "Shhh, you're only making things worse."

Rita slapped me before storming out of the banquet hall, to the amusement of the many "oohing" and "aahing" onlookers. I was alone for the ceremony after all.

The highlight of the inauguration was a protracted speech by the Lord Mayor of Dortmund, who had recently been appointed by the British.

"This is what we have created out of the ashes," the mayor said, hoisting his hands up in a V. "We hope war will never ever interrupt the smooth functioning of this beautiful complex."

After the inauguration, I couldn't wait to return to Lima. But my parents cajoled me into traveling with them to my father's hometown of Hollerath, a small hamlet on the German-Belgian border. *Père* had always relished the sweet fresh air, rolling hills and expansive forest of the picturesque Eifel region, populated by mostly subsidence farmers. He was simply a different person in the countryside of his birth, relaxed, more pleasant and happier. Most importantly, he reveled in the opportunity to converse in his Platt dialect, spoken only by Hollerathians.

As a child, I looked forward to visiting rural Hollerath. It was a needed escape from the tedium of city life. As a ten year old, fascinated by a variety of animals, I volunteered to shepherd for the entire hamlet, steering about 30 cows to an open grazing field. My granduncle owned two mules, named Fritz and Ella, which he had purchased from the army. I enjoyed being with the animals, and felt important when put in charge of them, taking the mules to the countryside water trough and keeping the cows from wandering into unfenced potato and oat fields.

I particularly relished sitting on the lush grass watching the innocent cows graze, their eyes lighting up as we came upon the palatable greenery. I remember the frail, staggering calves butting each other's foreheads playfully before snuggling next to their mothers. The cattle were gloomy and sluggish, trapped with organic feed in small ranches behind Hollerath homes, but snappy and playful in the open lush fields where they perhaps belonged. I appreciated being part of their short-lived freedom and joy.

There was considerable respect for farm animals in Hollerath for a lot depended on them. Most of the hamlet's necessities came from cattle, which provided milk, cheese and fertilizer, pulled the plows, and dropped a calf once a year before eventually giving up their hide and being turned into sausage for the dinner table. Everything bigger than a dog was shod and employed as a draft animal. It was the perfect food cycle.

The residents of Hollerath were as poor as Sahara dirt. Money was such a rarity that villagers got what they needed through archaic bartering or by producing things themselves, continuing to do so well into the war.

"Where is the water closet," I had once asked on my first visit.

Everyone laughed at the question.

"Walter, we have no water closet."

"The outhouse then?"

"There is no outhouse, either," my Granduncle explained. "Use the stable."

Life was simple, so were most Hollerathians.

The hamlet was graced with low homes, kept small to conserve heat and energy. Thus, when we drove into the hamlet in Père's small automobile, my cousin Edith Kühn's 3,000 square-foot, fairly modest, home looked like the White House.

The Kühn's family was fairly well to do. Edith's husband, Hans Joachim, was a master in sanitary installations, and Edith, who had inherited a large sum of money from her mother, was a well-known cook at a nearby dormitory vacation school. Edith was very close to the family. She was just as much a cousin as everyone else in the hamlet. The Kühn home had an indoor pool, and sat next to a large rock house built in 1597 in which my father was born.

Nearly the entire town was present at our annual family-wide dinner, whence I was deluded with a million questions about my adventures in South America. At the dinner table, adults sat attentive and amused, consuming my every word like gullible kids being told adventurous bedtime stories. As usual, I enjoyed being the center of attention.

"So how big are their farms over there?" one distant aunt asked.

"What do they eat?" another inquired.

Not surprisingly, all their questions seemed to revolve around farming.

"There are several farms in South America that are over a hundred thousand acres," I responded, to the sheer amusement of my audience as they whispered to each other.

"Walter, have you been drinking too much," one uncle inquired. "I mean, I don't know what you think, but we're not that stupid."

"I beg your pardon?" I asked, my voice a little taunt from impatience. "As a matter of fact, it's not uncommon for South American statesmen to own up to a million acres, if you must know. I kid you not."

"In that case, I just might accompany you the next time you travel to the West," the same uncle continued. "If that is not paradise on earth, only God knows what is."

We vacationed in Hollerath for two days.

Consisting mostly of vacationing Americans, the flight from Düsseldorf back to Perú via New York was peaceful until impassable snowstorms forced us to spend two days in temperate and snowy Iceland.

Contrary to *Mutti*'s incessant advice, I had purchased an Icelandic Airlines ticket because it was least expensive. Nevertheless, Iceland's terrain of mostly plateau interspersed with mountain peaks, ice fields and coast, deeply indented by bays and fiords, was most extraordinary. Everyone was blonde with blue eyes.

I found most impressive, however, Iceland's gracious and resilient history as narrated to us stranded passengers by an on-site tourist guide at the airport in Reykjavik, the northernmost national capital in the world. Icelandic Airlines organized the tour as compensation for the weather-incited travel delay.

"Iceland was settled by Norwegian and Celtic immigrants during the late 9th and 10th centuries A.D," the young, handsome tourist guide began, standing in the aisle as we wove through the city in a large tour bus. "This small island nation, the size of your state of Kentucky, boasts the world's oldest functioning legislative assembly, the Althing, established in 930."

The tour guide ceased his spiel momentarily as the bus jostled to a stop in front of a glamorous state capitol building.

"This is it. Our own version of the White House," the tour guide enthused, as the tour bus kicked back into gear.

"Tell you what, I'll explain why the U.S. has a large Icelandic immigrant presence. Would you like that?" he asked, in his slightly American accent.

Apparently, our tour guide had been educated in America.

The passengers nodded dryly. The tour was a little home sickening perhaps.

"The Askja volcano eruption of 1875 devastated the Icelandic economy, causing widespread famine. After the eruption of Mount Askja, the Oeskjuvatn Lake formed in a crater now simply called viti or hell. That's how bad the disaster was. Over the next quarter century, 20 percent of the island's population emigrated, mostly to Canada and the U.S," he explained. "But, literacy, longevity, income and social cohesion were and still are first-rate by world standards. We are very proud of our resilience, you see."

Our protracted flight to New York resumed the next day. Somehow I felt the burning voracity to remain in Iceland a little longer, but I succeeded at squashing such thoughts. The inarguably mammoth task of completing my aqua-therapy facility in Lima seemed more pressing and imperative at the time.

Shortly after landing in the "Big Apple," I boarded a connecting Panagra Airlines flight to Miami, and then to Perú.

It felt satisfyingly good to be back in my modest Lima house. My dog and plethora of friends had missed me so.

The Texas Two Step with Horses

> *I thought I knew Texas pretty well, but I had no notion of its size until I campaigned it. - Ann Richards (Former Texas Governor).*

I returned to business as usual, offering therapeutic swimming lessons to Lima's promising youth. Arturo Banderas, the banker, seemed enthusiastic to bankroll my hydro-therapeutic facility near Lima, but I needed additional training.

Affluent Lima families often transferred their polio-afflicted children to renowned Warm Springs, Georgia for hydro-therapeutic treatment. That changed when an association of such families invited a doctor from Warm Springs to Perú. A lovely home and a chauffeured automobile were afforded Dr. Jones, who frequented my swimming pool for clients. Dr. Jones fit the stereotypical description of a physician: nerdy, well-read eyes squinting behind half-rimmed spectacles perched atop an pinched nose.

"Congratulations Walter," he complimented, strolling around my outdoor pool during his first visit. "This is quite a brainy facility. Tell me, what's your invaluable secret?"

"Common sense," I replied. "But I'm very much interested in obtaining some training in hydratherapy at Warm Springs. Do you think that's a good idea?"

"To be frank, the difference between the miracles you're performing here and the gibberish they'll teach you there is quite negligible," he said, laughing. "But I guess such superfluous training wouldn't hurt."

"Thank you for your generous words, Dr. Jones. I figure some sort of certificate showing I have undergone special training would be comforting to my clients."

"Well, on that note, I must agree with you. Only God knows how many patients I would've lost had my huge, framed certificate not been hanging on my office wall in Georgia."

"Is there any way you can help?" I asked. "I do need to get invited to obtain a visa to America."

"You can come to Warm Springs anytime," he enthused. "Give me your information and I'll do the honor of sending the American Consulate a personal invitation for you."

Literally about five hours after Dr. Jones' arbitrary offer, the Association of Owners and Breeders of Peruvian Paso Horses called. Apparently, an American horse magazine had arrived via mail at their office. Of prominence was an article detailing increasing American interest in the Peruvian Paso horse, world popular as the smoothest gaited mount, thanks to its unique, inborn, four-beat lateral gait. The temperament of the Peruvian Paso is one of the world's best, due to a long-standing Peruvian tradition of breeding only animals with suitable disposition.

The Paso horse descended from the bloodstock introduced to Perú by the Spanish, blending the Barb, Friesian, Spanish Jennet and the Andalusian gaiting breeds. For centuries, no alien blood has been introduced into the Paso breed, and it is the only naturally gaited breed in the world that can guarantee its gait to 100 percent of its offspring. To cap the Paso's value, it's the only horse in the world born with *término*, a graceful, smooth movement in which the forelegs are rolled towards the outside as the horse strides forward, much like the arm movement of a swimmer. By all accounts, the result of these features is sheer riding pleasure, making the inimitable breed rather pricey, and well sought after.

As the only AOBBPH member who could speak and write English, I was asked to look into possibly exporting Paso horses to the U.S.

"It might be a good way for you to make quick money, Walter," the secretary advised. "Besides, I remember you saying you want to travel to Warm Springs. Think about it, you can kill two birds with one stone."

The offer seemed heaven-sent. I personally owned two Paso horses, but for some bizarre reason 12 seemed the target number. So, I began scouring for a business partner. I made the common mistake of assuming Texas to be the horse state of America. It was actually California. Thus, I wrote to the Texas Governor's Office, and was referred to the Good Neighbor Commission. The business hunt culminated with the San Antonio Chamber of Commerce.

One Gladys Coy was organizer of San Antonio's Battle of Flowers Parade on April 21, celebrated in memory of fallen Alamo heroes and the subsequent Battle of San Jacinto, where Texas won its independence from Mexico.

A colorful parade in Spain inspired the initial Battle of Flowers Parade in 1891. By 1895, the procession had developed into a weeklong rabid celebration called Fiesta San Antonio. In 1901, the parade introduced its first horseless vehicle. By 1958, the Battle of Flowers Parade had morphed into spectacular flower-covered floats with participants adorned in beautiful dresses, striking uniforms and colorful costumes.

Coy was always scouting for the glitziest of attractions and performances.

"What can I help you with, sir?" she barked in her heavy Texan accent the first time I called.

"I understand you have Texas Independence Day celebrations coming up very soon?"

"Yes."

"Well, I have these fine Peruvian Paso horses that have never been introduced to the U.S, but would certainly appeal to horse-loving Texans," I spieled.

Miss Coy laughed and continued.

"What is it about these Paso horses that you think Texans haven't already seen?" she inquired. "I have horse shows up to here, if you know what I mean."

"The Paso horse has the smoothest gait in the world," I said. "No annoying trotting whatsoever."

"Wow, Walter I'm sold!" she enthused. "Would you be a darling and send me a picture of these prized horses of yours?"

"Sure, it would be my pleasure."

So I sent Miss Coy photographs of my two white Peruvian Paso stallions.

"It's my intention to sell all 12 of these fine horses after the show," read an accompanying note with a final price list and the stallions' age, weight and size information.

Apparently, Gladys passed the information packet on to one Jack Sellers, a famous San Antonio horse aficionado, who drove King San Antonio during the Fiesta San Antonio celebration in an elegant, white Mardi Gras-like carriage manned by Palomino horses.

I had priced my pictured horses at $2,000. When Sellers saw the white Paso stallions, he assumed them to be white Lipizzaners, which were rare and literally priceless.

The white Lipizzaner stallion has galloped boldly through 400 years of European history into the hearts of millions of Americans. Walt Disney's motion picture, The Miracle of the White Stallions, depicting the rescue of the horses by General Patton's men during World War II, did much to publicize and boost sympathy for the doomed stallions.

In 1580, Archduke Karl, ruler of four Austrian provinces, established a royal horse-breeding farm in Lipizza, located in the hills of Karst, near Trieste. It was rugged, craggy country with little vegetation or water, but the Lipizzans thrived on it, lending to their endurance, strength and speed. They became almost exclusively the property of the nobility and military aristocracy. The stallions were trained for battle. Their great leaps and caprioles struck fear in the hearts of foot soldiers who opposed their well-born riders. World leaders ranging from Oriental Ghengis Khan to Arab and Tuareg emperors of the Sahara have prized the Lipizzaner horse ever since.

Three weeks later, I received a letter from San Antonio assuring me that Jack Sellers had placed an order for all 12 horses. My plan was to spend a week in San Antonio (for the duration of the celebration), sell the horses to Sellers, and then travel to Warm Springs, Georgia for hydra-therapeutic training.

American Foy Johnson owned *Expreso Aéreo Peruano*, a small air-cargo company, which boasted one airplane: a Flying Box Car Fairchild Packett. Johnson was a short, stocky and bald-headed man with stubby fingers the size of German sausages. A Cuban cigar clung forever between his bare lips. Johnson was a master businessman hence his success. He visited my swimming pool after learning of my project to export Paso stallions to Texas.

"You can save your spiel on hydra-therapeutic healing because I'm not here for that," he snapped after we shook hands. "I'm here to do business. I hear you are into trading Paso horses?"

"Yes. As a matter of fact I just secured an order in Texas for twelve animals," I replied, pulling two porch chairs near the pool to keep an eye on the swimming children. "I have six horses so far. Good thing you stopped by because I was in need of an investor for the completing six. I take it you might be interested?"

After glancing at the diminutive seat twice, Johnson sat, his obese behind nearly tearing the screeching chair apart.

"I'm in."

"Is that it?" I inquired. "I don't need to explain further?"

"You see, Walter, I'm a man of few words," he replied. "I know good business when I see it."

"Okay."

"Or is there any reason to be suspicious of this?" Johnson asked.

"No none at all," I said. "I'll go grab the paperwork I got from Texas."

I handed Johnson a copy of the correspondence from the San Antonio Chamber of Commerce. He was particularly pleased to see the letter acknowledging the 12-horse order had been placed.

On April 18, 1958, myriad Peruvians circled our Flying Boxcar at the Limatambo Airport to witness the loading and first-known commercial exportation of Peruvian Paso stallions from Perú to the United States, and the departure of our historically significant delegation. I was principal-in-charge and had three city government-assigned assistants, one of whom was son of our association's secretary. Donald Craig represented Expreso Aéreo Peruano and Carlos, a friend of mine who owned a respected Lima restaurant, handled food and accommodation for the trip.

The tiny hairs on the back of my neck sprung to life in excitement as the crowd cheered our every move. I felt like Superman or perhaps Noah as the tranquilized stallions were laggardly loaded onto the airplane in box stalls

We departed Lima late that afternoon, friends and relatives waiving as we climbed aboard.

Some indiscreet technical problems prevented us from performing a refueling touchdown in Panama, so instead we landed in Belize (at the time a British colony and thus the only English-speaking country in South and Central America). In Belmopan, the unloading of both animals and humans without a trespassing clearance was banned, so we fed the prized Paso horses aboard the plane. Eventually, we resumed our flight to Houston, Texas in the plane's classy and rather comfy cabin aptly seated for four.

The flight went favorably well until one of the stallions got restless and hysterical, kicking and shattering a plane window. The wind gushed in, causing the aircraft to seesaw uncontrollably.

"What the hell was that ya'll?" Donald yelled, in Texas drawl, springing from his reclined seat like Jack-in-the-box.

"Calm down, Cowboy Donald. It's probably just a little turbulence," I said calmly, mimicking Donald's accent. "Don't ya'll travel in airplanes in Texas?"

"Fuck you, Walter," he replied. "I heard a loud bangin' from there yonder."

Donald pointed animatedly at the backdoor leading to the horses. Soon the P.A. system crackled. It was the pilot.

"Hey gentlemen, I have reason to believe one of the plane's windows in the rear section may have popped open," he announced. "Walter, you're in-charge, would you be so kind and check on that please?"

"Perhaps you should go check it out Cowboy Donald?" the cook said, strapping on his seat belts before curling into his seat.

My assistants were so obviously terrified that the word "fear" may very well have been inscribed on their foreheads. Cowboy Donald, who once looked bear-like and menacing in his Texas boots, blue jeans and scowl to match, appeared as timid and threatened as the Texas Jaguarundi. The once infuriatingly loquacious cook now sat reticent, his petrified eyes as large as dinner plates. The third assistant, a Paso horse aficionado and expert from Lima, snoozed obliviously through the tumultuous fracas like an infant.

"You goddamned cowards!" I yelled.

I braved the plane's rocking, and dashed for the backdoor. Just as the pilot had predicted, one of the windows was smashed in, the pressurized gush of wind parting hair and exposing bare white skin on a few nearby horses.

"A horse's eyes are the keys to its soul," Normando had once taught me. "They have two blind spots, one directly in front of the horse when it's about four feet away, and the other directly behind it, about ten feet in length. Since a horse's eyes are located on both sides of its head, it's a wonder they aren't in a constant state of confusion. It's sort of like watching two things going on at the same."

As I checked on the utterly panic-stricken horses, I finally understood what Normando had meant. The Paso stallions were bucking and neighing loudly, their large, black eyes glassy with acute trepidation as the plane seesawed out of control, obfuscating hay and dust billowing about the diminutive stable.

I crawled slowly through a four-foot alley - between the row of box stalls and the plane's siding - to the shattered window, and stuffed it with some old cotton sacs. One of the horses lifted its front legs, one leg landing on my left shoulder. As I tried to remove the horse's leg his other leg landed on my right shoulder. I was looking in the eyes of a terrified horse in 10,000 ft of altitude. Once the destabilizing hole was plugged and the horse's legs off my shoulders, the airplane ceased rocking.

I had survived yet another life threatening test.

The pilot had not notified Houston International Airport of our arrival. We were low on fuel as a result of our earlier mishaps and unable to fly to another airport. After much ado, Houston granted permission for an emergency landing.

Houston authorities did not permit us to unload the horses, until they ran a few blood tests on the animals. Two astronaut-like dressed officers from the Texas Department of Agriculture boarded the plane to retrieve some blood samples from the horses. Three hours later, a large eighteen-wheeler flatbed truck wheeled in for the horses. We humans were sprayed with some pungent concoction, and our luggage fumigated before disembarkation.

"Just to let you know," a customs agent informed, as we waltzed across the landing field from the plane to the 18-wheeler truck. "As non U.S. citizens, you must pay a duty for importing breeding horses. Plus, you'll need a customs broker."

"What's a customs broker and why do we need one?" I asked. "We didn't plan for any extra expenses."

"The customs broker is the agent for the importer, who employs him," the agent replied. "He's frequently the importer's only point of contact with the U.S. Customs Service, and sort of advises on importing, preparing and filing entry documents, obtaining necessary bonds and arranging delivery to the importers' warehouse."

"So, basically we can't get out of here without first consulting a customs broker?"

"To cut the long story short, yes," he said, whipping a card out of his pocket. "You might wanna try them. I hear they're pretty good."

The agent handed me a card for R.W. Smith and Co. I called the Houston-based agency, and three inspectors were on-site almost immediately.

"Before you gentlemen start anything," I warned. "We really don't have the money for this. Why don't you call Jack Sellers in San Antonio. He is going to purchase the horses." They obviously did. A short while later one of the inspectors asked me.

"Are you Walter?"

Tomorrow Unfolds

"We called Mr. Sellers in San Antonio. As soon as we're done, y'all can go ahead and leave because Mr. Sellers has agreed to pay for our service by C.O.D when we arrive in San Antonio."

R.W. Smith and Co. assigned a young black truck driver to transport us (and the horses) to the Joe Freeman Coliseum in San Antonio, where Jack Sellers was waiting.

"You don't leave San Antone until you've collected the cash, okay," I overheard one of the inspectors warn the driver prior to our departure.

Halfway through the trip, the driver began to nod at the wheel, so I took over and drove all the way to San Antonio, which, apart from its Spanish architecture, seemed unimpressive by my expectations of America. Like most of its kind, the Freeman Coliseum was dome-shaped, located in a barren industrial zone in southeast San Antonio, "The Fiesta City."

With his dashing gray hair, impeccable coif and stocky build, Jack Sellers looked a little younger than most fifty-year-olds.

"Well, well, well, if it ain't Walter Meyer and them fine horses," he said, shaking my hand firmly outside the coliseum. "How are ya'll doin?"

"Fine. Just a little tired," I replied. "You have a place to keep the horses for a couple of days before the parade starts?"

"We can keep 'em right here on the coliseum premises," he said. "Can I see the horses?"

Smiling proudly, I swung open the truck's tailgate. Sellers turned red when he saw the Paso horses.

"These aren't Lipizzaner horses!" he yelled, storming off "What're you guys, some kinda dupes?"

Sellers soon drove off in a huff, and we were stranded with $24,000 worth of Paso horses.

"Okay guys, be quiet and don't wake up the driver," I ordered.

"What are you thinking?" asked Carlos.

"Just silently offload the horses."

We stashed the stallions into indoor stalls provided by the Freeman Coliseum management. Eventually, the deep-sleeping driver awoke to the noise of me slamming the tailgate shut after unloading the last horse. Perhaps disillusioned by a sudden new environment and loneliness, he scrambled out of the truck's passenger seat to approach us.

"Hey, hey, where the hell do ya'll think ya'll are going?" he yelled. "Money first, please!"

"Oh, the money."

"The broker said no animals get off the truck until ya'll give me two thousand dollars!"

"Don't worry," I said, handing the driver a promissory note. "That note says we'll pay your boss as soon as possible. The man that was supposed to pay us just ran away. Okay?"

"I'm sorry, but they won't accept that!" he persisted.

"I'm sorry, but there's little else I can do," I explained. "In two weeks, we'll sell these. When that happens, I'll send your boss the money. It's hard to abscond the law with so many horses."

Feeling cheated and left with unfavorable options, the long-faced truck driver eventually sped out of the Freeman Coliseum empty-handed. If his sullen demeanor was anything to go by, I bet he got fired upon delivering the bad news to R. W. Smith and Co. I would have been more sympathetic had I not been inundated in crisis of my own. I slept with the horses at the Freeman Coliseum. The others stayed at the Gunter Hotel. Three days later Cowboy Donald, Carlos and the Paso horse trainer returned to Lima.

I was alone in Texas with 12 stallions.

Many new adventures would develop in North America.

About the author

Walter Meyer now resides in Austin, Texas. He is proud to have earned a Ph.D. at the University of Texas and two additional Ph.D.s at other universities. He has taught, painted, farmed, and raised horses to name just a few of his adventures. These adventures will be narrated in a forthcoming sequel to this book.